Saving Shadow

Saving Shadow

Laura Beers

Phase Publishing, LLC
Seattle

Phase Publishing, LLC second paperback edition
July 2019

ISBN 978-1-943048-35-9
Library of Congress Control Number 2017951936
Cataloging-in-Publication Data on file.

More Romance from Phase Publishing

Also by
Laura Beers
A Peculiar Courtship
To Love a Spy
A Tangled Ruse
A Deceptive Bargain

Coming Soon
The Unfortunate Debutante

by
Rebecca Connolly
An Arrangement of Sorts
The Lady and the Gent
The Merry Lives of Spinsters

by
Emily Daniels
Devlin's Daughter
Lucia's Lament
A Song for a Soldier

by
Grace Donovan
Saint's Ride

Prologue
Italy, 1809

Lady Elizabeth Beckett pulled her brother's bulky wool overcoat tighter against her body in a vain attempt to ward off the night chill as she hurried along the quiet street. Her quick, darting steps sought equal amounts of speed and silence, and she regretted not trading her stylish kid ankle boots for something sturdier as she avoided another treacherous hole in the worn cobblestone.

Eliza suddenly froze, pressing herself against the cold stone of a building that offered meager concealment in its shadows. Some thirty yards ahead, Lord Jonathon Beckett stopped and glanced backwards, prior to ducking into an alley.

Tugging at the cloth cap concealing her chestnut brown hair, she hastened to follow her brother. She bunched his overcoat at the waist of her thin muslin dinner dress and ran towards the alley into which he had disappeared. Slowing as she approached the alley, Eliza paused at the corner, doubts once again rising in her mind.

What did she think she was doing? Jonathon would be furious if he even suspected she had followed him from their rented apartment, despite his refusal night after night to answer her questions about his nighttime departures. Overwhelming curiosity had compelled her to begin this impromptu pursuit, and she would now see it through despite the possibility of facing her brother's ire if she was caught following him.

After all, it was not as though Jonathon had reason to distrust her. They had worked together on sensitive assignments for almost a year now! Yet he still dismissed her questions and chided her to focus on her own tasks. Did he doubt her abilities? Her commitment?

Dangerous and important work was something of a family business, after all. Eliza's Uncle Charles served as England's chief spymaster and was responsible for all agents of the Crown. Jonathon had been recruited by their uncle four years before and had brought many sensitive missions to successful conclusions, both official diplomatic ones and undercover assignments. Eliza's father, the Duke of Remington, had begun to permit her to accompany her brother on diplomatic missions shortly before her seventeenth birthday, and Uncle Charles had seen a rare opportunity for her to use these diplomatic visits to gather intelligence for England.

Jonathon, who was five years her senior, was responsible for meeting with foreign governments, in lieu of the Duke of Remington, to continue to rally support for England in their ongoing war against France. Even though he would be in meetings during the day, the evening festivities were equally important to garner support and allowed them to exhibit English grandeur by their fashionable dress and jewels.

These diplomatic visits permitted Eliza to have access to a wide range of homes and offices throughout the world. As a young noblewoman, she had the advantage of being easily overlooked during dinner parties and official gatherings.

More importantly, unsuspecting servants often left her to wander unattended during the day, carefully avoiding gentlemen whose sole purpose seemed to be to flirt with her. She regularly found herself free to investigate offices and studies in embassies and homes, a veritable cache of poorly-guarded secrets.

She had also taught herself to pick locks, and with a few simple and easily-concealed tools, she could gain access to nearly any room she desired.

Eliza possessed a remarkable memory, and she quickly confirmed Uncle Charles' confidence in her by demonstrating she could locate a document, absorb its contents, and faithfully reproduce the information later with great accuracy. She would peruse the unguarded desks and bureaus of dignitaries, ambassadors, and even royal family members during her visits, and found a wealth of information available to her. Military communications revealing troop locations, personal correspondence between high officials, and even evidence of lovers' trysts and scandalous goings-on passed before the young spy's eyes.

After reading as much as she was able without being noticed or interrupted, she would return to the privacy of her chambers and copy down the information she had gleaned. When her brother found a free moment amid his meetings and other duties, she would pass him the handwritten pages, and Jonathon would secretly transfer the documents to other awaiting agents at his soonest opportunity.

If she found herself with the luxury of additional time, Eliza would also rapidly copy coded messages she discovered carelessly stuffed into drawers or left beneath other documents on a desk. She had shown an aptitude for deciphering codes while quite young, and she often as not was able to pass Jonathon already-deciphered messages along with the encoded texts she had copied.

The responsibilities of an agent had been exhilarating at first, but despite the constant risk of being caught in one of her acts of espionage, Eliza soon grew tired of merely handing off papers to Jonathon, then sitting demurely in her room waiting for the next assignment. Agents of the Crown were called upon to perform much grander deeds than clerical work, she knew, and she believed that this was a path to the adventure that her mundane life so desperately lacked.

So here she was, creeping along Florentine streets in the cold and dark, hoping that Jonathon would not detect her trailing him. Eliza admitted to herself that she did not fully know what she hoped to accomplish with this outing, but it certainly had been more exciting than retiring for the evening.

Eliza reached beneath her garments to grip a concealed dagger and edged around the corner into the alleyway. Her senses were immediately assaulted by the stench of rotting food and the pungent reek of urine. She pulled the collar of her overcoat up over her nose and pressed on, stepping around a pile of discarded waste.

She was vaguely aware of crumbling stone archways and a haphazard arrangement of architectural styles butting up against each other, but she focused on her path, taking care that her boots did not slip or make too much noise, and trying not to think about the contents of the dark puddles of rank liquid that dotted the alley.

Finally, Jonathon's silhouette took shape in the darkness ahead. Beyond her brother, Eliza could just make out a man gesturing wildly. She crouched and crept a few feet closer, taking advantage of a stone doorway recessed enough to allow her to remain hidden.

Eliza saw the other man repeatedly throw up his hands in obvious frustration, but she could only discern snippets of the heated conversation. It slowly became apparent that this man was a fellow agent and the topic was an upcoming mission. Although she wished she could hear the entirety of what was being discussed, she did not dare get any closer for fear of discovery.

Her legs started to ache from crouching so long, and she began to lower herself to a sitting position. As she pressed her shoulder against the doorway, staying quietly concealed, she heard muffled footsteps coming slowly towards her. Eliza pulled the coat's collar over her face and held herself motionless.

The footsteps passed by. She risked a look and saw the slowly receding form of a stocky man with tangled hair pulled back and tied at the neck. Eliza's eyes moved down the man's form as he crept stealthily on, and her heart leapt into her throat when she glimpsed the long, thin form of a stiletto pressed close against his thigh.

Jonathon's voice was louder now as he continued to argue with the agent, but neither man seemed to notice the threat moving towards them in the darkness. "Turn around," Eliza muttered under her breath. "Just turn around, Jonathon." Her mind raced. If she shouted a warning, the man might still attack and have the advantage. She must act.

Eliza carefully stood, steadying herself against the stone door frame and slipping off the unwieldy overcoat. The night chill pierced her thin dress, but she dared not risk entangling her arm.

She stepped clear of the doorway, feeling the dagger's familiar heft as she calculated the distance and angle to the creeping man. He was ten paces from Jonathon's back... nine, steadily closing in... eight. Her pulse pounded in her ears. She had spent hundreds of hours practicing with this dagger, and even killed small game in the presence of her uncle's game warden, but she had never anticipated she would ever have to attack a person. *Could I really...*

The stiletto in the man's hand began to rise, and Eliza's mind snapped into focus. She took a deep breath, planted her foot, and threw her dagger fiercely at the center of the shadowy form.

The blade found its mark and plunged deep into the man's back. He cried out in pain and shock, falling to his knees and twisting in vain to reach the dagger. Jonathon and the agent whirled around at the man's cry, pistols drawn, but the would-be assassin merely coughed and slumped forward onto a pile of excrement.

The two men raised their pistols in Eliza's direction and peered into the darkness. She remained motionless until Jonathon's voice rang out.

"Eliza?" Jonathon exclaimed in disbelief, lowering his pistol.

"Yes, it is I. How you did not notice that man approaching you with a stiletto is beyond me," she said, rubbing her arms to ward off the chill. She stooped to retrieve the overcoat from the ground and quickly put it on. Eliza winced as a stench hit her, realizing too late she had dropped the coat into some foul substance, but it was too cold to remove it again.

Jonathon replaced his pistol in the waistband of his trousers as he walked over to the dead man. He placed his foot on the man's back and yanked out the dagger. He crouched down and wiped the blade clean of blood using the man's coat, then paused to examine the weapon, running his thumb slowly over the jewels embedded in the ornate hilt. He approached his sister and held the dagger out to her.

"Father's dagger?" he asked through gritted teeth.

"Yes," Eliza confirmed, taking the weapon and placing it into a pocket of the overcoat.

Jonathon let out a gruff sigh which sounded more like a growl. "And are you wearing my overcoat?"

Eliza raised her eyes to Jonathon's face. Even in the darkness, she could see the firm straight line of his lips and his eyes blazing with fury. "Are you angry?" she asked, slowly wringing her hands together. "I have just saved your…"

Jonathon put his hand up to silence her. He looked ready to explode into a rebuke, when the other agent stepped close to Jonathon and touched his shoulder. The agent leaned in to murmur something into Jonathon's ear, and Eliza's eyes widened as she caught sight of the man's muscular chest beneath his open white shirt. She glanced up, taking in the long brown hair that hung down the sides of his face and partially concealed a shabby beard.

Both men directed their gazes at her, and from the bleak expressions on their faces, neither appeared eager to start a conversation. Looking away, her eyes flicked past her brother to the place where the dead man lay. The agent stepped forward, blocking the dark form of the corpse, and spoke in a deep voice.

"Eliza, is it?"

"Yes, it…" she began, when Jonathon suddenly grabbed her arm and began pulling her out of the alley.

"Who is that? Why did you not introduce me?" Eliza asked, glancing over her shoulder at the man who remained standing in the alley.

"He is not someone you need to know," Jonathon said firmly.

"Why not? Is he an agent?" she prodded.

"Yes, he is an agent."

"Why was he so upset with you?"

"He was voicing his concerns about his new assignment."

"What is his new assignment?" Eliza asked curiously.

Jonathon stopped for a moment but did not release his grip on her arm. He sighed and tilted his head towards his sister, then continued hastening them along the street. "If you must know, Uncle ordered him to impersonate a French Navy officer in hopes of locating their eighty-gun ship, the *Franklin*."

"Oh, that sounds dangerous!" Eliza said. What a mission! Though she could guess at his concern. His life would be forfeit if he were discovered as a foreign spy.

Being forced to keep pace with Jonathon's rapid, determined strides was becoming tiring. Eliza was tall for her age, but she could not hope to match her brother's stride for long. She tried to pull her arm free from his iron grip. He slowed his pace, but he did not stop.

Soon they turned onto a familiar street and approached their apartment. Two uniformed guards armed with pistols turned towards them. Jonathon finally released Eliza and held his hands up in front of him to show he was not a threat.

"Lord Jonathon, is that you?" the shorter of the guards asked in surprise as he lowered his pistol.

"Yes. My sister and I decided to go for a stroll before we retired for the evening," Jonathon said lightly.

"The streets are a dangerous place at night, my lord! Next time you go for a walk, please inform us and we will accompany you," said the taller guard, pulling open the gate to allow them entry.

Eliza and Jonathon thanked the guards and proceeded up the path to their apartment. Jonathon threw open the door to their lavishly-decorated drawing room, dimly lit by a low fire in the ornate marble fireplace, and stood aside for his sister to enter. Along one wall, there were large floor-to-ceiling windows that overlooked Cascine Park, but were draped with heavy silk curtains.

Wrinkling her nose as she took off the overcoat, she placed it on a side table, then settled herself onto a floral upholstered armchair and waited for Jonathon to start yelling. She did not have to wait long.

"Are you mad?" Jonathon exclaimed.

"Hush, Jonathon. The servants might overhear you," Eliza admonished, glancing over her shoulder.

"I do not give a damn about the servants," he growled, as he began to pace in front of her. "Do you know what could have happened to a seventeen-year old girl on the streets of Florence in the middle of the night?"

Eliza kept her back straight and her hands folded primly in her lap as Jonathon continued to rant. She opened her mouth to defend her actions several times, but each time her brother simply shouted louder about the dangers of leaving the apartment unescorted. She clenched her jaw and continued to endure the tirade, wondering whether the servants had been awakened by the noise.

She was so tired of this, how Jonathon coddled her, how he refused to let her make choices that concerned her future. This night had been the most exciting in months, but Jonathon would now ensure that she never left their apartment alone again. It had been an exhilarating taste of freedom, but she knew Jonathon would not understand.

Her brother's firm voice broke into her thoughts. "If you sneak out one more time, I will send you back to Uncle Charles' estate. Do

I make myself clear, Eliza?"

She clenched her hands tighter. Uncle Charles was wonderful, when he was there, and his household staff was kind, but the thought of going back to Uncle Charles' estate to be forgotten by the family was not something she would accept. She had been given reprieve by going on these diplomatic missions, and she would not go back willingly. Her espionage efforts as part of these visits had proved she was meant for greater things, and she would not, could not, return to the quiet life of a young noblewoman.

"No," Eliza replied sternly.

"I beg your pardon?"

Eliza fixed her brother with a penetrating glare, gratified to see a flicker of uncertainty in his eyes. "I said *no!*"

Jonathon looked confused and started to speak, but this time she put her hand up to stop him. "You may try to send me back to Uncle Charles' estate, but I will not go. If you lock me in my room, I will escape." Her eyes never wavered from his face. "Have you already forgotten what happened tonight? You would have been killed but for me!"

Jonathon groaned and ran his fingers through his hair in frustration. "Eliza, be reasonable, for heaven's sake! Tonight, you were fortunate. You might be the one lying in that alley had events been even a little different!"

Rising from her chair, her eyes blazed. "Clearly, I was the only one prepared to deal with these 'events', as you call them. Uncle Charles knew that I could be trusted with the responsibilities of an agent, and now it is plain that I would do just as well as a field agent."

"You have no idea what you are saying, Eliza! You, my little sister, killed a man not even two hours ago, and you are still treating this as some kind of game. There is so much you do not know."

"Then teach me!" she exclaimed, throwing up her hands in frustration. "From now on, I want a say in which missions we undertake. I will continue to decipher codes when I receive them and I will break into offices, but I want to deliver the papers with you. I want to be a field agent and your partner."

"No," Jonathon said flatly. "Women, much less girls, cannot be agents. You are the daughter of a duke and you must abide by certain rules. I am sorry, Eliza, but that is the way it is."

"I will turn eighteen next week, and I have access to the inheritance that Grandmother left me. It is enough money that I can live comfortably for the rest of my life, and I do not care one whit for society and its rules."

"Why are you acting so irrationally?" Jonathon asked in confusion. "This is not like you at all."

Eliza smirked at her brother. "I have been working as an unofficial agent for almost a year now, deciphering codes and stealing information all over Europe. Whether you will admit it or not, I may as well already consider myself a field agent. I just want to accompany you when you meet other agents."

"Absolutely not."

"And *why* not?" she challenged.

"Because you are too valuable to be wasted in the field!"

Eliza was taken aback at this. "What do you mean?"

Jonathon started pacing in front of her. "Your mind is what makes you such an asset to the Crown. You can decipher enemy codes from all over the world, and when you search offices, you do not need to remove any papers to make copies of them. You have singlehandedly determined the locations of half a dozen French frigates by creating a mathematical algorithm. And I could go on." He stopped pacing and turned towards her. "Field agents we can find and train from ranks of the military and elsewhere, but you, Eliza, you are special. What you do, no one else can do." His eyes had softened and now begged her to understand. "Uncle Charles, no, *England* cannot risk anyone learning about your abilities, so please just forget about endangering yourself and meeting other agents."

Eliza had never given much thought to her own value to the Crown; she knew her skills provided an important service, but Jonathon's words made an impact on her. Still, she knew she must stand firm or risk losing this opportunity and perhaps her future altogether.

"What if…" she bit her lip. "What if I stayed in the shadows like I did tonight?"

Jonathon shook his head. "No. I will not be able to protect you if you are out of my sight."

Eliza glared at him. "I seem to recall someone else in need of protection tonight."

Jonathon collapsed onto the burgundy velvet sofa and leaned back with his hands over his face. "I owe you thanks for stopping that man, but that does not mean I want you following me around. You are my younger sister, for heaven's sake!"

Her temper flaring, she put her hands on her hips. "From now on, I will follow you every night you go out. I will stay hidden and observe unless something goes wrong, but then I will step in and protect you like I did tonight."

Jonathon moved his hands and gazed up at the white paneled ceiling, refusing to look at her. "I could lock you in your room."

Eliza gave him a smug smile. "You could try, but I would still follow you."

Jonathon rubbed his eyes and spoke with a strained voice. "Fine. I will write to Uncle Charles, but I know he will not like this. He might ask you to come home."

She shook her head adamantly. "There is nothing for me in England now that Kate is married to that vile Lord Camden, and Luke is managing the estate in Scotland."

Jonathon finally leaned forward and looked seriously at his sister. "My job is to keep you safe, and I cannot do that if you sneak around after me. You may have dangerous talents, but you are still my sister and I love you. I cannot bear to think of losing you."

Eliza sat down next to Jonathon on the sofa. "I cannot lose you either, but I know I can do more than what you and Uncle Charles permit me. You have seen me hunt game in Uncle Charles' forest, and I am quite good at staying hidden. Besides, I can defend myself. My dagger is not the only weapon I can use," she said confidently.

Jonathon sighed. "You do realize you killed a man tonight?"

Eliza's gaze flicked away. "He was going to kill you."

Jonathon closed his eyes and leaned his head back again. "And what happens the next time? Are you prepared to continue killing in the name of the Crown?"

Eliza bit her lip as she stared at the floor. Could she keep killing? Even though she had killed a man tonight, she did not mourn his death or feel any guilt. In truth, it hardly felt real. A shadowy enemy had tried to hurt her brother, and she had struck him down with no more hesitation than she would a wild dog or a poisonous snake. Perhaps all those years of hunting in her uncle's forest had prepared her for working as a field agent? "Yes, I would kill again if I had to."

Jonathon's mouth tightened into a grim line. He seemed about to say more on the subject, but instead he merely stated, "You will need to wear warmer clothes if you are to be running around at night."

If this was sarcasm, Eliza decided to ignore it. She tapped a finger on her mouth in contemplation. "I will find some trousers, a shirt, and some work boots. I am certain one of the maids can tailor them to fit me."

Jonathon suddenly placed his hands on her shoulders and forced her to look at him. "You must promise me that the moment you feel your life is in danger, you will stop being a field agent."

Eliza returned his intense gaze and nodded. "I promise."

Worry lines were etched between his brows as his eyes searched hers. "I am serious, Eliza. The minute being a field agent becomes too much for you to handle, you must leave this work immediately. Becoming distracted out there, even for a moment, could mean your death. Promise me."

"I promise, Jonathon," she reassured him.

Jonathon held her gaze for a moment longer, then dropped his hands in defeat. "I am not happy about this, Eliza. I hope you understand what you are asking." He stood abruptly and departed the room without a backward glance.

Staring after him for a moment, she retrieved her dagger from the smelly overcoat and walked towards her bedchamber. She could hardly believe she had stood up to Jonathon, but more importantly, she was amazed she had won.

She gently placed the dagger under her pillow as she had for the past seven years. She always kept it hidden from Uncle Charles' staff for fear they would take it away from her. Eliza did not see her father often, and the dagger let her pretend he was always near, protecting and guarding.

Before climbing into bed, she walked over to the large window and stared into the night. The sky was filled with twinkling stars, and the words of William Shakespeare flowed into her mind. *It is not in the stars to hold our destiny, but in ourselves.* Tonight, she had changed her destiny. She would no longer be controlled and sheltered, but would lead a life of purpose and excitement.

Tomorrow she would purchase men's clothing and begin to accompany her brother on his missions. She would learn all she could from Jonathon and the other agents. Eliza smiled. She would become the best agent the Crown had ever seen. *What a grand adventure this will be!*

Chapter One
London, England, 1813

Lady Elizabeth Beckett sat at her dressing table in her room, gazing at her reflection while Martha, her lady's maid, finished weaving pearls through her hair. Rich chestnut brown hair was piled high on Eliza's head and cascaded down her back as soft curls in the front framed high cheekbones, a pert nose, and full red lips... the effect was stunning, and she was quite pleased with her appearance tonight.

She was aware that she had grown into an attractive woman, and her beauty and her lineage as the daughter of the Duke of Remington meant that dealing with suitors was a continuous chore. At first, such attentions had been flattering, but Eliza had become frustrated by the lack of sincere intentions towards her. Sadly, most of her suitors appeared to be more interested in a marriage of convenience than falling in love.

After a few seasons, Eliza stopped trying to secure a love match and instead focused her energy on developing social connections that would benefit her. She had perfected her role as a jovial, carefree lady who enjoyed the frivolity of balls, house parties, and all types of social gatherings. She knew intelligent women were often derided as bluestockings by members of the ton, so she downplayed her intellect in conversation.

The titled men she associated with wanted a woman that looked beautiful on their arm and was demure in nature, so she played to their vanity, laughing and flattering, biting back the witty retorts that filled her mind. As a result, she was a popular guest and secured invitations to many homes, which in turn allowed her to accomplish secret missions for the Crown.

Eliza rested her chin on her hand and sighed. On the outside, she had everything… money, beauty, social standing, an endless stream of suitors… but inside she felt jaded. Her work as an agent brought her in regular contact with the worst members of society, and it always amazed her what men were willing to do to gain money and power, no matter who they were. Evil made no distinction based on class, and she had seen terrible things done by both poor and rich.

Despite all this, serving as an agent of the Crown gave Eliza a measure of control over her own affairs that would be otherwise impossible. She relished the freedom and danger that her job afforded her, and unless she wanted to stop working as a spy, she must continue playing the carefree young noble. So, she needed to go to the ball tonight as planned.

"You look beautiful, my lady." Martha broke through her introspection.

Eliza smiled up at her. "I only look beautiful because of your handiwork." Standing, she walked over to her bed, where Martha had laid out a pair of long, white kid gloves.

"Are you all right, my lady? You seem distracted," Martha said. "Perhaps you are thinking of a certain gentleman?"

Eliza stopped putting on her gloves and rolled her eyes. "I can assure you that I have not found any gentleman that has captured my attention."

"I know it is not my place," Martha paused, then continued, "but you have seemed sad lately, and the bad dreams are becoming more frequent."

"I know, and I am sorry if I have kept you awake at night," she sighed.

Martha shook her head. "You misunderstand me, my lady. I simply mean to say that maybe it is time to entertain gentlemen callers again. They could take you to the opera or on carriage rides around Hyde Park, and it might lift your spirits."

Eliza wrinkled her nose at Martha's suggestion. "I have entertained callers for four seasons, and I am tired of that charade. Most of those gentlemen went to my father after a few outings, more interested in how much my dowry was than whether I was happy. Men are not interested in love and faithfulness. They are only interested in the appearance of wedded bliss with their wives while they keep mistresses in a house across town."

"My lady! Not all men are so base. Your brother and uncle are not like that."

"True, but Jonathon is not married, and Uncle Charles still mourns the loss of his wife from twenty-five years ago. He must have loved her very much," she said longingly.

"I doubt Lord Beckett has even considered remarrying with his busy schedule," Martha pointed out.

Eliza paused to consider. Uncle Charles was indeed quite busy as the man responsible for all the agents of the Crown, a position of the highest trust that he had held for over two decades. "Perhaps you could say that my uncle is married to his job."

Martha smiled. "Well, I trust that your brother will continue being a good man when he finally decides to marry."

"I believe he will," Eliza said, leaning against her bed. "But I really have no desire to marry. I do not want a man to dictate what I can and cannot do…" she stopped, her eyes wide. "I am so sorry, Martha! I cannot believe I said that to you. That was most insensitive."

Martha paled slightly and slowly sat down in a nearby chair. Her eyes focused on the floor. "I know you did not mean anything by that, my lady. If not for you, I would still be at the mercy of those vile men."

Eliza gazed compassionately upon her maid, one of the few people she considered a friend. She was saddened to recall how Martha had been tricked at an early age, sold to a man named Mr. Aaron Wade, and subjected to unspeakable degradation.

"I can scarcely bear to think of what you had to endure for those five years." She crouched down next to Martha's chair. "I promise you that Mr. Wade will be brought to justice."

"Thank you." Martha smiled gratefully at her employer and friend. "Now please stand up before you wrinkle that new gown. I do not want to have to press it before you go," she said with a shaky laugh.

Eliza stood and smoothed out her ball gown. She remembered how furious she was when Uncle Charles told her that she could not just kill Aaron Wade for his crimes. Her uncle wanted her to gather evidence against Mr. Wade, then arrest him for kidnapping and enslaving young women. She had tried to fight her uncle's decision, but he was the Chief Spymaster, and his word was law.

A loud knock snapped Eliza out of her dark thoughts. Martha rose to answer the door, but before she could reach it, the door burst open to reveal Lord Jonathon Beckett. Martha stiffened and lowered her eyes.

"Jonathon, you cannot just barge in here! You scared Martha... *again*." Eliza tilted her head towards the trembling maid.

Walking slowly over to Martha with his hands in front of him, Jonathon moved quietly as though he were soothing a frightened horse. "I am terribly sorry, Martha. We have known each other for years now, and I should know better than to burst in like that."

The frightened maid kept her eyes lowered. "I apologize, my lord."

Jonathon smiled reassuringly. "You have nothing to apologize for. I hope you know that you are always safe and welcome here or in any of our homes."

Martha hesitantly met Jonathon's eyes. "I do believe that." She took a deep breath. "Old habits die hard, I'm afraid..." Martha's voice trailed off.

His face darkened, but he nodded to reassure her. "I understand."

After a moment, Martha turned to Eliza. "Can I do anything else for you before the ball, my lady?"

Smiling fondly at her, Eliza replied, "No, Martha. You have already done enough. I will be home late tonight, but I will ring for you when I need to undress. Until then, go lie down or peruse a book from Jonathon's library. I am certain he has one or two good books in there." Eliza recalled that Martha was the daughter of a vicar and had been blessed to have a mother who taught her to read.

"Actually, I have quite an impressive collection of books in my library. I do not know what any of them are, but I am told there are many impressive volumes," Jonathon said.

Eliza laughed. "Who told you that you have an impressive collection of books?"

Jonathon did not entertain many visitors, so it was a safe guess that Father had told him that he had an impressive library. On Jonathon's twenty-first birthday, Father had given him this townhouse on Grosvenor Street, a coveted address among the ton. The townhouse had been in the Beckett family for generations, and the library was filled with books collected over the years by various family members. Unfortunately, Jonathon's work as a diplomat and agent rarely permitted him to remain at home long enough to enjoy any leisure time in the library.

Attempting to turn the conversation in another direction, Jonathon remarked, "Eliza, you are looking beautiful tonight. Perhaps you will receive another marriage proposal?"

She merely shook her head at her brother, and Martha took the opportunity to excuse herself from the siblings and their banter. Eliza knew Jonathon was teasing her, but she fell silent as she thought again about marriage. She was in a unique position, even among nobles, in that she had access to her own fortune. A rarity for a woman, even the daughter of a noble, this freed her from the necessity of finding a wealthy husband to secure her future.

More importantly, this freedom had also allowed Eliza to develop into one of the most successful agents in the service of the Crown. Jonathon and Uncle Charles, who had recruited her in the first place, may have been the only two people in England who knew that she worked as an agent, but hundreds in Europe and beyond told tales of the notorious spy known as *Shadow*. *Shadow's* legend had grown over the past several years, though Eliza doubted anyone suspected that she was a woman; agents had always been men who secretly served the Crown.

She certainly enjoyed much about her lifestyle, both lifestyles, and the many advantages her wealth and position brought. Her father had never complained about bills he received for expensive ball gowns, and though she could have paid for them herself, she was content to let her father provide her with the latest fashions.

Eliza was very pleased with her ball gown this evening. The servants had collected it earlier that day from the dressmaker, another splendid creation from the highly sought-after modiste Madame Lanchester. The pale gold and generous, rounded neckline of the gown served to accent her olive skin, while ground rubies were stitched along the net overlay of the muslin bodice.

Jonathon's rambling broke into her thoughts. "So, we are getting in and out this time?"

"I am sorry, Jonathon. What are you going on about?"

Jonathon gave her a lopsided grin. "Time to stop staring at your new dress. We need to talk about the mission tonight." Jonathon took a seat on the mahogany settee and crossed his legs.

After a moment's consideration, Eliza decided her brother looked very handsome tonight in a black tailcoat that highlighted his tall, muscular build. His deep brown hair was a little longer than the current style, but it did not hide his strong jaw and his engaging smile.

It also served him in his work as an agent. Jonathon's contacts were often to be found in taverns in questionable areas of London, and perfectly-groomed hair might actually invite danger. With that thought, she grew serious and began to review the plan for the evening's mission.

"You will play the rogue, and I will play the overbearing sister who tries to dissuade you from embarrassing the family with your childish behavior. Then we will sneak into Lord Vernon's office and see if he is involved in Mr. Wade's business. I will review the documents, then we will get out. No one will be the wiser." Eliza joined her brother on the settee and reached for her white satin slippers with the gold fringe.

Jonathon groaned loudly. "I do not want to play that role again." He stood and walked over to the stone fireplace. "What if you swoon and I carry you to the study to recover?"

She shook her head. "No, the footman would direct you to one of the fainting rooms. The only way we can access the study is if we are in a compromising situation that might reflect poorly on Lord Vernon."

"Fine, we will do it the way we always have. This will not help my reputation, you know." Jonathon pointed towards the door to indicate to his sister that it was time to depart for the ball.

"Perhaps…" Eliza reached for the silk reticule that Martha had placed on the table by the door, glancing inside the small bag for a moment. "Perhaps, as this is an engagement party for Lord Vernon's son, the best time to strike would be during the announcement, when the guests are distracted." She glanced around the room once more, then stepped into the hall.

Jonathon followed his sister, but stopped her at the top of the stairs that led down to the entryway. He gently placed his hand on her arm. "Please be careful tonight."

She gave Jonathon a teasing smile. "Do not worry about me. I have my dagger if it really comes to that." Eliza patted her thigh. She always felt safer having her dagger close to her, even though it would not be easy to retrieve from her long dress.

Jonathon was still holding onto her arm, and she noticed for the first time an apprehension in his eyes as he searched her face. Did he know something about this assignment that she did not? Jonathon never worried about her when they had to search a house. After all, what could really happen? They might be caught and dismissed from the party. Surely, he would not be...

Then it hit her; France. Eliza closed her eyes. She did not want to think about her last trip to France. Six dead sailors, warm blood dripping from her hands... No, she did not want to think about that at all.

Her eyes snapped open. "Why are you warning me to be careful? Is this because of what happened in France last month?"

Jonathon grimaced as she wrenched her arm away from him. "I just thought..."

"I did what had to be done." Her eyes dared him to argue.

Jonathon spoke calmly. "I know. You saved me and a whole team of agents that night. We all owe you our lives. But Eliza, I worry that it has affected you more than you have acknowledged. I heard that horrible dreams afflict you every night now." The worry etched onto his face was evident. "You know you can always come talk to me about anything." Jonathon hesitated, then continued. "What really happened that night?"

Eliza lowered her eyes from Jonathon's intense gaze. If she revealed that, then he would insist she retire as an agent forever. She forced a smile. "I am fine. Martha should not have told you about my dreams."

Jonathon clenched his jaw and looked away. "Mr. Larson told me about them."

Her loyal butler and friend had betrayed her trust? Her eyes widened in shock.

Jonathon continued before she could react. "Before you get upset with him, you should know he told me because he loves you." Jonathon lowered his voice. "We all love you."

Eliza did not want to spend another moment thinking about that ill-fated night in France. She had long ago separated her life as Lady Elizabeth from the necessary actions of agent *Shadow*. That was the only way she could cope with the killing that was so often required of her.

Taking a deep breath, she forced her face into an expressionless mask. "We should go, Jonathon. We have a job to do." She spun on her heels and started down the stairs.

Jonathon did not move. He could tell that Eliza was hurting, but she refused to confide in him as she once had. He was her brother, her partner, her best friend... but she had begun to withdraw from him after that mission in France. Something had happened, something that had drastically altered his sister.

Mr. Larson had been with them in France, but he also refused to divulge any details about that night. In fact, it had surprised Jonathan that Mr. Larson had even mentioned her dreams, as he was fiercely loyal to her. What could have alarmed such an experienced agent?

Jonathon watched his sister descend the stairs. He loved working with Eliza. If he had to be honest, he would acknowledge that his sister was the best agent working for the Crown.

Her peculiar mind allowed her to piece together information and decipher enemy codes faster than any agent he had ever seen. She could shoot a pistol, wield a sword, and throw a dagger with deadly accuracy. Her skill with the dagger was only surpassed by her skill with the longbow, and that skill had saved many agents' lives, including his own.

Yet Eliza had grown distant of late, and her smile did not reach her eyes anymore. She always claimed she was fine, but he knew it was an act. Jonathon forced a smile of his own and started down the stairs to catch up with his sister. He had a plan to help her, and it was time to put that plan into action.

Chapter Two

$\mathcal{B}$enedict, the Earl of Sinclair, was bored. He chuckled to himself as even he recognized the irony that he was bored. He was leaning against an ornate white pillar drinking a glass of champagne in Lord Vernon's ballroom, observing the candle sconces that illuminated the cream walls with gold embellishments. Large floor-to-ceiling windows ran the length of the ballroom and two oversized doors opened to a well-manicured courtyard.

At any point, he could end his self-imposed boredom by playing cards upstairs or dancing with one of the ladies that continually glanced his way, but he preferred to be alone. Lord Vernon's ballroom was so blasted hot even with the doors wide open. Benedict decided to step outside and take advantage of the cool night air, as he placed his glass onto the tray of a passing servant.

Walking out into the lighted courtyard, he found a bench towards the back of the garden. He sat down and placed his elbows on his knees. He was vaguely aware of the soft music drifting out of the ballroom. This wasn't supposed to be his life, it was supposed to be his brother's life. Benedict was supposed to live the quiet life as the second son of the Marquess of Lansdowne. Rubbing the back of his neck with his hand, he grimaced. *Well, the quiet life of a spy.*

Oh, how desperately he missed his brother, Henry. Benedict was gone for months on end for his work as an agent of the Crown, but when he came home, he spent all his time with Henry. In the morning, they would tour their lands and meet with the tenants. More times than not, they found themselves working alongside their tenants to repair roofs, build fences, or tend to the elderly. If there was remaining time in the day, they would fence until they collapsed from exhaustion. Although, he always found time to harass his brother about the new lady that caught his fancy. He smiled fondly as he thought of his brother.

Then his smile faltered as Benedict dropped his head in shame. Six months ago, he received a letter from his father informing him that Henry was dead, and he was now the heir. His father told him to report home immediately and take his rightful place as the Earl of Sinclair. It was all business with his father, the Marquess of Lansdowne. Well, to be fair to his father, he wanted to settle his estate since he had taken ill.

After he received the letter, he chose to ignore Father's summons. He did not want to go back to his ancestral home, Chatsworth Manor. How could he go home to an estate without Henry? How could he go riding on their lands without Henry? Most importantly, how could he take over for Henry, without being reminded daily that he was replacing his brother?

In the end, it did not matter. A month ago, he was injured on a mission, forcing him home to recover. His mission involved following an English merchant ship to France that had abducted fifteen women off the streets with plans to sell them to the highest bidder, supposedly a brothel. Five agents were assigned to board the ship and rescue the women. It was supposed to be an easy mission, but it quickly turned deadly.

Without realizing it, he rubbed his right leg where he had been stabbed. He had been attacked from the side, and he did not even have a chance to defend himself. The sailor stabbed him in his right thigh and was getting ready to plunge the knife into his chest, when he just collapsed on top of him. Fortunately, an agent, code name *Shadow*, had been providing support from a nearby rooftop, and saved him by shooting an arrow into the sailor's back.

Benedict acknowledged he had been given a second chance at life, and he was going to make the best of it. His father was dying, and soon he would be the Marquess of Lansdowne. As he reviewed the accounts and ledgers of each of his seven estates, he was astonished at how much wealth his family had obtained. Father had done an impressive job of increasing their wealth and holdings over the years. Now, it was his turn to continue the family legacy.

However, it was not the life he wanted. He wished to remain an agent of the Crown. He was grateful that Lord Charles Beckett agreed to let him pursue one more mission before he had to retire, now that he was the heir to his father.

His mission was to gather proof against his stepbrother, Aaron Wade, for the murder of Henry. Benedict knew Aaron had a hand in Henry's death, but he needed to prove it. He would gather proof and then see his stepbrother hanged for his crime.

Rising from the bench, he straightened his black coat. As he was approaching the refreshment table, he heard Lord Jonathon Beckett's voice over the crowd. He turned towards the sound of his friend's voice and noticed that Jonathon was talking to a small group of men.

He broke through the group as Jonathon was saying, "…so then my sister decided that it would be easier to catch frogs with her pillowcase." The group of men started laughing and Benedict assumed that the story must be about Jonathon's younger sister, Eliza, since she always did the most amusing things. His friend used to read her letters aloud to him when they were at Oxford.

Before Lord Jonathon continued with the story, he stopped and glanced over at Benedict. "Lord Sinclair, is that you?" Jonathon's face broke out into a huge smile and embraced him. "I haven't seen you in years. How are you?"

Benedict smiled, because he had just accompanied Jonathon last month on a mission in France, but they must be discreet. "I'm doing well. I see that your sister is up to her usual tricks," he said good-naturedly.

Jonathon laughed. "No, I am sharing the story of when Eliza read a book about how frogs could be used for medicinal purposes."

Chuckling, Benedict rubbed his chin knowingly "Ah. If I remember correctly, that was when she was fifteen." Jonathon nodded and then quickly provided introductions to the group.

Suddenly the group parted, and the most beautiful woman Benedict had ever seen slid in, and placed her hand into the crook of Jonathon's arm. She was dressed in a beautiful gold gown that hugged her curves perfectly, and sparkled red when the light reflected off the bodice.

When she turned towards him, her green eyes latched onto his, and for the briefest of seconds, time stood still. She seemed oddly familiar to him, but he was certain he had never seen her before. As they proceeded to gaze at each other, he heard Jonathon discreetly clear his throat, and she averted her eyes.

The loss of her gaze seemed to pierce his very soul, and Benedict could not deny the instant connection he felt towards her. He found himself longing to learn all that he could about this young woman.

Jonathon provided the introduction. "Lord Sinclair, may I introduce you to my sister, Lady Elizabeth Beckett." She gave him a slight curtsy.

Benedict was shocked to discover that this enchanting young woman was Jonathon's adventure-seeking sister. His years of etiquette training kicked in, and he executed a perfect bow. "It is a pleasure to finally meet you, Lady Elizabeth."

She raised an eyebrow. "Why would you be finally meeting me?"

Jonathon spoke up. "I used to read your letters aloud to Lord Sinclair when we were at Oxford." Glancing at her, he grinned. "The situations you got yourself into were quite hilarious, and I just had to share it with my roommate."

Her lips curled downward in a frown of displeasure. "Lord Sinclair, I apologize that you were subjected to learn about the adventures of my youth. I did not realize Jonathon was reading my letters to other people."

Benedict did the one thing that would make this situation worse. He laughed. "I am sorry, Lady Elizabeth, but your adventures were quite humorous." He held up one finger. "First, I recall you somehow managed to burn a barn down during a rainstorm." He held up another finger. "Secondly, you tried to train a donkey to do tricks." He held up his third finger. "Then, you made wings out of your bed linens so you could fly out of your second story window." He held up a fourth finger. "And lastly, you tried to make your own perfume and your estate had to be evacuated."

Bending over with laughter, Benedict realized that Jonathon and the rest of the men were laughing, as well. The only person that was not laughing was Lady Elizabeth. In fact, she did not look pleased by the memories that he shared.

She squared her shoulders and spoke over the laughter. "First of all, the burning of the barn was when I was fourteen, and I knocked over a candle in the barn while I was reading. All the other ideas came from books that I had just read."

Benedict stopped laughing, but his eyes still twinkled with merriment. "I'm sorry, my lady, but I really did love hearing about your adventures. You were like a breath of fresh air."

Visibly relaxing, she returned his smile. "I am glad that I could amuse you, my lord."

Another dance started and the men in the group left to claim their dance partners. Benedict looked around to see who would claim her for a dance, and when no one appeared, he asked, "Do you not have a dance partner for this set, Lady Elizabeth?"

She glanced at her brother, and he shrugged. Benedict did not know what was being communicated between them. Her gaze flickered back to him. "Jonathon and I were sitting this dance out. We are anxiously awaiting Lord Vernon's announcement."

"You are anxiously awaiting Lord Vernon's announcement that his selfish, thirty-four-year-old son has agreed to an arranged marriage?" he said sarcastically.

"Of course, Lord Sinclair." Her eyes danced with amusement as she leaned in towards him, with her hand at her mouth like she intended to tell him a secret. "As Socrates said, 'By all means, marry. If you get a good wife, you'll become happy; if you get a bad one, you'll become a philosopher.' So, in a few years we will see if Lord Vernon's son becomes a philosopher." Eliza smiled and leaned back.

Benedict chuckled. "I will look forward to that discovery."

Her smile became strained but stayed in place. "I do pity the recipients of an arranged marriage. Marriage should be based on love, not business."

Nodding, Benedict agreed. "Although, my parents started in an arranged marriage, and they eventually evolved it into a love match."

Smiling sadly, Lady Elizabeth glanced towards the dancers briefly. "The majority of arranged marriages that I know of have not gone well, and I would prefer to marry a man I love *before* we marry."

"People in our stations tend not to marry for love, but there are exceptions." He reached for her gloved hand and brought it up to his lips for a kiss. "The course of true love never did run smooth."

She flashed him a brilliant smile. "You are familiar with William Shakespeare."

Benedict puffed out his chest at her reaction. He would continue to quote Shakespeare if she would continue smiling at him like that. He needed to release her hand but found he did not want to, so he said the next best thing. "Since I am already holding your hand, may I escort you to the dance floor?" A corner of his mouth quirked up. "Unless you really are trying to secure good spots for Lord Vernon's announcement?"

Jonathon let out a bark of laughter, but covered his mouth with his hand. "Eliza, go dance with Lord Sinclair. I will be right here when you get back."

She allowed Benedict to escort her to the dance floor where the music had already begun. When they reached the other dancers, he placed his hand on her waist and started leading Elizabeth in the waltz. He noticed that she seemed to stiffen when she put her hand on his shoulder.

"I hope I did not embarrass you back there with your brother. I just find it refreshing to hear that other people believe that love is a requirement for marriage," he said while trying to engage her in another conversation.

Elizabeth observed him almost as if trying to gauge his sincerity. "Sadly, I do not have a favorable opinion of marriage." Her eyes then refused to land on his face. "It is common knowledge that my father lives with his mistress, Lady Anne, and my mother just recently found a new man to entertain her during the Season." Benedict's eyes grew wide as he realized the implications.

While he was trying to think of something to say, Elizabeth spoke up again. "Some of my friends are in arranged marriages and none of them are happy. A few of their husbands even refused to give up their mistresses after the wedding. My twin sister Katherine is married to a cruel man, but it is all right, because he is a wealthy earl," she said with thinly veiled contempt.

He heard what she said, but had to address the most interesting piece of information she had revealed. "You have a twin sister?"

"Yes, but we are no longer close," she said, her voice drifting off.

Benedict realized he needed to refocus the conversation, or this dance was not going to end well. "I'm sorry about your friends and your sister. A wife should be cherished, loved above all else," he said deliberately.

He noticed that he had Lady Elizabeth's full attention again. As his eyes roamed her expressive face, he marveled at her lovely olive skin, with a light sprinkling of freckles on her nose. Her alluring lips curved upward at the corners, almost begging to be kissed. Still, her best feature was her wide, mesmerizing green eyes as they gleamed with cleverness, and perhaps, adventure.

"May I call on you tomorrow?" He realized he had asked her a question when she started shaking her head no.

"I apologize, but I do not receive callers anymore," she said while glancing in the direction of her brother.

Benedict decided to change tactics. "Then I will call on Jonathon tomorrow and hope that you are home." He gave her a charming smile that he knew worked on the ladies. Lady Elizabeth's eyes landed on his smile and she quickly looked away. Her cheeks were turning pink and it appeared that she was blushing.

"I do not live with Jonathon anymore," she said softly.

"Where do you live then?" Benedict pressed. He realized that the song was almost concluded, and he needed to secure where she lived quickly.

Lady Elizabeth stopped the dance by dropping her hands from him as she stepped back. "Thank you for the dance, Lord Sinclair."

She bobbed a curtsy to him and spun around before he could formulate a response. She quickly but gracefully walked to her brother and grabbed his arm. They walked off towards the ballroom's exit.

He was left staring at the retreating figures. Why would the question of where she lived have unnerved her? He would call on Jonathon tomorrow and figure out where his sister lived. Benedict laughed to himself. Maybe he should bring flowers to Jonathon? After all, he wouldn't want to disappoint him.

Chapter Three

$\mathcal{J}$onathon noticed that Eliza was walking towards him with a determined stride. She appeared to be deep in thought by her furrowed brow, then her blazing green eyes latched onto him. She forcefully placed her hand in the crook of his arm and led him towards the ballroom exit.

"So, how was the dance with Lord Sinclair?" Jonathon prodded with humor in his voice.

Eliza's eyes flickered to him then straight ahead again. "I made a mistake," she mumbled. Jonathon was intrigued, because his sister rarely made mistakes. He hoped by staying silent she would continue her confession. He did not have to wait long. "I told him I did not live with you."

Jonathon stopped abruptly which caused her to drop his arm. "You told Benedict about Beaumont Castle?" he asked in a hushed tone. Not even the family knew that Eliza had bought Beaumont Castle and had spent the last couple of years restoring it to its former glory.

She rolled her eyes. "No, of course not. I just told him that I did not reside with you anymore."

"Why would you just announce that you do not live with me anymore?" Jonathon pressed. How did his friend gain her confidence so soon?

Eliza opened her mouth then shut it without revealing anything. She put her hand on her hip. "Lord Sinclair asked if he could call on me tomorrow, and I told him I did not receive callers anymore. He just kept smiling at me, so I confessed I did not live with you." Jonathon had to strain to hear what she said. She started chewing on her bottom lip, which he knew his sister only did when she was deep in thought or distressed.

It was obvious that his friend had unnerved her. As much as he wanted to tease her, he needed to calm her down. They still had to sneak into Lord Vernon's study, and she needed all her wits about her. Jonathon placed his hands onto her shoulders.

"I will talk to Benedict and ask him to keep our living arrangement to himself. You can trust him, Eliza."

She looked hesitant but mumbled her thanks. Jonathon dropped his arms, and Eliza started walking towards Lord Vernon's office without even checking to see if he was behind her. Jonathon chuckled. *Oh yes, this will be fun to watch*, he thought, as he quickened his stride to catch up to his sister.

Lady Eliza kept shaking her head and thinking about what a fool she had been. How could she have told Lord Sinclair that she did not live with Jonathon? Even her father was not aware that she lived at her own place!

When she gazed into Benedict's dark blue eyes, she felt an unfamiliar feeling of complete trust. His eyes were so inviting, almost encouraging her to reveal all her secrets, so she told him that she did not live with her brother. She could have lied, but she did not feel impressed to lie to him. Well, at least she did not tell him where she lived. That would have been a huge mistake. Besides, Jonathon would talk to Benedict and tell him to keep her living arrangement undisclosed.

Why did he have to be so dashingly handsome? There should be a law preventing men from being that good looking. Eliza blushed as she remembered placing her hand on his broad, muscular shoulder during their dance. Benedict's dark brown hair was cut fashionably short with long sideburns which led down to a masculine, square jaw. Her mind jumped to daydreaming about what his firm lips would feel like pressed against hers. "What is wrong with me?" she mumbled under her breath.

"What was that, Eliza?" Jonathon asked from somewhere behind her.

She stopped short and Jonathon ran into her. She had forgotten about her brother following her. Eliza shook her head. She needed to play a part tonight, and a smitten girl was not the role. She took a deep breath and cleared her mind of Lord Sinclair, and his tall, muscular body. Ultimately, it took her a few deep breaths before she cleared her mind. Now she was ready to be a spy again.

"I am ready," Eliza stated as she looked around the corner to confirm the hallway was clear, minus the footman guarding the study door. "Lord Vernon's office is around the corner."

"Are you sure that is his study?" Jonathon asked.

"Yes. I paid a parlor maid to tell me where the study was," she replied. She pulled a guinea out of her reticule and closed her hand around it. "Let's go, my roguish brother," Eliza teased.

She elevated her voice to make sure the tall, liveried footman could hear every word. "I cannot believe you were dancing with her! Do you know what Father would say if he saw you even talking to her? You have a betrothal agreement with a nice girl from Bath. What would she think of your behavior?" Eliza acted like she was fuming at Jonathon. Her voice was echoing through the wide hallway that housed the family portraits, but not enough to attract attention from the other guests.

She had to grip Jonathon tightly as he started to sway back and forth. "H-h-h-heeeey! I think my fiancéeee... would be pleased that I got my flirting out of the way before we walk down the aisle, don't ya?" Jonathon asked while slurring his words and grinning like a drunken fool.

Rolling her eyes in mock disgust, she guided him till they were standing close to the footman. Eliza gave the footman an apological smile. "Sir, do you have a place that I can lecture my brother about propriety in private? I would hate to make a scene and take any attention away from your master's ball." She tried to look as embarrassed as possible as she pretended to plead with the footman. "My brother is inebriated, and I am afraid his voice will carry when we start discussing his behavior. We would make haste and depart, but my mother is refusing to leave until after the announcement." Eliza rambled on to give the impression she was nervous. "Please sir, I do not know what else to do." Furrowing her brow, she reached out to hand the footman the gold coin.

The footman gasped when he saw the guinea she handed him. He immediately deposited it in his pocket and looked up and down the hallway to confirm there were no witnesses to what he was about to do. The footman procured a key from the same pocket and quickly unlocked the door.

He stepped aside, so they could walk in and loudly whispered, "You have five minutes. Please lower your voices, or we will be discovered."

Slowly closing the door, she mouthed, "Thank you." Nodding, he gave her a sympathetic smile.

Eliza briefly took in her surroundings. With drapes drawn open, the moonlight illuminated the middle of the room where the large mahogany desk was sitting. She quickly went to the front of the desk and quietly started to open all the drawers.

They still had to convince the footman that they were in a family dispute, so she loudly said, "Do you know how angry Father will be if you do anything that would break the betrothal agreement?"

She hoped that Jonathon would take up the conversation from there while she focused on rifling through all the paperwork in the desk drawers. Right on cue, Jonathan started ranting about how he could oversee his own life and no one, not even Mother or Father, would force him into a life he did not want. Eliza stopped listening to Jonathon and focused on her task at hand.

As she was rummaging through the documents in the desk, she found nothing to tie Lord Vernon to Mr. Wade. She found many accounts and ledgers, but it was not what she was looking for. She needed to find an inventory list or something to imply he could be an investor of Mr. Wade's ships. Eliza kept rifling through papers. She only had a few minutes left before the footman would discreetly ask them to leave and to take their argument elsewhere.

Eliza decided to see if Lord Vernon had a secret compartment in the bottom drawers of the desk. She knocked on the bottom panel of the right drawer, and it sounded hollow. There was a false bottom! She grabbed the gold letter opener from the top of the desk and forced it between the bottom and the side of the interior desk drawer. She slowly forced the false panel up.

In the hollow area, there were a few sheets of paper. Grabbing the documents, she read them with haste. When she finished absorbing all the information, she placed them back in the hollow part of the desk and lowered the panel. She made sure each paper was put back exactly where it had been, as if undisturbed.

Eliza signaled to Jonathon that she was done. She walked over and raised her voice to be heard over Jonathon's ranting. "Mother will be ready to go now."

She quickly opened the door and observed the footman who was still standing guard. He looked up and down the hall and motioned for them to come out of the study. Eliza gave him a hesitant smile. "Thank you, sir. You have been most helpful."

Grabbing Jonathon's arm, Eliza pulled him forward out into the hallway. Jonathon swayed back and forth and was mumbling something about how he didn't care about his inheritance anymore. They would stop the farce as soon as they rounded the corner. She wanted to ensure the footman would have no doubts about why they went into the study.

As they turned the corner, she released her grip on Jonathon's arm and ran straight into a wall. Wait, no, it was a man's chest. She tilted her head up and realized she had run into Lord Sinclair. *How did I not see him?*

His arms came up and steadied her. "I apologize, Lady Elizabeth. I did not expect anyone to come around the corner."

Eliza blushed as she realized his hands were lingering on her arms. "No harm done, my lord. We were looking at the family portraits in the next hallway."

Lord Sinclair lowered his hands from her arms and gave her a crooked smile. "I'm surprised you were looking at the family portraits when earlier you seemed overjoyed to hear Lord Vernon's announcement." He had a mischievous twinkle in his eyes as he awaited her answer.

Placing her hand on Benedict's arm, Eliza quirked a smile up at him. "I must have left quite an impression on you if you remembered our previous conversation so well." She winked at him and his eyebrows shot up presumably at her brazenness.

As she started walking away, she heard him clear his throat as he gently grabbed her arm to stop her departure. He leaned down and whispered in her ear, "Rest assured, you definitely have left quite an impression on me."

His breath tickled her skin, and she found she was having difficulty concentrating on his words. In fact, she was so distracted by Benedict's nearness that she seemed to have lost all rational thought.

The cause of her distraction straightened and dropped his hand from her arm, then started to walk down the hallway they had just vacated. Jonathon caught his arm and whispered something to him as Benedict's eyes darted to Eliza. Jonathon slapped him on the back and walked over to his sister to offer his arm. Benedict ducked his head and disappeared around the corner.

"What was that all about?" Eliza glanced behind her shoulder to see if he would suddenly reappear.

Jonathon shrugged. "Benedict is planning on searching Lord Vernon's study. I told him we found everything that we needed, but if he wanted to continue searching, then there was a secret compartment in the bottom desk drawer on the right."

"He is an agent of the Crown?" Eliza asked.

Jonathon nodded in the affirmative. "We have gone on a few missions together. He is a good agent."

"Intriguing," she muttered.

Eliza realized that she was still smiling as they waited in the line for their carriage to take them back to Jonathon's townhouse.

Chapter Four

Eliza woke up to the drapes in her room being thrown open and sunlight flooding in. She grabbed a pillow and threw it over her face. She had stayed up till early morning recreating the papers that she saw in Lord Vernon's study. She left them on the front table with a note to send to Lord Charles Beckett's office at first light.

"Good morning, Lady Eliza," Martha said in cheerful voice. "Your brother is waiting for you in the dining room. He received a note telling you that Lord Beckett is expecting you at his office at two this afternoon."

Throwing the pillow off her face, she rolled out of bed. Her white lace overlay, high-waisted afternoon dress was laid neatly over the settee. She stood and began the usual ritual of donning the attire laid out for her, with Martha assisting her with all the buttons up the back of her dress. Then, Martha manipulated her hair up in a simple, but stylish chignon. The finishing touches left ringlets framing the sides of Eliza's face.

"How was the ball, my lady? You made no mention of it when you returned home last night," Martha asked as she finished Eliza's hair and stepped back to admire her handiwork.

Eliza turned in her chair to look at Martha. "The ball was very…" she hesitated. "It was unexpected."

Martha's lips curled up knowingly. "You met someone."

"I met lots of people last night," Eliza said nonchalantly. "I did get introduced to Lord Sinclair who was Jonathon's roommate at Oxford." She started rubbing her favorite rose-scented cream on her hands as she tried to distract Martha from this line of interrogation. "I should hurry if I want to have a chance to eat something before we depart to see Uncle Charles."

"Is he handsome?"

Eliza's thoughts started betraying her as she remembered her body tingling when he whispered in her ear. She thought of his dark blue eyes and how they seemed to captivate her. She realized that Martha was still awaiting her answer. "I suppose, in a rugged sort of way," she admitted.

Martha started giggling. "You are blushing like a brand-new debutante. He must have left quite an impression on you."

Eliza decided to confide her feelings in her friend. "I felt this instant connection with him. It was as if I have known him for years and not just a few hours," she said. "It was all so confusing." She grabbed Martha's hands. "And when he spoke to me, I felt like the most important person in the world."

Martha smiled and patted her hands. "He sounds wonderful."

Retrieving her kid gloves from the table, Eliza remarked, "Oh, and he is also an agent." Her voice was casual, even though it was a very important fact.

Martha's head jerked up as she picked up Eliza's discarded nightgown from the bed. "He is?"

"Yes, but I probably will not see him again," Eliza said honestly.

"Why not?" Martha pressed.

"Well, Jonathon told me that Lord Sinclair is the future Marquess of Lansdown, and he must retire as an agent since Uncle Charles does not allow heirs to work for the crown," Eliza informed her.

"I think you would make a lovely marchioness," Martha teased.

Eliza let out an amused laugh. "I admit that he is undeniably handsome, but that is all there is to it. I have no intention of pursuing a relationship with him, or anyone."

Martha pursed her lips disapprovingly. "That is a shame."

Seeing Martha's disappointment in her, Eliza defended her position. "I know you think I should be more open to marriage, but I have a great life. I am a spy and no one dictates what I can and cannot do. Why would I give that up?"

Martha lowered herself down on the settee. "I just want you to be happy."

Eliza waved off her concern. "I am perfectly content," she lied, as Martha frowned at her response. "Besides, I do not think I could ever fully share the details of my past to anyone," she said adamantly. Eliza knew she had done too many horrible things, and she killed too many men to think she could ever lead a normal life as a wife and mother.

Martha gave her sympathetic smile. "You will when the right man comes along."

"I used to think that way, but now I am more realistic," Eliza said while walking to her bed. "Regardless, if I ever told Lord Sinclair about slitting that man's throat in France, he would look at me with utter disgust."

Martha sighed in frustration. "And why would you think that?"

"Because I look at myself like that," Eliza replied honestly, as she reached for the dagger from under her pillow and placed her foot up on the settee next to Martha. She strapped her dagger to her right thigh and shoved her dress down.

"You did nothing wrong. I wish you would stop blaming yourself…" Martha started.

Eliza put her hand up. "I do not want to discuss it."

Martha frowned. "You never want to discuss that night. That is part of the problem. I wish you would confide in someone else about what happened."

Eliza started pacing in front of Martha as she tried to displace her frustration over this topic. "And what would I say? That I remember every sight and smell associated with that night in France? Or that sometimes I hear a noise, and it takes me back to the moment right after I slit that man's throat, when my hands were covered in blood?" She stopped pacing and met Martha's gaze. "I know, I should mention that I have not felt truly safe since I left that rooftop."

Arising from the chair, Martha embraced Eliza. "I'm sorry. I wish there was a way I could help you."

"You are helping me by being my friend." Eliza allowed herself to be embraced then she turned to walk out the door. She stopped and slowly turned around to face her maid and friend.

She hesitated before she asked, "Do you honestly believe that a man could overlook all that I have done, and still love me?"

Martha nodded. "Yes, the right man would."

Eliza offered up a halfhearted smile and hurried down to the dining room to join her brother for breakfast.

Jonathon lowered his paper as his sister glided into the room.

"Good morning, Jonathon," Eliza said as one of the footman held out a chair for her. The footman pushed in her chair as another footman brought her a plate with some eggs, bacon, and a pastry.

"Is it still considered morning?" he asked jokingly. "Did Martha tell you that we need to leave soon to see Uncle Charles?"

Eliza picked up her fork. "Yes, I will be ready to depart after I eat. After meeting with Uncle Charles, I was going to head back to Beaumont Castle. Martha is packing up my trunk and Mr. Larson is making the necessary preparations. Do you mind if we use your carriage to travel home?"

Jonathon waved his hand as if dismissing the notion. "Of course, you can instruct the driver to take you to Beaumont Castle. I will rent a hackney if need be."

He returned to reading the newspaper while his sister took a few minutes to enjoy breakfast. When she was finished, she wiped her mouth with her napkin. "Did you have a chance to review the documents before they were sent to Uncle Charles?"

Jonathon put the newspaper down and gave Eliza his full attention. "No, I did not. I only woke up a short bit ago myself."

Eliza started listing what she discovered by reading the papers. "The first paper was an inventory list for Mr. Wade's ship, the *Deceiver*. Most of the items that were listed are quite common commodities and nothing that would cause suspicion. Although, half way down the list there was a line item of the number twenty-six."

"Twenty-six?" Jonathon repeated back.

"Yes, twenty-six."

"Twenty-six what?"

"Since we know that we are dealing with Mr. Wade, I suspect it means twenty-six girls." Eliza did not think that this number was an error on the inventory list, because every other item was clearly outlined.

"That is impossible. Mr. Wade has never taken that many girls at one time, it would be too risky. Where would he even stash them before setting sail? His normal pattern is taking ten to fifteen girls at a time, and he only takes girls that could go missing without too many inquiries." Jonathon leaned back in his chair.

Eliza took a moment to ponder what Jonathon said. "I agree with you, but Mr. Wade is getting bolder. We have already freed fifty-seven girls that he had abducted or bought from someone else." She stopped her train of thought and shuddered. *Who would sell a loved one to a life worse than death?* Taking a moment to compose herself, she continued. "He might decide that trying to sell ten or fifteen girls at a time is not working. If he can abduct twenty-six girls, then that is a huge profit for him."

Jonathon grabbed the newspaper and started rifling through the sections as if he was searching for something. He landed on a page towards the back, then he folded the previous pages behind it, and leapt out of his chair. He walked over and leaned against the table next to Eliza and extended the paper towards her. "This article is about how fourteen girls have been reported missing. When the first few girls were reported missing, the magistrate did not take it seriously since it was assumed the girls ran off to get married."

Eliza perused the article and realized that all these girls came from respected families. They would not have been reported missing if they ran off to get married. It would have created too much scandal for the families. "Someone is targeting aristocratic families. It must be Mr. Wade, but that would be quite the stretch for him. Poor girls go missing all the time from the slums, and no one seems to care, but kidnapping daughters of the peerage is extremely risky," she stated.

Jonathon nodded. "Right now, the number of abducted girls is fourteen. If our theory holds true, then Mr. Wade must abduct twelve more girls." Jonathon reached for the newspaper from Eliza. "Did it say how these girls were abducted?"

Eliza did not have to check before answering. "Yes, they were abducted off the street while they were shopping. Witnesses reported the girls were thrown into a waiting black carriage, but they were inconsistent on their descriptions of the assailants. In all cases, the girls were only accompanied by their lady's maid." She made a mental note to carry her overcoat pistol with her when she went to visit her modiste, Madam Lanchester. "The article did suggest Ladies take extra precautions when leaving their homes and to take along extra footmen if possible."

Jonathon put the newspaper down and walked over to the window. Eliza wanted to continue discussing the papers that she found last night. "If there truly are twenty-six abducted girls, then we have time. The documents stated the *Deceiver* is not scheduled to set sail for three weeks. The map that I found had a coastal city in France circled that I believe is the rendezvous point for the ship. If our thesis is correct, we can try to stop the ship before it even leaves England. If not, we can talk to the French ambassador for permission to board the ship when it arrives in France. Monsieur LeBlanc is very helpful with these types of missions." Eliza smiled when thinking of her French friend.

Laughing, Jonathon turned towards his sister. "Monsieur LeBlanc," he stated sarcastically, "is only helpful because he is in love with you."

Eliza blushed at the memory of Monsieur LeBlanc's blatant flirting attempts. "He is a nice man and has made no inappropriate advances towards me."

She decided not to tell Jonathon the full truth of what had transpired the last time she had seen the French ambassador. Monsieur LeBlanc had declared his undying love for her and proposed marriage. She had graciously turned him down and Monsieur LeBlanc claimed he would wait for her to change her mind. It had been over a month since she had seen him, so she assumed he had directed his undying love towards another eligible lady.

Looking up, Eliza saw her brother smirking at her. She just shrugged because there was no use in denying Monsieur LeBlanc's feelings. Jonathon laughed. Eliza arose from the table, but she wasn't finished talking about the mission.

"The last paper in Lord Vernon's desk was a list of expenses that he was responsible for. On the top of the page it listed a solicitor, a Mr. Paul Warner. This is not the same solicitor that Mr. Wade has used before. I want to break into Mr. Warner's office and see if we can find any more investors for the *Deceiver*."

"Need I remind you that Wade's last solicitor was pulled from the River Thames a few weeks ago?"

Eliza pursed her lips. "We do not know for sure that our searches in Mr. Mundy's office led to his death."

"He did die shortly after we arrived back from France," Jonathon pointed out as he came around the table.

"True, but he had to know the moment he affixed his business with Mr. Wade that he signed his own death warrant," she said with a shake of her head. She was genuinely baffled by anyone who would willingly choose to work for Mr. Wade, since he was not one to leave any loose ends.

"Let us go see Uncle Charles. I think a night time trip to Warner's office would be a grand idea, but first we need to update our uncle."

Walking to the grand entryway, Eliza reached for her thatched straw hat, which was turned up in the front and lined in pink lace. After securing the hat on her head, she headed to the waiting carriage with Jonathon following behind.

Chapter Five

Jonathon's carriage pulled up in front of a nondescript, two-story white brick building on the outskirts of the fashionable part of town. The building appeared to be run down and in dire need of a paint job. A few raggedy looking men were loitering outside, but Eliza was acquainted with them and knew their real identity. They were agents assigned to protect the building.

They were met inside by a well-groomed young man who greeted them from behind a desk. The young man, who was obviously new since they didn't recognize him, did not rise, but calmly waited for them to approach the desk with only one hand visible. His other hand was presumably under the desk holding a pistol, in case he encountered any type of danger. Anytime someone walked into the building, all the agents were on full alert.

Jonathon smiled in his carefree manner as he announced, "Lord Jonathon Beckett and Lady Elizabeth Beckett to see Lord Charles Beckett."

The young man visibly relaxed and stood up with a pistol in his right hand, confirming Eliza's instinct. "Lord Charles Beckett is expecting you. Please, follow me."

They followed the young man up the stairs which fed into a large open room with small offices along the walls. They passed through and into a corridor that led to the imposing red door of Lord Beckett's office.

A balding receptionist sitting at his desk saw them approach, and Eliza smiled tenderly at her uncle's loyal assistant, Mr. Frank Weber. "Lord Beckett has been anxious for you to arrive."

"How do you do, Mr. Weber?" she asked politely.

"I am well, Lady Elizabeth," Mr. Weber said, smiling brightly.

"That is good to hear." Eliza returned the smile as they were ushered into the office and Mr. Weber closed the door behind him.

Lord Charles Beckett was in the middle of writing something and kept his head down. He pointed his finger up to indicate he needed a minute. Once he was done, he put the feather quill down and stood.

"It is good to see both of you." He moved around the massive oak desk, and gave Eliza a kiss on the cheek. He indicated that they should sit at two of the upholstered chairs that sat against the wall nearby. Returning to his chair, he sat down. "I received the papers that you sent over this morning. What are your thoughts?"

Eliza smiled lovingly at her tall, distinguished-looking uncle who still boasted a full head of auburn hair, neatly waxed into position. Her favorite thing about her uncle was that he wasn't one to waste time with idle chitchat.

Jonathon jumped right in. "We believe that the number twenty-six on the inventory list is actually the number of women that Mr. Wade is currently in the process of abducting." Jonathon then spent the next few minutes filling him in on what they discussed earlier in the dining room.

Uncle Charles sat quietly for a minute, then bobbed his head in agreement. "I concur. I have had a few agents trying to figure out who was abducting those girls. I will give them your assessment and see if we can start building proof that Mr. Wade is behind this. Since we have a few weeks till the ship departs, I want to work on building a case on all the men that are helping to finance this nasty business of selling women."

"Or I can just kill Mr. Wade?" Eliza offered, hopefully.

Her uncle dropped his head and sighed loudly. "No, Eliza. We have been over this before. You cannot just kill a man in cold blood. We both know Aaron Wade has committed heinous crimes, but we need proof to bring him in. We cannot just make him disappear. That would cause too many questions." He leveled his stare at her. "Do not let your hatred of Mr. Wade cloud your judgement."

Eliza gave her uncle a slight nod acknowledging his advice. She did hate Mr. Wade. In fact, she loathed him after Martha shared the details of her abduction by him and her years of working in a brothel. How was it fair that he was walking the streets, when he had forced so many women into a living hell?

She had to admit that Mr. Wade was an exceptionally shrewd businessman. The Crown had previously seized possession of three of his ships, but he successfully proved that someone else had rented his brig's services and he had no knowledge of the crimes. Aaron Wade always seemed to manipulate his paperwork to implicate his business associates as the true criminals.

Uncle Charles seemed to accept her silence as confirmation that she would comply with his request. He gave Jonathon a side look. Eliza glanced between the two of them and grew suspicious. She suspected something was going on between them. Uncle Charles focused back on his niece. "I have decided to assign Jonathon to another case."

Uncle Charles extended a dossier to Jonathon while he explained the extent of his new mission. "Lord Pembrooke is the English ambassador to Spain. He has gone into hiding and no one knows where he is, but he claims he has documents that expose a high-ranking individual as a traitor. He managed to get a letter out, and it just made its way to my desk. His life has been threatened, and his concern is that someone may come after his daughter, Lady Hannah, to use as a bargaining chip. We will take Lady Hannah and place her into our protection. She is currently residing at her country home in Bath, and I want you to go and retrieve her immediately."

Jonathon nodded his head. "Consider it done."

Uncle Charles seemed pleased with Jonathon's answer, and his attention returned to Eliza. "I have decided to assign you a new partner, at least until Jonathon completes his new mission."

She arched an eyebrow in disbelief. "A new partner?" Jonathon had always been Eliza's partner from the moment she became an agent to the Crown.

Pressing forward, Uncle Charles added, "Yes, your new partner will be Lord Sinclair." He flickered his eyes towards Jonathon. "Are you familiar with him?"

"You want me to partner with Lord Sinclair?" Eliza asked hesitantly.

Jonathon must have mistaken her hesitation for apprehension about getting a new partner as he tried to reassure her. "Lord Sinclair is a good man, and as I told you before, you can trust him."

Eliza's instinct told her that she could trust Benedict, but it did not mean she wanted to be assigned his partner. "Why do I need to be assigned a new partner? I can bring in Mr. Wade on my own," she insisted.

Uncle Charles shook his head firmly. "No, I want you to have a partner. Lord Sinclair is one of my top agents and will ensure your safety."

"I can protect myself," she said adamantly.

"I know you can, but please appease me."

Eliza sighed. "May I ask why you selected Lord Sinclair as my partner?"

"Yes," Uncle Charles said as he intertwined his fingers together and rested them on the desk. "He strongly maintains that his stepbrother, Mr. Aaron Wade, had a hand in his brother's death. I have allowed him to pursue that investigation. Since then, he has started uncovering information that Mr. Wade has been using his ships for illegal activities. You both have been working on parallel investigations, and I feel that it would benefit everyone if you worked in partnership. I am confident that both of you can bring Mr. Wade to justice."

"As you wish," Eliza said, knowing it was a losing battle to refuse to partner with Benedict.

Uncle Charles nodded his approval. "Excellent." His face softened as he gazed at her, and she could see his eyes were filled with compassion towards her. "I want you to trust Lord Sinclair, Eliza. He is a good man, and he will never betray your trust. I would not partner you with anyone that I did not trust implicitly."

She was surprised by her uncle's comments about Lord Sinclair. He always urged her to trust no one, yet he just told her to trust this man completely. "Will you reveal my code name to him?" Eliza asked.

"Yes," Uncle Charles said.

Before she had a chance to respond, a loud knock interrupted the conversation. Mr. Weber opened the door and announced, "Lord Sinclair to see you, my lord."

Eliza reached up to smooth out her hair and straightened her hat. She saw from the corner of her eye that Jonathon was watching her.

He had the nerve to smile at her. She rolled her eyes at him, but then she took a moment to smooth out her dress.

Lord Sinclair was curious as to why Lord Charles Beckett had sent a messenger over to request his presence this afternoon. He was up most of the night trying to figure out the importance of the inventory list that he reviewed in Lord Vernon's office.

Who was he kidding? He was up most of the night thinking about Lady Elizabeth, or Eliza in his head. He kept thinking about how her gold dress clung to her body, displaying her delicate curves, and how she kept him on his toes throughout their conversation.

Once he was done with the meeting with Lord Beckett, he was planning to call on Jonathon's townhouse. With any luck, he might discern where Eliza lived within a few hours. He could not wait to see the surprise on her face when he called on her unexpectedly. He chuckled to himself.

Lord Sinclair walked into the open door and gave a slight bow to his chief. "It is good to see you, Lord Beckett."

The chief stood up from behind his desk. "It is good to see you too, Sinclair. It has been a few weeks." He tilted his hand towards two people sitting down. "I know you are familiar with Lord Jonathon, but have you met my niece, Lady Elizabeth?"

Benedict's head jerked around and he found himself locking eyes with Eliza. He was planning to tear the town apart to find out where she lived, yet here she was, in this office with him. The very woman who had dominated his thoughts now sat before him and raised an eyebrow as she waited for his response. Obviously, he had looked too long at the object of his desire.

"Yes, I was pleased to make Lady Elizabeth's acquaintance last night," he managed to say. Eliza put her fingers to her mouth to hide her smile. She seemed to be amused at his reaction to seeing her, but what was she doing in Lord Beckett's office?

Lord Beckett cleared his throat. "Excellent. Please have a seat." Benedict sat down in the chair next to Jonathon. "I want to get down to business." He looked over to his niece, then back to Benedict. "It appears that your stepbrother has abducted fourteen girls from aristocratic families, and we suspect he plans on abducting a total of twenty-six. Eliza and Jonathon believe that is what the line item of twenty-six meant on the inventory list." He picked up a paper on his desk and handed it to Benedict. "Do you recognize this list?"

Looking at the list, Benedict was shocked. He turned to Jonathon. "Did you go back in and take this out of the desk?" He was surprised that his friend would make such a basic mistake as leaving a trail.

Jonathon shook his head. "No, Eliza recreated it this morning. She remembered what was on the list and was able to recreate it."

Benedict shook his head. He had remembered a few of the commodities, especially the suspicious line item of twenty-six, and most of this list did look familiar, but how could anyone remember such an extensive amount of information perfectly? "That is impossible. There are over forty different line items of commodities. How do we know that she remembered all of them correctly?"

Lord Beckett, Jonathon and Eliza exchanged amused looks. Lord Charles Beckett spoke up first. "Lady Eliza has a very peculiar mind, and she remembers things easily. I have no doubt that she copied that inventory exactly as listed. Furthermore, she copied the map and the expense report." He handed over the two pages for him to review, "She concluded that Mr. Wade is using a new solicitor. The next step will be to break into Mr. Warner's office and try to find any paperwork on the *Deceiver.*"

Benedict was amazed at the papers. They were nearly perfect copies of the documents he read last night. How could someone recreate these from only looking at the papers for a few minutes? He looked over at Eliza and she seemed to be studying him for his reaction.

Clearing his throat to get Benedict's attention, Lord Beckett continued. "I have decided that you and Lady Eliza will be assigned as partners on this mission."

Benedict's eyebrows shot up. "Lady Elizabeth is an agent?" This piece of information confused him. "I was under the impression that the Crown did not employ female agents?"

Lord Beckett's eyes darted to his niece then landed back on

Benedict. "Technically, Lady Eliza is not an official agent. She is…" He hesitated before saying, "She is more of a consultant to the Crown."

"A consultant?" Benedict asked, still perplexed. What did a consultant do for the Crown? Then it dawned on him that Eliza must be his replacement, since he was about to retire. "Am I to train her then?"

Jonathan laughed loudly. "I think some training might suffice. What do you think, Eliza?"

Her mouth held a slight quirk. "What kind of training are you offering, Lord Sinclair?"

Benedict turned his full attention onto Eliza. "I know working as an agent sounds exciting, but have you considered all the risks that are associated with being an agent?"

She started laughing but threw up her hand to muffle the sound. Jonathon and Lord Beckett were also discreetly laughing. Lady Eliza managed to stop laughing at him and rewarded him with a brilliant smile. "I assure you that I am aware of the risks, my lord."

Benedict could not comprehend what was so amusing about this situation. Why was Lord Beckett allowing his niece to dabble in such dangerous work as spying? Stopping, he reevaluated his position. If he was to partner with Eliza, then he would be able to spend a lot of time with her. He could teach her how to shoot a pistol and throw a knife. It would put him in the perfect position to possibly court her in the future.

Yes, he would love to partner with her, then when she got bored he could go back to working on getting his stepbrother sent to Newgate. After all, it would only be a few days, maybe a week, till she realized how dangerous being a spy could be. "I think it is a grand idea to partner with Lady Elizabeth," Benedict announced.

Eliza had a surprised look on her face. "You do?"

"Yes, and I can also teach you how to defend yourself by shooting a pistol or throwing a knife." He spoke to her like talking to a young child that had no idea of the dangers behind these weapons.

Eliza's whole face lit up. "You would do that? You would teach me how to shoot a pistol, and throw a sharp pointed thing?"

Benedict puffed out his chest. "That is called a knife, and yes."

He would teach her anything if she kept smiling at him like that. He noticed that Jonathon was covering his mouth to hide his laughter. Was Jonathon laughing at him, or at his sister trying to be an agent?

Lord Beckett finally spoke up. "That is enough. If I understand your position correctly, you believe that Lady Eliza is training to be a new agent?" He was encouraged to continue when Benedict nodded his head. "I apologize for the confusion, but she has been an agent for quite some time."

"But I thought you said she was a consultant to the Crown?" he asked.

Lord Beckett nodded. "Yes, because the Crown does not allow Ladies to officially become agents."

"What exactly does a consultant to the Crown do that is different from being an agent?" Benedict saw Eliza from the corner of his eye, and it appeared that she looked amused by this question.

Jonathon spoke up. "A consultant actually does more for the Crown than a regular agent."

Benedict turned in his seat towards Jonathon. "What do you mean Lady Elizabeth does more than a regular agent?"

Lord Beckett's face took on a somber expression. He glanced at his niece and she nodded back at him, as if she was granting her permission for him to say something. "What I am about to reveal to you cannot be spoken of again. You are one of my top agents and having you partner with Lady Eliza is the greatest compliment I can give you." Lord Beckett's gaze bore into Benedict. "Lady Eliza's code name is *Shadow*."

Chapter Six

Eliza watched Lord Sinclair as a range of emotions skirted all over his face. After a few minutes, he finally spoke. "I do not believe it..." he said, his voice trailing off. Benedict glanced at her, and obviously did not see a glimpse of a spy in her, because his next words betrayed his thoughts. "Impossible. There is no way a woman could be *Shadow*." He had the nerve to turn to Jonathon, looking for confirmation.

Jonathon put his hands up in front of him. "Benedict, you need to stop making a fool of yourself. Eliza is *Shadow*."

Benedict raised his brow. "No, I do not believe it. There is no way Lady Elizabeth can be *Shadow*." He paused before stating, "*Shadow* knows twenty languages."

Eliza casually shrugged one shoulder. "I only know five."

Seeming to acknowledge her response by glancing her way, he continued with another fact. "*Shadow* has been known to crack foreign codes in less than a few minutes."

Eliza gave him an amused smile. "No, the shortest time it took me to crack a code was about five hours." She looked towards her Uncle Charles for confirmation, and he nodded back.

"*Shadow* has successfully pinpointed the location of French frigates just by looking at maps," Benedict said.

"That is not completely accurate. I did look at maps, but I created a simple mathematical algorithm to locate the frigates," Eliza volunteered.

"*Shadow* has written unbreakable codes for the War office," he rattled on.

Eliza's face lit up. "Now, that is accurate."

"*Shadow* has killed over one hundred men and is more of an assassin than an agent," Benedict stated firmly.

Feeling the blood drain from her face, she nevertheless met his gaze. "No. That number is not accurate," she said weakly.

Benedict continued to focus on her. "My apologies, Lady Elizabeth. I'm just repeating what I have heard about *Shadow.*"

"You can stop repeating what *other* people are saying," Jonathon growled.

Eliza took a deep breath before she addressed Benedict's concerns. "As I have stated, most of what you have heard about *Shadow* is not entirely accurate."

He directed his attention back to Lord Beckett. "If what you are saying is true about Lady Elizabeth being *Shadow*, then why do you need me to partner with her?"

Lord Beckett's lips were pressed together tightly for a moment and a muscle ticked in his jaw. Eliza could hear the irritation in his tone as he spoke. "Well, for many reasons actually. Normally, Lady Eliza partners with Lord Jonathon, but I assigned him to another mission. Since you and she have been working parallel investigations, I thought it was best to bring two of my best agents together. More importantly, I want to ensure that my niece has a partner that will protect her at all costs."

Benedict rubbed the back of his neck with his hand. "My lord, I do not know if this is a good idea. Is it even proper for me to partner with a female agent?"

Jonathon scoffed. "This is just for one assignment, Benedict."

Sensing his hesitation, Eliza decided she should try to reason with him. "Lord Sinclair," she ventured as she gave him her best smile, "we have a common interest in taking down your stepbrother. He is a vile, deceitful man, and I will not rest until he can be brought to justice, or killed."

"Eliza..." Uncle Charles' voice held a warning.

Eliza frowned at her uncle and turned back to Benedict. "I know I am not your typical agent, but I am good at what I do. So, I am asking you if you can overlook what you think you know about *Shadow* and partner with me?"

Benedict took a deep breath, but maintained his eye contact with her. "I don't know," he said hesitantly.

"And why not, Lord Sinclair?" Eliza asked defiantly.

"You are the *Shadow.*"

"And?" she pressed.

Benedict shook his head. "That is not a small thing."

Eliza narrowed her eyes at him. She was furious, but yelling at Lord Sinclair would not solve anything. Straightening her spine, she turned back to her uncle. "As I stated before, it is not necessary that I have a partner, but since you are adamant that I do, I will ask Mr. Larson to help me with this mission." She arose from her chair. "Gentlemen, if you will excuse me, I have work to do."

All the men quickly rose from their chairs and Jonathon went to hold the door open for her. Eliza gave him a tight smile as she headed out to meet Jonathon's carriage. As she was heading out of the building, she was fuming. She was a renowned spy, and no one, especially not Lord Sinclair, would make her feel inferior. She laughed wryly to herself. The arrogant fool *actually* thought he was going to train *her* as a new agent. "What a pompous idiot!" she thought, fisting her hands as she walked.

Shaking her head at her own naivety, she wondered, what else did she expect? Did she really think he would rejoice at discovering he was partnering with a woman? He didn't even seem to believe she could be *Shadow.* "I'm going to bring down Mr. Wade, with or without Lord Sinclair," she muttered to herself.

Jonathon slumped back into his chair after escorting Eliza out of the room. He recognized how upset she was about Benedict's treatment towards her, but she buried her emotions well. Lord Beckett and Jonathon turned their attention to Benedict, who had his shoulders hunched and his gaze was lingering on the floor.

Jonathon wasn't sure what to say. He was furious at his friend for his reaction to Eliza when she asked him directly to be her partner. She put herself in a vulnerable position, and he turned her down. Jonathon wanted to hit something. No, Jonathon wanted to hit Benedict. He jumped out of his seat and started pacing back and forth in Uncle Charles' office.

He decided to direct his fury onto its source and bellowed out, "How could you treat her that way? She saved your life in France! Instead of thanking her, you blame her for being born a woman!" Jonathon chastised.

Benedict's eyes widened. "I know I acted poorly, but it was quite a shock. A warning would have been sufficient. After all, your sister is the most notorious spy in England, hell, maybe in the world." He jumped up from his chair. "How could you possibly allow your sister to be an agent?"

Jonathon narrowed his eyes at his old roommate. "You have no idea how clever she is. Eliza is a better agent than the both of us combined."

Straightening his waistcoat, Benedict pressed his point. "I have no doubt that Lady Elizabeth is intelligent, but to allow her to be a spy? Do you not realize what would happen if she was discovered?"

"First, I did not make her a spy, my uncle did, and secondly, she is well protected," Jonathon said as his hands clenched into themselves.

"How can you protect her when you are not with her? Your sister sits in the dark, waiting to kill people," Benedict countered.

"My sister is always guarded, and she is very well skilled with the sword and longbow."

"You are a fool to think Lady Elizabeth would live if confronted by a man who knew she was a spy. He would kill her without hesitation."

Jonathon smirked. "She saved your life, did she not?"

"Yes, but…" Benedict started.

Cutting him off, Jonathon added, "And she has saved my life on more than one occasion. Eliza has proven she can defend herself."

His friend shouted over him. "Women are not meant to be spies."

Jonathon balked. "And why is that?"

"Being a spy is incredibly dangerous. We both have been nearly killed on multiple occasions."

"Eliza can defend herself just the same as you or me," he said determinedly.

Benedict shook his head in obvious frustration and said sarcastically, "Fine. Your sister is smart and she can defend herself. She can also kill loads of men. I have only killed a few men, and I have a tough time living with that. Your sister literally stays in the shadows and waits for opportunities to kill people, hence her code name *Shadow*!" he scoffed. "Whether you like it or not, your sister has become a notorious assassin!"

Pulling back, Jonathon threw a punch at Benedict's face. Benedict's head whipped back and he doubled over while covering his nose. "You punched me? What the bloody hell is wrong with you?" he said as shock resonated in his voice.

Jonathon stood over his former classmate, trying to curb his temper. "She is my sister and she is not an assassin. She is an agent just like you and me," he asserted.

Benedict kept his hand to his nose as he straightened up. "She is not like one of us. If what they say is true, then she has killed hundreds of men…"

"Enough!" Jonathon interrupted. "I have been with Eliza on every mission, and she has only killed a small number of men."

"Do you hear yourself?" Benedict said in disbelief. "Lady Elizabeth should never have been put in a position to kill anyone."

"My sister wanted to be a field agent. It was her choice," Jonathon exclaimed.

"I do not understand how the Duke of Remington even allows his daughter to work for the Crown, in any capacity," Benedict said turning towards Lord Beckett.

"You do not get to have an opinion on whether Eliza should be an agent or not," Jonathon said annoyed.

"No? Well, at least I am looking after her best interest," Benedict roared back at Jonathon.

"And I'm not?" Jonathon asked.

"Every country in the world is trying to kill *Shadow*. You have given your sister a death sentence."

Jonathon shook his head. "No, I have not."

"You need to convince Lady Elizabeth to stop working as an agent," Benedict said adamantly. "If not, it will only be a matter of time before she will be discovered and killed."

Jonathon lowered his gaze as his friend's words sank in. He ran his hand through his hair before he turned his attention back to his uncle, who was quietly observing their fight. "Benedict does not deserve to be Eliza's partner. I will stay on as her partner, and you can assign him to retrieve Lady Hannah."

Lord Beckett sat back in his chair with lips curved upwards. Jonathon had not even an assumption as to what his uncle was thinking as he leaned forward in his chair and rested his hands on his desk. He focused on Benedict, who was clearing blood from his nose with his blue waistcoat sleeve. "Lord Sinclair, you have been one of my top agents for years, but I think it is time for you to retire." Benedict opened his mouth to argue, but the chief put his hand up to stop him from talking. "My niece has been working on bringing your stepbrother to justice longer than you, and I believe she is the better agent. I will assign her another partner, and you can enjoy more time with your ailing father." Lord Beckett began to rise from his desk to indicate the meeting was over. "If you will excuse me..."

"Wait." Benedict slammed his hands on the desk. "So, that's it?"

"Yes, Sinclair. That's it," Lord Beckett confirmed.

"Is this because I think Lady Elizabeth should stop being an agent?"

Jonathon and his uncle exchanged a pointed look. "Actually, Jonathon and I agree with you that it might be time for Eliza to stop going into the field."

"Then why have you not told her that?"

Lord Beckett leaned back in his chair. "That is complicated. No one can really *tell* Eliza what to do. Besides, she would go after your stepbrother with or without my permission."

Jonathon leaned against his uncle's desk. "I believe that we can convince Eliza to stop working as a field agent once we bring in Mr. Wade."

"Then what?" Benedict scoffed.

Jonathon glared at him. "What do you mean?"

"What do you want Lady Elizabeth to do after Aaron has a noose around his neck?"

"She would continue working as an agent in the safety of her home," Lord Beckett informed him.

"Is that what she wants to do?" he prodded.

Jonathon was fed up and threw his hands in the air. "Why do you care what Eliza would want to do in the future?"

"It seems that you two are doing an excellent job at deciding what Lady Eliza wants to do. Why not just ask her? Maybe she wants to stop being a spy?"

Lord Beckett pointed a finger at him. "No, the Crown needs her. She is my top agent and is invaluable."

Benedict put his hands up in front of him. "I believe Lady Eliza has a right to determine her own future."

Jonathon scoffed. "Trust me when I say that my sister already controls her own future."

Uncle Charles folded his arms across his chest. "Lord Sinclair, it is clear you do not have the slightest notion of what *Shadow* has accomplished as an agent." He paused a moment. "You have been one of my top agents for years, but you could learn a lot from Eliza. Maybe I should assign my niece to train you?"

Raising an eyebrow, Benedict replied, "I do not need any training, since this is my last mission. My only focus is to bring Aaron in for murder."

"If that is true, then partnering with Lady Eliza is your best option," Uncle Charles chided.

Running a hand through his hair, Benedict sighed. "Fine. Would it still be possible to partner with Lady Elizabeth?"

Lord Beckett huffed. "No."

"No?" Benedict asked.

"Yes, my answer is no." Lord Beckett sat back in his chair and looked at Benedict like he was a half-wit. "Contrary to what you might believe, I love my niece. I recruited Lady Eliza as an agent, because she has a remarkable mind. She can decipher enemy codes and write new codes faster than I have ever seen. Furthermore, her contribution has saved thousands of English lives, and the life of our prince regent." Lord Beckett shook his finger at Benedict. "She even saved your life." He paused before continuing, "I will not have her partner with someone who does not understand how valuable she is."

Benedict slowly sat down in a chair. "She did save my life, and I did not even thank her." He sighed and roughly rubbed his brow with his hand. "I want to make amends with Lady Elizabeth." He paused and focused on Jonathon. "Did you know that I planned on visiting your townhouse after this meeting to discern where she lived?"

Jonathon saw his uncle glance at him with shock written all over his face. Uncle Charles was the only other person in the family that knew Eliza didn't live with Jonathon.

"I just did not expect her to be in the meeting, nor did I expect her to be *Shadow*," Benedict said, hoping he sounded contrite, but leveling a gaze at Lord Beckett since he did not really intend to back down. "Sir, what can I do to change your mind?"

Bringing his hand up to his chin, Lord Beckett seemed to consider the agent for a few moments. "Nothing."

Benedict bowed his head in defeat.

"But if you can convince her to be your partner, then I will allow it," he continued with a smile.

Benedict's head shot up. "Thank you, my lord. You will not be disappointed. Lady Elizabeth and I will make a wonderful team."

"Do not thank me yet," Uncle Charles chuckled. "You still have to convince Eliza to partner with you."

Jonathon pushed off from the desk and grumbled, "I guess I will take you to her castle." He was not ready to forgive his friend's mistakes.

"Lady Elizabeth owns a castle," Benedict smiled. "That does not really surprise me."

Jonathon turned to his uncle and smirked. "Perhaps I should just give him directions and let him try to travel there by himself." His uncle shot him a warning look.

Benedict curiously looked between Jonathon and their chief. "Why can I not go by myself?"

Lord Beckett took his eyes off Jonathon and glanced at Benedict. "You would not even make it to the front door without the code." He turned back to Jonathon and pointed his finger at him. "You will make sure Sinclair arrives unharmed at Eliza's door."

"Yes, Uncle," Jonathon mumbled under his breath. "Did you bring your carriage?" he asked Benedict.

"Yes, it is in front."

"Good. Eliza took mine." He put his hand out to indicate they should exit the room. Jonathon started to follow when his uncle called him back.

Uncle Charles leaned forward in his chair and put his elbows on his desk. "Jonathon, do not get Benedict killed. I believe he and Eliza could make an effective team in more ways than one," he said with an amused smile.

Jonathon nodded his head as he turned to catch up with his friend.

Chapter Seven

So far, the trip to Eliza's castle had not been enjoyable at all. Jonathon refused to speak and was staring out the window. Every time Benedict attempted to say something, his friend would only communicate with a grunt or nod. They had been traveling in his crested post-chaise for about thirty minutes, leaving the crowded streets of London behind, and now trees and lush green fields surrounded them.

Once they arrived at the castle, Benedict knew he would need to solicit his friend's help. It had been about five minutes since his last attempt to speak with Jonathan failed, so he needed to change tactics. He had been a cad to Eliza, and he did not think he could just use his charm to get back into her good graces. Somehow, he needed to convince her to partner with him. He needed to have a plan and the only plan that made sense was to work with Jonathon.

"Jonathon, I am sorry." Benedict tried again.

Jonathon tilted his head. "For what?"

Benedict knew he was on shaky ground here. Jonathon was talking to him again, but one wrong word could send him back into silence. "I am sorry for being rude to Lady Elizabeth, and implying you did not protect her," he said.

Jonathon's lips flattened as he stared at Benedict, and he could feel the tension radiating off him. Slowly, Jonathon's shoulders relaxed. "And I'm sorry about your nose." He took a deep breath. "You will need to apologize to Eliza for being rude, but you were right about me not protecting her. I was the one that allowed her to start working in the field." Jonathon started staring out that blasted window again. Frowning, Benedict wondered if he should pull the shades down to force his friend to focus.

Without looking away from the window, Jonathon spoke again. "Eliza cracked her first French coded message when she was twelve. Uncle Charles left the code on his desk in his study, and she found it. It took her two days to decode the message. The war department had been trying to crack the code for weeks."

Benedict sounded doubtful as he asked, "She just picked up a coded message and deciphered it?"

Jonathon nodded in response to his question. "Eliza's mind absorbs everything. I cannot explain it. Uncle Charles recognized that she had a remarkable mind and started grooming her while she was very young to become an agent. He gave her basic codes that had already been deciphered and taught her the patterns in the codes. He spent hours teaching her what to look for, and she thrived on the attention. When she found the French coded message, she thought it was another test, so she went into the library and would not leave till she figured it out. When Uncle Charles returned home and found the coded message was gone, he went in search of Eliza. She had just finished decoding the message, and she was so happy that she was spinning in circles." Jonathon chuckled to himself.

"Lady Eliza knew French at twelve?"

"Fluently."

Still doubtful, Benedict wondered how a twelve-year-old girl could decode a French message. "How did Lord Beckett know that she decoded the French code correctly?"

"Uncle Charles took it over to the war office and told them that he broke the French code. They took it and verified its authenticity. Eliza had decoded the message accurately."

Shocked, Benedict asked, "How did the war office react to a twelve-year-old girl cracking the code?"

Jonathon crossed his arms over his chest. "They never knew. Uncle Charles brought back the coded message without an explanation. The war office probably assumed his office agents cracked it."

Curious about Jonathon's implication that Eliza lived with her uncle, Benedict asked, "Why was Lady Elizabeth living at Lord Beckett's manor?"

Jonathon furrowed his brows. "You caught that, did you?"

"I am a spy," Benedict said with a smirk.

Jonathon's lips briefly turned upwards at his comment, but then it was gone. "Mother kicked Eliza out of the abbey when she was ten, and she was sent to live with Uncle Charles," Jonathon informed him.

"What?" Benedict was taken aback. How could a mother kick their child out of the house at ten years old? What could Eliza have done that was so bad that it would warrant that punishment?

As he sat pondering that revelation, Jonathon opened the carriage door, and yelled to the driver to turn onto a dirt road that was coming up. Benedict looked out his window to see an overgrown dirt road leading towards a heavily wooded area.

As they continued on the uneven road, the trees opened up to reveal on the horizon a rectangular shaped, two-story stone castle with protruding turrets rounding out each corner. It appeared that the castle's architecture dated back hundreds of years, but modern touches had been added, such as the large windows spread along the castle's exterior.

While Benedict was trying to get a better view of the medieval castle, he noticed the carriage was slowing down. As it rolled to a stop, Jonathon opened the door and stepped outside. Following Jonathon's lead, he stepped out and noticed a man on top of a horse approaching them. As the man drew nearer, he saw that the man was holding a pistol in his right hand but lowered it when he saw Jonathon.

Waving to the man as he approached the carriage, Jonathon loudly exclaimed, "The valley gets more sun on the east side." Benedict recognized that this must be the code.

The rider waved his hand with the pistol in it. "It is good to see you, Lord Jonathon. I did not recognize the carriage, so I had to be prepared." The rider then tucked the pistol into the top of his trousers.

Jonathon nodded. "I was worried about that, which is why I got out of the carriage to greet you." He put his hand out towards Benedict. "Roger, this is Lord Sinclair. He is Lady Elizabeth's new partner."

Roger acknowledged him by giving him a quick nod then turned back to Jonathon. "Did you get assigned to a new case?"

"Yes, I will be gone for a short time. I will make sure that Lord Sinclair knows the code, but have some patience with him in case he forgets. My uncle does not want him to be shot."

Roger laughed. "Lord Beckett does not want him to be shot, but do you or Lady Elizabeth want me to shoot him?"

Jonathon had the nerve to shrug. "Feel free, but don't kill him."

Benedict curiously watched this interaction but said nothing. Jonathon was obviously familiar with Roger, and had even informed him that he got a new assignment. Roger must be an agent. Did Lord Beckett send agents to guard Eliza? He needed to ask Jonathon the next time he had the chance.

Roger laughed. "I will inform the other guards that Lady Elizabeth has a new partner," Roger said as he glanced towards Benedict. "I will notify the castle of your impending arrival, Lord Sinclair." Roger then reared his horse back in the direction of the castle and rode off.

Jonathon watched him for a moment then walked back to the carriage. As he started to open the door, he stopped and looked back. "You will need to remember the code that I just revealed." Benedict repeated the code verbatim and Jonathon nodded his head in approval. "Good. You must say that every time you come out to Beaumont Castle. It would also be best to ride out by yourself when you come to visit Eliza. The less people who know where she lives the better," Jonathon warned as he hopped back into the carriage.

Following Jonathon, Benedict hit the roof to let the driver know to continue on the road. He observed a few men on horseback patrolling the grass fields surrounding the castle. "Are all these men agents?"

"Former agents."

"And all these former agents are guarding your sister?" Benedict asked, intrigued.

Jonathon gave him a disbelieving look. "Of course, they are guarding my sister. Eliza is an asset to the Crown." Jonathon looked like he wanted to start yelling again, and Benedict braced himself for the onslaught. Instead, Jonathon took a deep breath before he started speaking again. "Eliza has made a lot of enemies both foreign and domestic. As you are aware, there is not one country in the world that would not want to acquire *Shadow*, dead or alive. Most countries have a price on her head because they fear her."

A surge of protectiveness washed over Benedict, unlike anything he had ever felt before. "I thought you said no one knew your sister was an agent or her identity?"

"No one does." Jonathon gave him a cocky smile. "Besides, you made it quite clear that no one would believe a woman could be *Shadow*."

Benedict rolled his eyes at Jonathon's insinuation. "What if someone does figure out that she is *Shadow*?"

Suddenly somber, Jonathon replied, "That is why Eliza is watched at all times. If anyone discovered who she is…" Jonathon's voice broke, but he seemed to swallow his emotions. "Uncle Charles and I have made precautions that point to me as being *Shadow*. However, I do not believe it will ever come to that. Besides, as far as anyone is concerned, my sister does not work for the Crown in any capacity."

Benedict nodded his head in agreement. He truly hoped that no one could ever implicate Eliza or Jonathon as *Shadow*, or else it would be a certain death.

The carriage rolled to a stop in front of Beaumont Castle. As his hand went to the lever on the carriage door, Jonathon put his hand on Benedict's shoulder. "Get Eliza to trust you," Jonathon advised, as he locked eyes with his friend. "Something happened last month in France that has deeply affected her. She will not talk about it." Jonathon winced. "I am hoping you can help her, because she still refuses to tell me what happened over there." Jonathon slumped back into the carriage seat.

Benedict did not know what he should say. He was not even sure that Eliza would agree to partner with him, so he decided to be honest. "I will try my best." Jonathon gave him a tight nod in response.

Stepping out of the carriage, he gazed at the oversized wooden main door of Beaumont Castle, then he noticed that Jonathon hadn't stepped out of his carriage yet. He stuck his head back in. "Are you coming?"

"No, I am heading back to town. I have some business to attend to." Jonathon rested his head back on the plush velvet seats.

"By business, you mean an evening at Whites?" Benedict joked.

Jonathon smiled. "Possibly. When you are ready to leave, use my carriage and horses that Eliza borrowed earlier. I do not feel like waiting for my carriage to be hooked up, and your carriage is fancier." He shrugged. "Besides, I really do not want to be there when you apologize to her. She is not the easiest person to talk to when she is upset."

Benedict did not like this at all. He was hoping Jonathon would help him convince Eliza to partner with him. Now he needed to come up with a new plan, and fast. He yelled up to the driver to take Lord Jonathon back to town, then turned back towards the massive door and knocked.

Chapter Eight

Benedict was frustrated. He had knocked three times with no answer. How long had he been waiting? It was probably only ten minutes, but it felt like hours.

He took a moment to admire Eliza's castle. The castle was surrounded by overgrown green fields, but along its walls, it boasted a well-kept landscape. He did not want to trample on her flowers to peep into her windows to try to get anyone's attention, so Benedict decided to knock louder this time. A loud metal screech followed the knock and it went on for a few moments.

As the door opened, a tall, older gentleman with salt and pepper hair stood in front of him. Even though the man was older in years, he appeared to be physically fit. He was wearing tan trousers with a tucked-in white shirt, and the sleeves of the shirt were rolled up to his elbows. His face was pink and Benedict could see sweat beaded on his forehead.

"Lord Sinclair, we have been expecting you," he said dryly, as he used his shirt to wipe away the sweat from his forehead.

Benedict waited for the man to step aside to let him enter but the man didn't move, so Benedict asserted, "I am here to see Lady Elizabeth to discuss an important matter. Is she receiving callers?"

He had no idea who this man was. Was he the butler? Another former agent? How could Eliza let a man dressed in tan work trousers receive callers for her? While Benedict was continuing to form conclusions about who this man was, the man in question decided to step aside for him to enter.

Benedict stepped into a narrow, two-story entryway that housed an elaborate wooden staircase, residing on the left side of the stone and pine paneled room. As the man closed the front door behind him, he proceeded to lower a portcullis. Benedict watched as the iron gate was lowered by chains attached to an internal winch. He had never seen a functioning portcullis in a home before, albeit a castle, and he found himself to be quite enamored by it.

After the portcullis was closed, he turned to address Benedict. "My name is Mr. George Larson. I run Lady Elizabeth's household."

"You are the butler?" Benedict's eyebrows shot up. There was no way this man was a butler. He was not even properly dressed for the job.

"Yes and no. I run the household, but Lady Elizabeth does not have a need for a traditional butler. In fact, you are the first real visitor we have received at Beaumont Castle."

Benedict was curious about this man, this... protector. "Are you a former agent as well?"

Mr. Larson eyed Benedict like he was trying to size him up. "I am."

"Interesting," Benedict said.

The moment dragged on as no one spoke, and Benedict heard the sounds of swords clashing. Mr. Larson acknowledged the sound by tilting his head towards the direction of the noise. "Lady Elizabeth has been fencing for the past hour. Would you like to accompany me to the courtyard?" Mr. Larson preceded him through the castle as the sounds intensified.

Benedict was curious. To be honest, he was more than curious. He had never seen a woman wield a sword before. He was also anxious to see Eliza again. He needed to convince her to partner with him. His attention was elsewhere, and the next thing he knew Mr. Larson slammed him against the wall, his forearm at his throat.

Mr. Larson leaned close and growled out his words, "If you ever upset my Eliza again, I will kill you."

Taking in Mr. Larson's blazing eyes, Benedict knew he was in earnest. How close was Eliza to her butler? His voice came out sounding strained because Mr. Larson's forearm was still pressing against his windpipe. He croaked out, "I'm here to make amends with Lady Elizabeth."

Narrowing his eyes menacingly, Mr. Larson sported a deep scowl on his face. Slowly, he relaxed his arm from Benedict's throat, but he did not remove it. "Lord Beckett sent over a message informing me that you were assigned to be Lady Eliza's partner, but I can make you disappear easily enough. Do I make myself clear?"

Instinctively, Benedict knew that Mr. Larson was just being overly protective of Eliza, and hurting this man would ruin his chances of convincing her to be his partner. He decided to reason with Mr. Larson. "I know I made a mistake, but I am hoping I can convince Lady Elizabeth to partner with me. I give you my word I will not upset her in any way."

Benedict's response seemed to satisfy Mr. Larson, because he dropped his arm and stepped back. He still wore a scowl on his face. "Be warned that I will be watching you very closely." Mr. Larson then strode towards the courtyard, leaving him behind. Pulling down his blue waistcoat, he adjusted his white cravat and trailed after him.

The distinctive sounds of sword fighting echoed off the stone walls as Benedict stepped out into the interior courtyard. They stayed close to the wall to avoid distracting the opponents during their match. The two fencers were dressed in tan trousers and white shirts, while thick gloves covered their forearms and pads protected their chests. They were using the traditional small sword for fencing and were aggressively thrusting and then retreating from each other.

Benedict's eyes quickly landed on Eliza, even though a mask covered her face. He noticed her brown hair was pulled into a tight bun at the base of her neck. He also could not help but admire her beautiful figure, because the trousers fit her tall, trim body quite nicely. He saw through Eliza's wire mesh mask that her face was pink from exertion, and she was smiling. In fact, her whole face radiated happiness.

He was amazed with her fencing skills. She not only was holding her own against her partner, but at times, she could have won the match if it was a competition. Benedict quietly acknowledged, "She is well trained."

Mr. Larson nodded in the affirmative. "That she is."

Both men watched while Eliza and her partner sparred with impressive skill and technique. They would randomly say things to each other, but Benedict could not hear exactly what was being communicated. Her laugh echoed throughout the interior courtyard at something her partner said. He thought that was the loveliest sound he had ever heard. He wanted to make Eliza laugh like that.

Benedict realized his hands were balled into fists. He was jealous of her fencing partner. No, that was ridiculous. Benedict glanced at Mr. Larson, who met his gaze and then made a show of glancing at his balled fists. Mr. Larson gave him a smug smile and went back to watching the sparring match.

"Halt." Mr. Larson's voice echoed throughout the courtyard. Eliza and her partner stopped in mid-swipe and put their swords vertical in front of their bodies, concluding their sparring match.

Eliza felt better. She always felt better after fencing. Glancing over at her partner as she pulled off her mask, she could see he was trying to catch his breath. She always worried that the men went easy on her. If she wanted to get better, then she needed real competition. Eliza would rather lose than be given a pity win. She addressed her sparring partner when she said, "Thank you, Spencer."

She wiped the sweat off her forehead with the back of her glove. Turning to face Mr. Larson, she saw Lord Sinclair standing next to him with a peculiar look on his face, and she sighed inwardly. Obviously, her brother had brought Lord Sinclair to Beaumont Castle. She raised her hand in greeting to him.

"It is good to see you, Lord Sinclair."

Benedict looked surprised by her comment. "It is?"

Eliza smirked. "No, but a lady must always be polite." She heard Mr. Larson snicker. Spencer came up and relieved her of her mask and sword as she gave him a gracious smile and thanked him. She started pulling off her gloves as she approached them. "Is Jonathon with you?"

"No, he dropped me off and headed back to town. He informed me that he had an important meeting," Benedict said.

Eliza smiled knowingly. "Ah, a meeting at Whites, I imagine."

"My thoughts exactly," he said while returning her smile.

Still angry with Lord Sinclair, she did not want to exchange pleasantries. "Why exactly are you here, Lord Sinclair?" Eliza handed Spencer her gloves and protective padding.

Benedict gave her a charming smile that Eliza suspected was being used to disarm her, but she continued to wait for a response from him. She was not going to make this easy for him, because she assumed he was here to apologize and attempt to partner with her.

"I apologize for my earlier behavior at Lord Beckett's office," Benedict said, his eyes searching hers.

"Thank you. I appreciate your sincere apology." Dropping eye contact with him, Eliza turned to walk inside. "I hope you have a nice drive back to town," she said over her shoulder.

"What? No. I wish to speak to you further, Lady Eliza." Benedict quickly caught up to her.

Eliza feigned ignorance. "What would you wish to talk to me about?" She put her hand to her heart. "I am just a *woman*."

"I see that you have not really forgiven me," Benedict muttered.

"Of course not, my lord," she said with contempt. "What would you have me say?"

Benedict lightly grabbed her arm and ushered her into the nearby drawing room. "I would like us to be partners," he said frankly.

Eliza decided not to reject him right away. She was curious about his change of opinion, since he was so negative before. "Why?"

"Why not?" he shrugged.

She let out a genuine laugh. "That is what you came up with? You are hoping to convince me to be your partner by asking me why not?" Eliza noticed that Benedict had not removed his hand from her arm, and she found it oddly comforting.

He carried a humbled expression on his face. "I was a fool."

One side of her lips curled upwards. "I am not going to argue with that."

Benedict dropped his hand from her arm. "Lady Elizabeth... I... I really am sorry," he fumbled out, pausing and obviously searching for the right words. "I insulted you, and I did not show you the respect you deserved." His eyes were filled with remorse as he continued to gaze at her. "I did not react well when I learned you were *Shadow,* and for that I am truly sorry." A very slight smile twitched the corner of his mouth. "In my defense, most women of your station are proficient at embroidery and the pianoforte, and not archery, fencing, and spying."

Eliza arched an eyebrow. "You will soon discover that I am not like the other girls you are acquainted with," she said, challenging him to deny it.

His smile grew wide. "I am well aware that you are unlike any other female that I know, which is why I need your help." He furrowed his brow, as his eyes flickered away from her. "Lord Beckett told me that if you do not agree to partner with me, then I am officially retired as an agent." He clenched his jaw and leveled his stare at her. "Which means I would have to investigate Aaron on my own, without the resources of the Crown."

Eliza's heart stirred with compassion. She was aware that he wanted his stepbrother in Newgate, just as much as she did. The reason he did not agree to partner with her before was due to her being a woman. Had his position changed? "But I am just a *woman*," she mocked.

Benedict's eyes flitted with emotion as he stressed, "No, you are not just a woman. You are *Shadow*, a spy that drives fear into the hearts of men in every country. Some people consider *Shadow* a myth, a legend if you will." His voice grew emotional as he added, "A legend that saved my life." He reached for her hand and brought it to his lips. "I made a grievous error when I failed to thank you for saving my life, and I would like to rectify that right now." He placed a lingering kiss on her hand and gave her a look of such adoration that her resolve began to weaken. "Thank you, Lady Eliza, for saving my life in France."

It took a moment for Eliza to recover from Benedict's warm lips on her skin, but she needed to act unaffected by his charms. She refused to act like a simpering woman. "Did you finally accept that I am *Shadow?*"

"I still find it hard to believe that someone so young could be *Shadow*. You have accomplished so much for one so young."

"You called me an assassin," she reminded him.

He winced. "Yes, I apologize for my bluntness. Jonathon and I had a long talk and he explained to me that I was misinformed."

Eliza gave him a tight smile. Sadly, Benedict was remarkably accurate with the number of men that she had killed over the years, but he would never know that. "Are you sure you can work with a female agent?"

Rubbing the back of his neck with his hand, he looked over her shoulder. "Working with a woman has never been the problem for me."

"So, the problem is working with *me?*"

"Yes," Benedict confirmed.

"Oh?" she questioned as she turned to walk away.

He reached for her hand to prevent her from fleeing. "No, you do not understand," he said cautiously. "The reason I did not want to work with you, is not because you are a woman, but because you are the most beautiful woman I have ever met." Eliza gave him a puzzled look as he continued, "You drive me to distraction. In fact, all my thoughts since last night have been about you."

Her face was getting overly warm from blushing, but she could not seem to look away from Benedict's handsome face. "Are you in earnest?"

Dropping her hand, he gave her a crooked smile. "Yes, I am in earnest. I could not wait till I could see you again." He glanced around the room and proudly announced, "And I discovered where you lived."

Eliza let out an amused laugh. "Not really. My brother did drop you off."

"True, but I would have eventually discovered Beaumont Castle," Benedict chuckled.

"How so?"

"I would have charmed Jonathon into revealing its location."

Her face softened at his humor. "And how exactly would you have charmed my brother?"

Benedict pretended to be deep in thought. "I would have brought him flowers and taken him on a carriage ride through Hyde Park."

"And if that did not work?" Eliza laughed.

Crossing his arms, he replied, "Then chocolate. I remember that Jonathon always had a sweet tooth at Oxford."

Putting her fingers to her lips, she pretended that she was mulling over his plan. "That plan sounds flawless."

Benedict smiled down at her. "Please say that you will partner with me?" He studied her face with amused eyes. "I think we could make a great team."

Tilting her head, she considered his proposal. "Yes, I will agree to partner with you, but only because we both want to see Mr. Wade in Newgate."

"Thank you." He stepped a little closer. "And I promise I will try to behave myself around you," he said smoothly, his deep voice sending chills up her spine.

As Benedict stepped closer to her, she felt an intense longing to be close to him. She felt strangely safe and calm in his presence. Hope bloomed anew in her heart. Perhaps he might be the one that could help her overcome her past?

Before Eliza could find any words to express what she was feeling, someone cleared his throat loudly. Eliza and Benedict jumped apart. Looking in the direction of the offending noise, Eliza saw Mr. Larson leaning against the door frame with his arms folded over his chest. He had a deep scowl on his face. *He wasn't angry with her, was he?*

Mr. Larson pushed against the door frame and walked further into the room. "Lady Eliza, I noticed that you have forgiven Lord Sinclair. Is it safe to assume he is your partner?"

"Um… yes. We were just discussing our partnership," Eliza confirmed as her face grew quite warm. How much had he witnessed?

Mr. Larson chuckled under his breath. "Yes, I could see you two were discussing a lot of things."

Eliza ducked her head to hide her red cheeks. Just then, she remembered that she was wearing trousers and a shirt, and it was an excellent excuse to step away for a moment. She started edging away from the men. "Gentlemen, if you will excuse me, I will go upstairs and change." Before she left the drawing room, she turned back around. "Would you like to go for a walk after I change, Lord Sinclair?"

Benedict bowed in her direction. "I would be delighted."

Nodding, she walked swiftly out of the room, trying not to run. The faster she got away from Lord Sinclair, the sooner she could think. Her emotions were in constant disarray around him, and her poise shattered.

As Eliza burst into her room, Martha was laying out a white walking dress and a dark blue spencer for her. Promptly removing her sweaty clothes, Eliza went over to her water basin to splash cool water on her face. She dried her face with the towel and proceeded to dress herself.

Martha came over and started buttoning up the back of Eliza's dress. "You mentioned Lord Sinclair was handsome, but that did not do him justice."

"I suppose," Eliza said casually.

"You are not fooling anyone, Lady Eliza. By the way Lord Sinclair was looking at you when he was apologizing, I thought he was going to kiss you."

Eliza jerked around. "What? You saw that?" She was mortified. Who else witnessed her weakness towards Lord Sinclair?

Martha put her hands on her shoulders, turning her back around and finished with the buttons. Walking over to the dressing table, she indicated that Eliza should sit. She made quick work of providing her with a more fashionable hair style. While Martha put the final pin into Eliza's hair, she spoke up. "I was curious as to what Lord Sinclair looked like, and I heard he had arrived, so I snuck down the stairs and peeked into the drawing room."

Eliza looked at her maid's reflection in the mirror. "You went downstairs by yourself?" Eliza was more than surprised. Martha had not gone downstairs without her, or a housemaid, since Eliza brought her back to the castle over two years ago. Martha was still skittish around men and felt uncomfortable walking around the castle without a companion of sorts.

Martha shrugged. "I wanted to see the man you are so clearly smitten with."

"I am not smitten with Lord Sinclair," Eliza denied. Martha's expression indicated she was not fooled. Eliza decided she should be honest with her feelings. "I am not sure what I am feeling, but whenever Lord Sinclair is near me, it seems like I lose rational thoughts."

Martha kept nodding, indicating she should keep talking. "He makes me so angry and then directs his charming smile on me, and I find myself returning his smile. Do you remember when I told you that he refused to work with me because I was a woman?"

"Yes, I remember the conversation we had only an hour ago," Martha replied teasingly.

Standing, Eliza walked to grab her bonnet from the bed where Martha had laid it. "Then Lord Sinclair just shows up, asks for my forgiveness and wants to partner with me. He insults me, makes me laugh, and then begs for my forgiveness. It is very confusing to me." Eliza put her hand to her forehead.

Martha smiled knowingly. "But you are not smitten with Lord Sinclair?" she prodded.

"No," Eliza said. "I just find him... irritating."

She didn't want to talk to Martha anymore. She wanted to run back downstairs to see Benedict. What was wrong with her? Eliza had been around attractive men before. Handsome, titled men had asked her father, the Duke of Remington, to court her and none of them even interested her. Furthermore, none of those men had insulted her. Yet, none of those men distracted her just by being in the room.

As Eliza was preparing to walk out, Martha said, "Lord Sinclair seems like a kind man. Maybe you can confide in him? After all, he is your partner for the time being."

Eliza shrugged. "I am not sure about that."

Picking up Eliza's gloves, Martha handed them to her. "Who better to help you than a fellow agent?"

Eliza gave her maid a tentative smile and headed downstairs.

Chapter Nine

Today has been a day of uncomfortable situations, Benedict thought, while he waited for Eliza to come downstairs to join him for a walk. He discovered that Eliza was *Shadow,* the agent who saved his life over a month ago, and then proceeded to insult her and his good friend, Jonathon. Luckily, he was able to convince her to partner with him professionally, yet he could not dislodge the memory of dancing with her and holding her close during the waltz.

Now, he was sitting in Eliza's drawing room, which was the goal for the day, and Mr. Larson was sitting across from him, staring at him like he was going to steal something. Benedict decided to start up a conversation with Mr. Larson, since it was apparent that Eliza held him in high regard. He cleared his throat.

"How long have you worked with Lady Elizabeth?"

Grumbling, Mr. Larson reached down, removing the pistol from the front of his trousers and laid the pistol on his lap.

Benedict groaned inwardly. This was the second time that Mr. Larson had made death threats against him. Perhaps he should switch tactics. "Have you taught Lady Elizabeth how to shoot yet?" he asked while motioning to the pistol. If not, maybe he could teach her how to shoot a pistol.

Mr. Larson leveled a stare at him like he was a dim-wit. "Lady Eliza already knew how to shoot a pistol before I met her." Success! Mr. Larson talked to him. He was pleased by his victory, but it was short-lived. Mr. Larson pointed his finger at him. "In fact, she could share a few pointers with you."

"I know how to shoot a pistol," Benedict answered confidently.

"Not as well as Lady Eliza," Mr. Larson said smugly. "She could outshoot you or anybody else with her eyes closed."

"I highly doubt that," Benedict said as he recalled a mission last year.

It was a foggy evening on the docks, but he could make out the flicker of a candle in the distance next to his target. He lifted his pistol and released the trigger, and almost immediately a distant groan was heard. He had hit his target, over twenty meters.

Which was why Lord Beckett had specifically assigned him to that mission, due to his exceptional shooting record. Benedict was startled out of his thoughts by a loud sigh from Eliza.

"And why can I not be a better shot than you, Lord Sinclair? Is it because I am only a woman?" she questioned from somewhere behind him.

Benedict's eyes narrowed briefly at Mr. Larson, who was looking quite pleased with himself. Standing up, Benedict turned towards his new partner, knowing that he had better say something fast that would rectify this situation. "I meant to say that I hoped you would give me some pointers on how to shoot more efficiently," he replied, flashing his most disarming smile.

Eliza raised an eyebrow at Benedict indicating she was not fooled. "Please do not insult my intelligence, Lord Sinclair." Tilting her head towards her protector, she added, "Please stop baiting our guest."

"I do not know what you are referring to, my lady," Mr. Larson replied innocently.

Eliza gave Mr. Larson a half smile which seemed to indicate that she did not believe his innocent act for a minute. "Lord Sinclair and I will take a turn around the fields," she informed him.

Mr. Larson rose from his chair and walked over to Benedict. He leaned in to ensure only Benedict could hear what he was about to say. "I will be watching you at all times."

Benedict responded in turn. "I would expect nothing less from you."

Leaning back, Mr. Larson started to walk out. As he passed by Eliza, her hand went to his arm. Her face softened as she smiled up at him and mouthed, "Thank you." He gifted her with a smile and departed from the room.

Laura Beers

Turning her full attention towards Benedict, Eliza smiled politely. His breath hitched at her beauty. She had on a very flattering dress, and her chestnut brown hair had been restyled, but her cheeks were still pink from her earlier fencing match. He liked her in a dress, but he realized he preferred her in trousers.

He shook his head. He needed to keep his wits about him if he wanted to bring his stepbrother to justice. Maybe partnering with a beautiful, tempting spy was not the best choice.

Eliza was watching him while he was having these improper thoughts and furrowed her eyebrows. "Is everything all right, Lord Sinclair?"

Running his fingers through his hair, Benedict chuckled. He could not tell her what he was really thinking. "I wanted to thank you again for agreeing to partner with me. There is nothing more important to me right now than bringing in Aaron for murdering my brother."

She smiled graciously. "I think we both will rest easier when Mr. Wade is in Newgate."

Benedict leaned back against the back of sofa. "If I may be so bold, why did you agree to partner with me even after I soundly insulted you?"

Eliza bit her bottom lip for a moment as she appeared to be pondering his question. "To be honest, I do not rightly know. We both have a personal stake in bringing down Mr. Wade, but I could have taken him out on my own." Her eyes twinkled with amusement and one side of her mouth tipped up in a wry smile. "I suppose there is something about you that gives me pause."

Benedict's lips curled into a smile. "Is that good or bad?"

The corners of Eliza's mouth were pressed firmly down like she was trying to repress a smile. "I have not decided yet, my lord."

"Please call me Benedict," he said, straightening from the sofa.

"What?" Eliza was surprised by his request.

"I would like you to call me Benedict."

She shook her head. "That would be extremely improper to call you by your given name, my lord."

"We are partners, are we not?"

"True, but..."

83

"And partners work closely together."

Eliza raised an eyebrow. "What is your point?"

"My point is, I will be calling you Eliza, so it is only fair that you call me by my given name."

"Lord Sinclair, you cannot be serious...."

"Benedict," he interrupted as he stepped forward.

Eliza's eyes grew wide as she took a few steps back, creating more distance between them. "Lord Sinclair..." she trailed off.

Benedict sighed and rubbed the back of his neck with his hand. "To be honest, I do not like being called Lord Sinclair. The title belonged to my brother when he was alive, and it is a constant reminder to me that I have replaced him."

Her lips flattened. "I am sorry for your loss."

"So, we are in agreement then?" he said as one side of his mouth curled upwards. "When we are alone you will call me Benedict."

"But it is still improper," she said hesitantly. He could tell that she was swaying in his favor.

"Eliza," he said as he walked towards her. She took a step back and found herself against a wall. He continued his advance until he was right in front of her. As he placed his hand on the wall behind her, he slightly leaned in, and she sucked in a breath. "You and I are partners for the foreseeable future, and it would be easier on me if you would call me Benedict. Do you not agree?"

"I suppose," she said softly.

"Benedict," he said teasingly. "Will you say my name?"

She shook her head, but her eyes never left his and it appeared she was stifling a smile. "I fear you are a conceited man since you so desperately want to hear your own name."

He leaned closer. "I'm waiting."

Eliza rolled her eyes. "Fine," she said, pausing for a moment, her lips curling in amusement. "Benedict."

He gave her a crooked smile. "Was that so hard?"

Her eyes were roaming his face as she asked, "Do you always insist on your partners calling you by your given name?"

"No, I just wanted to hear my name on your lips," Benedict replied honestly.

"And do you always brazenly flirt with your partners?" Eliza asked, her eyes twinkling.

Benedict could see she was trying hard to pretend she was unaffected by his nearness, however, the blush on her cheeks gave her away. He chuckled. "No, my dear. You have bewitched me, and I find myself longing to be near you." With his free hand, he slowly caressed his fingers down her right arm.

Eliza's arm erupted with goose bumps, but her voice remained steady. "Well, I assure you, my lord, that I did not cast a spell on you."

He kept glancing at her lips. "How could you not?" His words came out breathless.

Her blush deepened, and she had not pushed him away yet, which was a good sign. Benedict noticed her eyes kept darting to his lips. All he had to do was lower his head. It would not take long. Would she welcome his kiss? He could not take his eyes off her lips and slowly started to lower his head.

Eliza quickly retreated away from the wall, knocking down a nearby table in the process. "Are you ready for a walk?" She spoke hurriedly and breathlessly as she righted the table.

Benedict stood there for a moment while he was recovering from what had just happened. Maybe Eliza was not as affected by him as he was by her? After a moment, he pushed off the wall and went to meet her at the door. As she was putting on her gloves, he leaned down to her ear and whispered, "Next time I will not let you get away so easily." His lips lightly brushed her ear as he whispered to her.

Eliza's breath hitched as her cheeks flamed bright pink. Slowly, she brought her face up to meet his and her eyes landed on his lips. For a brief moment, she swayed towards him, and he was encouraged to start leaning in. Just before his lips captured hers, she stiffened and took a step back. Putting her fingers to her lips, she quickly walked out of the room. Benedict watched her flee, and he was satisfied that she was more affected by his charms than she let on.

He chuckled to himself. *Working with Eliza was going to be an adventure of a lifetime*, he thought, as he followed her.

The new partners strolled towards a wooded area near the north side of Beaumont Castle. She decided not to wear her bonnet, and she lifted her face to feel the warmth of the late afternoon sun. Turning her head, she caught Benedict staring at her, but he quickly diverted his eyes forward.

"Lord Sinc... Um, Benedict..." Eliza fumbled out.

"Yes?" he replied, smiling. He seemed pleased that she had used his given name.

"Tell me about your family," she pried as she veered them towards a break in the trees.

He clasped his hands behind his back. "My family is a topic I generally avoid." He did not speak for a few minutes then sighed. "My mother passed away during my birth, thus I have no memories of her. My older brother Henry was murdered by my stepbrother Aaron, and my father is on his deathbed. Soon I will be the last remaining member of my family."

Eliza's heart surged with compassion towards him. "I am sorry for all of your losses. Was your family close?"

Benedict's lips tightened into a straight line. "Henry was my best friend, and we were inseparable even as boys. My father did his best to spend time with us, but he was exceptionally busy with his duties as a marquess. Like other aristocratic families, my father shipped us off to Eton as soon as we became of age," he said. Although his voice was firm, his eyes betrayed his sadness.

"I am sorry. I should not have pried into your family circumstances." She gave him an apologetic smile.

He unclasped his hands from his back and turned towards her. "You have no reason to apologize. As a young boy, I longed for a relationship with my father, but it was never reciprocated. Now that my father's days are limited, I feel sadness for what could have been." They resumed their walk in silence, and Eliza glanced over at Benedict as he seemed to be wrestling with himself over his past.

She stopped, even though they had just resumed their walk, and touched his arm. Benedict gave her an inquisitive look. "Regardless of your past with your father, it is not too late to make amends. If you would rather be with your father right now, then I can bring Mr. Wade in for both of us."

"Are you trying to get rid of me already?" he teased.

Eliza's eyes widened. "No, I meant that you might..." she started to explain.

He chuckled as he laid his hand over hers. "I am just teasing you. I swore to my father that I would bring Aaron to justice before he died, and I intend to do just that."

Benedict raised his hand, and she slipped her hand off his arm. "That is very noble of you." She walked over to a birch tree and leaned against it. "Now how exactly did you get such a wonderful stepbrother?"

Benedict's lips slowly curved into a smile. "Now, my stepmother was a welcome addition to my family. My father married Jane about ten years ago, and she is a good woman. In fact, Jane has faithfully nursed my father through his sickness as she did with her previous husband."

"Is Jane close to her son?" Eliza pressed.

He shook his head. "After Jane married my father, we had all hoped to have a close relationship with Aaron." Benedict looked at her. "Did you know that Aaron is my age?" Eliza shook her head no. "We should have been friends, but instead he grew distant towards me. He hated that he did not carry a title. Every time the use of my title would come up, he would roll his eyes or make a joke. He hates the peerage, and he kept trying to get me to turn against Henry for being the heir. Aaron used to say, 'Why should Henry, who was born two years before you, inherit all that your father has, and you get nothing?'"

"Was Mr. Wade a second son?" Eliza was curious about what fueled Wade's hate of the nobility.

"No, he was the first born of a vicar. His father was the second son of an earl and became a vicar as his profession. My stepmother Jane was the daughter of a viscount. Aaron grew up around extreme wealth, but his family only lived on a modest income from his parsonage. He was greedy and wanted more from life."

Eliza listened intently to what he was saying. She knew from her experience as an agent that greed could corrupt almost any man. She was curious to learn more about Mr. Wade. "So, what happened?"

Benedict leaned up against a tree across from her. "About five years ago, Aaron decided to branch out and make his own way in the world. Father wanted Aaron to succeed, because he knew it was important to Jane. He invested a small portion of money with Aaron to help him start a business. Aaron wanted to buy ships and use them to create a merchant empire." Running his hand over his chin, he looked distraught. "A year ago, Henry started hearing rumors that Aaron had branched out into illegal avenues, so Henry hired a Bow Street Runner to investigate our stepbrother. Soon after, we received confirmation that Aaron had a reputation for buying and selling anything that could make a profit."

Eliza knew this part of the story. "He buys and sells women."

Lowering his eyes, he said in a strained voice, "Amongst other things." Benedict brought his eyes up while he continued his tale. "Henry was furious when he found out and told Father. They summoned Aaron to the estate, demanding that he stopped his illegal activities or they were going to turn him over to the authorities. Aaron mocked them and said there was no proof that he had done anything wrong. Father had him thrown out of the house and told him never to come back." His brow was furrowed as he finished speaking.

"How did Jane take that news?"

"I'm sure she cried for Aaron, but she supported my father. I believe my father and Jane have grown to love each other."

Benedict pushed off from the tree started to walk past her. Eliza placed her hand on his sleeve to stop him and asked, "How was Henry killed?"

He glanced down at her hand for a moment, and she started to remove it, thinking she had been too bold in her show of support. Before she had a chance, his hand was on top of hers, and he held it firmly in place. "I was on a mission six months ago when Henry was killed. He was thrown off his horse and trampled to death." Benedict gave a humorless laugh. "Henry was an accomplished rider, and he would never have been careless enough to be thrown off his horse."

"Did the magistrate open up an investigation?" Eliza inquired.

"He did." Benedict clenched his jaw, a muscle twitching just below the ear. "Aaron told the magistrate that he went out and tried to catch Henry on his morning ride, but found him unresponsive. Everyone knew that Henry went on a morning ride whether rain or shine."

"What was the reason Mr. Wade gave for wanting to catch up with Henry?"

He scoffed. "According to Aaron, he just wanted to apologize to Henry for the misunderstanding of his business dealings and plead for his forgiveness."

"The magistrate did not find it unusual that Henry died, and his estranged stepbrother was the one who found him?" Eliza asked curiously.

"Everyone found that suspicious, but there was no proof that tied Aaron to killing Henry. The magistrate apologized, and said legally his hands were tied unless new evidence was brought to light. Father tried in vain to convince the magistrate to charge Aaron with his murder, but there was no proof. It was ruled a suspicious death," Benedict said, in a resigned voice.

Eliza tilted her head, as she observed the profound sadness that reflected in his eyes. She desperately wanted to help bear his burden and wipe away some of the pain he was feeling. She waited till his gaze met her eyes, and she placed her other hand on top of his hand. "Together, we will bring Mr. Wade to justice and make him pay dearly for what he did to Henry," she said determinedly.

Benedict's eyes started filling with tears. "Henry was my best friend. There is not a day that goes by that I do not recall how I failed my brother. I failed to protect him." He sighed mournfully, shaking his head, "I failed to tell him how much he meant to me."

Eliza withdrew her hands, and Benedict felt an overpowering feeling of emptiness wash over him by the sudden loss of contact. A moment later, her gloved hands went around his neck and pulled him into an embrace. His arms immediately circled around her waist, as he pulled her tightly against him. Her touch had a strange calming effect on him that gave him a temporary, but much-needed respite from his grief.

"I am sorry about Henry," Eliza whispered against him. "In no way did you fail him. How could anyone have known that Mr. Wade was such a threat against your family, or that he would stoop so low as to murder his own stepbrother?"

"I should have known," Benedict said, his voice hitching.

89

Eliza slightly leaned back, gently placing her hand on his cheek, and her eyes were filled with compassion and genuine sympathy. "You are a good man, but even you cannot foresee the future. No one could have predicted that Mr. Wade would have become such a despicable excuse for a human being." She tenderly wiped a tear from his cheek and returned his embrace.

Benedict realized that this was the first time he had confided to anyone about his brother's death. Even though he had only known Eliza for two days, he trusted her completely. How long they stood amongst the trees hugging each other, he did not know. All he did know was she was allowing him to embrace her for as long as he wanted. Benedict knew he needed to release her, but he found he did not ever want to let her go. He marveled at how perfectly she fit into his arms.

Glancing up, he saw the sun setting and knew it was time to head back. He was surprised that Mr. Larson had not already come hunting for him since they were gone for so long. He reluctantly dropped his arms from her waist and stepped back. "Thank you, Eliza." He reached for her hand and intertwined their fingers.

As they slowly made their way back to the castle, they remained in comfortable silence. He did not feel the need to force a conversation with her. Benedict felt content for the first time since he'd heard about Henry's death. While he glanced down at his new partner, he squeezed her hand and her whole face lit up when she smiled up at him. He had never believed in love at first sight, but Eliza had made him a believer.

Chapter Ten

Eliza woke up drenched in sweat. Someone was shaking her. Someone was trying to kill her. Her hand shot under her pillow to grab her dagger. It was not there. Why was her dagger missing? She started fighting back against her attacker. He was saying something. Why was he telling her to wake up? Eliza realized that someone was trying to wake her. She opened her eyes to see Mr. Larson leaning over her, with his hands on her shoulders, and he was still shaking her. He stopped when he realized she was awake. His face was etched with concern.

"You were screaming again."

She closed her eyes in mortification. *When would these horrific dreams go away?* "My hands were dripping with blood," she said as she sat up in bed and pulled her knees towards her. "He was laughing at me as blood was splattering out of his mouth."

Martha walked over to the bed with a new set of linens. "Lady Eliza, I need to switch the sheets on your bed, then we will put you in a new nightgown."

Eliza slowly arose, and Mr. Larson escorted her to the blue velvet settee at the end of her bed. Once she was seated, he sat next to her as he had done repeatedly for the past few weeks. "Eliza, dear, you need to stop punishing yourself. What happened in France was not your fault," he said, his voice filled with compassion.

She looked at him with a tear streaked face. "He was laughing at me and I... I slit his throat." Eliza leveled her stare at the floor. "What kind of monster am I?" she questioned as a sob escaped her mouth.

"You are not a monster," Mr. Larson reassured her, pulling her into a hug. "I failed you that night. It was my job to protect you, and you ended up saving me."

Resting her cheek on his shoulder, she relaxed into his embrace. "You are like a father to me. I would give my life to save you."

Her protector sounded pained as he said, "Do not say that. I'm supposed to protect you, remember?"

When she finished changing the linens, the maid stepped away from the bed. Mr. Larson released Eliza. "I will step outside while Martha helps you with your nightgown. Do you want me to come back in after you change and sit by your bed till you fall asleep?"

She shook her head as she looked at him. "I am sorry for waking you up again. Please go back to bed. I will be fine."

He put his hand on her shoulder. "Are you going to be all right for the rest of the night?"

She nodded reluctantly. "I rarely have a second bad dream after I fall back asleep."

Mr. Larson removed his hand, but still looked concerned. "You are having these dreams every night now."

Eliza hugged herself. "I just cannot get those images out of my head. My hands and clothing were dripping with blood and the sailor's lifeless, bleak eyes piercing up at me."

Giving her a sympathetic look, he assisted her up from the settee, then he excused himself so Eliza could change her nightgown. Once she changed, she got back into bed and lowered her head onto the pillow as her hand instinctively went to grip her dagger. Her hand only met the sheets, and she could not locate it.

Before she could ask about it, there was a knock on her bedroom door. Martha opened it, and Mr. Larson stepped back into the room. Walking over to the bed, he handed her the dagger.

"Thank you," Eliza said as she put her trusted dagger under her pillow and laid her head back down.

She closed her eyes as her thoughts strayed towards Benedict. She reminisced back to their previous conversation about losing his brother, and his strained relationship with his father. She started wondering if she could ever fully confide in him about her past as he had confided in her. Tears welled up in Eliza's eyes as she imagined the look of disdain he would have on his face as she told him the truth of the things she had done as *Shadow*. No, she could never tell him the full truth of what she had become. Eliza felt so alone as she softly cried in her pillow till sleep overtook her.

Benedict arrived at Beaumont Castle mid-morning and found himself overjoyed at the prospect of seeing Eliza again. Last night, she had invited him to stay for dinner, then they spent hours discussing their favorite books and poems. She shared stories of how she used to play with her siblings in the forest near the abbey, but he recognized she never spoke about the time when she lived at her Uncle Charles' manor.

In turn, he regaled her with stories about his youth with Henry and how they would spend hours riding around their properties, and the mischief they always ultimately found. It was the perfect evening.

Benedict knocked on the door just as Mr. Larson opened it and ushered him in. "Good morning, Lord Sinclair," he said energetically.

The older man's suspicious behavior immediately put Benedict on guard. *Why was he being so cordial to him?* His eyes narrowed as he thought about reaching for the knife concealed in his right boot. Mr. Larson put his hand out to indicate he should follow him into the dining room. Benedict decided to do his bidding for now, because he needed to have a plan of action in case Eliza's protector tried to poison him at breakfast. He walked into the room and saw Eliza sitting down at the table, absent-mindedly staring at her food.

As he came closer, she glanced up and smiled. "Good morning, Benedict," she said pleasantly. Mr. Larson's eyebrows shot up when Eliza used his given name, but she did not seem to notice.

"Good morning, Eliza. Did you sleep well?" Benedict pulled out a chair next to her and sat down. He leaned closer and asked flirtatiously, "Was everything all right after I left, or did you miss me too much to sleep?"

Eliza's cheeks turned a bright pink which he found adorable. After a moment, she said softly, "I did not sleep well last night due to a bad dream."

Mr. Larson placed a plate in front of him piled high with eggs and muffins. Benedict looked back at him with shock. "How much do you think I eat?"

"I just want you to feel comfortable," the older man smiled.

Benedict was now even more suspicious that something happened. Yesterday, Mr. Larson had gone out of his way to make him feel as uncomfortable as possible at Beaumont Castle. In fact, he literally pushed him out the door last night.

"I see that you are ready to go riding," Eliza said, acknowledging Benedict's riding outfit of buckskin breeches, a white shirt, and knee length riding boots. "Let me go retrieve my riding gloves while you finish breakfast." He rose quickly and pulled out her chair for her. She politely thanked him, then quickly walked out of the dining room.

Sitting back down at the table, Benedict turned his full attention to Mr. Larson. "Did something happen last night?"

Glancing over at the doorway that Eliza just departed, Mr. Larson came around the table to where Benedict was sitting and leaned against the edge while folding his arms. "Eliza has been having bad dreams about what happened in France last month."

"Those dreams are common amongst agents," Benedict pointed out.

"True, but this is different."

"How so?"

"I have seen this reaction from men coming back from the war. It appears that their minds cannot cope with what they have seen or had to do, and they keep reliving a specific experience."

"How long does it take for them to recover?" Benedict asked.

Mr. Larson shrugged. "It varies, but some never do."

"What are Eliza's dreams about?"

Shaking his head, the older man frowned. "That I cannot tell you. I should not have even told you about the bad dreams, but it is getting alarming." He winced as he said, "She wakes up screaming and is drenched in sweat every night now. The whole household has not had a good night's sleep in a month, and some nights she has multiple episodes. Martha, her lady's maid, is afraid to wake her up when she is in that state, because once she tried it, and Eliza almost stabbed her."

Benedict's eyebrows shot up. "She almost stabbed her? How did Eliza get a knife in bed?"

"She sleeps with one under her pillow." Mr. Larson seemed surprised at the question. "You do not sleep with a knife under your pillow?"

Shaking his head, he answered matter-of-factly, "No, I sleep with a pistol next to my bed."

Mr. Larson nodded his approval. "Well, I have to remove the dagger before I try to wake her up. When I start shaking her to wake up, she thinks I am attacking her, and she goes on the defensive. Yet, when I do not shake her, she will scream for hours." He sighed deeply. "I do not know how to help her anymore." Straightening up, he frowned. "I was hoping she might confide in you."

Benedict was not sure about that. "Jonathon told me that Eliza has not even told him about that night."

"True," Mr. Larson said, "but I have seen the way she looks at you. I have no idea why, but she trusts you." The older man shook his head in disgust. "I really have no idea what she sees in you."

He smiled at Mr. Larson's attempt to insult him once again. "Maybe she trusts me because I am such a handsome man?"

Mr. Larson loudly snorted. "Obviously, you do not own a mirror, Lord Sinclair." With that final insult, he headed out the door.

Starting in on the pile of food on his plate, Benedict pondered what Mr. Larson had revealed to him. Jonathon had also asked him to get Eliza to trust him the day he dropped him off at her Castle. How would he get her to confide in him about what happened in France?

Benedict hoped she would share her secrets with him, because he found he wanted to know everything about her. Her likes and dislikes, what makes her happy, even her fears. He knew it would be a challenge get Eliza to open up to him, but it would be worth it.

Eliza stepped back into the dining room wearing her dark green riding habit. When Benedict saw her, he stood, pushing his chair back from the table. She took a moment to admire him and his rugged physique, and realized he was positively the most handsome man she had ever met. Though his manner was charismatic and courteous, his entire presence emanated a sense of danger and adventure. She was exceedingly grateful that this man was her partner, and not fighting for the enemy. Every time he was in the room, she found her defenses were weakened, and she highly doubted she could take on Benedict the spy.

"Are you ready?" Eliza asked as he walked closer, hoping her voice would not betray her thoughts.

Benedict stopped his approach in front of her, leaving very little distance between them, and lifted an eyebrow. "Am I ready for what exactly?"

Eliza rolled her eyes mockingly. "To go riding, of course."

Giving her a crooked smile, his bemused eyes stared at her searchingly. His hand reached out and slowly started caressing her forearm. "I am, but we could stay and amuse ourselves in other ways."

Without thinking, she clasped her ungloved hand over his mouth. "Do you have a death wish, my lord?" She nervously glanced over her shoulder. "Mr. Larson would shoot you on the spot if he heard you making such lewd suggestions." She could feel Benedict's lips as they curled into a smile, and she immediately redrew her hand, as if his lips had burned her. What was she thinking putting her hand on his mouth?

"What exactly did you think I was alluding to?" He had the nerve to feign shock, as he placed his hand on his chest. "After all, I thought discussing poetry in the library was something you might enjoy."

"You thought no such thing, and you know it," Eliza stated as she boldly met his gaze. Benedict was toying with her, and she needed to show him that she could match him wit for wit.

He chuckled. "And how would you know what I was thinking?"

Amusement twinkled in her eyes and played with the corner of her mouth. "I am a spy." As she spun to walk out of the room, she said over her shoulder, "I know everything." She heard him chuckle as he caught up with her.

It wasn't long before they both were cantering their horses in the open fields around the castle. Strands of Eliza's hair had started to come loose from her bun, since she chose to forego wearing a riding hat. Her cheeks were flushed with excitement, because riding was one of her favorite pastimes.

"Are you up for a race?" Eliza challenged Benedict as she reined in her horse.

He pulled up next to her. "What do you have in mind?"

Eliza pointed to a heavily wooded section of her property behind her castle. "First one to the trees, wins."

"Sounds fair."

Eliza started counting. "One... two... three!" she shouted as she kicked her horse into a run.

Chapter Eleven

$\mathcal{A}$ few minutes later, Eliza arrived at the trees and reined in her horse. She turned to watch Benedict, who was close behind. She was pleased to see he had a bright smile on his face. She dismounted and secured her reins while waiting for him to do the same. Once the horses were both settled, Eliza started walking through the trees with Benedict following.

"I want to show you something," she said over her shoulder.

They walked for a few minutes as the sound of running water trickled through the trees. Eliza had discovered there was a babbling brook that ran through her property. She spent so much time here at first that she had asked Mr. Larson to move a bench to this location, which allowed her to sit and enjoy the tranquility of the forest. Eliza sat down on the iron bench near the stream's edge.

"It is beautiful here," Benedict said after a few moments, while claiming the seat next to her.

She murmured her agreement. "It is. I spend a lot of time here." He slid closer to her and put his arm on the back of the bench. She allowed herself to relax against his shoulder, as they both sat in quiet meditation, while birds chirped merrily in the trees.

Benedict's voice broke into her thoughts. "What happened in France, Eliza?"

She felt the blood drain from her face, but she quickly recovered. Not wanting to answer that question, she tried to distract him. "Which time, Benedict? I have been to France many times over the years," she said nonchalantly while watching the sparrows dance in the birch trees.

"I am asking about what happened last month," he pressed.

Eliza laughed it off. "Why would you want to know about our last mission? You were there too, were you not?"

"True, but I was on the ship."

She kicked a pebble with her boot. "Yes, Jonathon told me you were on the ship. I am glad I was there to help you."

"Speaking of Jonathon," Benedict hesitated, "he implied that something horrible might have happened in France that you have not told him."

"Why exactly do *you* want to know?" Eliza asked defensively while she tried to stand, but he reached for her hand, stalling her efforts.

"It sounds to me like you are afraid to talk about it," he challenged.

Refusing to take the bait, she squared her shoulders. "I am not afraid of anything."

Benedict raised his brow in disbelief. "Can you tell me about France then?"

"I do not want to talk about that," she answered coldly.

He clenched his jaw. Obviously, he was disappointed with her answer, but she did not want to discuss with him what had happened in France. He let out a sigh. "How about we start with an easier question?" He paused, then asked, "Why did you become a spy?"

Eliza shrugged. "What else was I to become?"

"What does that mean?"

"Sometimes I feel that I was born to be a spy."

"Why?"

"It is a long story," Eliza answered in a dismissive tone, hoping that it would discourage Benedict.

Instead, he intertwined his fingers with hers, relaxed back into the bench and seemed to be waiting for her to start the story. "I am ready when you are," he said patiently.

Eliza stared at their hands for a moment, then gazed into his blue eyes. His eyes were filled with warmth and compassion, and she knew she could trust him with her story. She took a deep breath to gather her courage.

"I was born with a mind that remembers everything. When I read books, it is like the pages are permanently sketched in my mind. Miss

Sharp, my governess, encouraged my reading mainly because she did not know what else to do with me. I read almost every book in the library at the abbey, then I started taking books from my father's estate."

"What kind of books would you read?"

"Anything I could get my hands on. I especially love poetry, philosophy, and history," she rattled off.

"When did you start reading those books?" Benedict sounded skeptical.

"I do not know exactly when, but I would guess around six or seven." Eliza raised an eyebrow in response to his shocked expression. "You do not believe me?"

His lips curled up. "No, I believe you, but I am just surprised you were able to comprehend what you were reading. When I was that age, I was still playing pranks on our nursemaid to avoid schooling."

"That does not surprise me in the least bit," she grinned.

He let out a slight chuckle. "So, you started stealing books from your father's library. Is that why you were kicked out of the abbey?"

Eliza's head whipped around. "How did you know my mother kicked me out of the abbey?"

"Jonathon mentioned it in passing."

She started biting her lower lip and her eyes flickered to her hands in her lap. "I was hoping to skip over that part of my life."

Benedict gently placed his large hand over hers, making her feel safe. "Is that why you became a spy?"

"No, but it set the wheels into motion," she said, shaking her head.

His hands were warm and broad and still encompassing hers. "If you would not mind, I would like to hear about what happened. Unless it is too painful for you to discuss?"

Eliza sighed inwardly, knowing she had never shared with anyone what happened with her mother. It was time to put her trust in someone and her instinct told her to trust Benedict. Without glancing at him, she started sharing her story.

"Every year, my mother and father throw a lavish ball at the abbey, and it is the one time of year that they are civil to each other.

Only the elite of the ton get invited to my mother's ball. When I was ten, I snuck downstairs after Miss Sharp fell asleep to watch the dancing. While I was walking by the library, I heard some men discussing John Milton's *Paradise Lost*, and I joined their discussion for over an hour. Some men had not read *Paradise Lost*, so I started reciting the chapters for them."

"You read John Milton at age ten?"

She smiled smugly. "No, I read *Paradise Lost* when I was nine."

"I was at Oxford when I had to read John Milton's works, but I confess I did not enjoy it," Benedict admitted.

Eliza smiled understandingly at him. "It is complex, but there are some profound truths in John Milton's works."

"What happened after you recited *Paradise Lost*?"

She frowned as she continued, "My mother walked into the library, found me conversing with the men and ordered me to bed. The next morning, Mother and Father had a horrible fight and Mother wanted to send me away to a boarding school. Later, Mother came into the nursery and told me that I had embarrassed the family by being a bluestocking." Pausing from her story, Eliza leveled her stare at the ground. "Just when I did not think it could get any worse, she told me that I had disgraced the family, and she hated me for it." Tears welled in her eyes. "My own mother told me she hated me."

Releasing her hand, Benedict handed her his handkerchief. She used it to wipe the tears away. "Your mother probably did not mean it."

Eliza let out a slight huff. "Oh no, she meant it. Luckily, I was sent away to Uncle Charles' estate, and he reassured me that my mind is what made me special. He allowed me to read any book from his extensive library, and he brought in tutors that taught me French, Italian, German, Russian and Latin. Furthermore, I had tutors for mathematics and logic. I received an education that rivaled Oxford or Cambridge," she announced proudly.

He nodded and smiled. "It sounds to me like you received a better education than those institutions offered."

Smiling appreciatively, she drew a large breath, her voice soft and resigned. "I was happy at Uncle Charles' estate, but I had no friends my age. The household staff was kind to me, but I was incredibly lonely when the tutors went away for the day, so I befriended the game warden on my uncle's property. Mr. Morton had a small cottage, and I spent most of my free time with him. He even took me hunting pheasants and deerstalking with him, which is where I learned how to shoot the longbow and throw a dagger." Eliza glanced down at her hands which were wringing the handkerchief.

Benedict spoke when she paused her story. "When did you learn how to shoot a pistol?"

Eliza's head popped back up. "Jonathon taught me years ago. Mr. Morton already taught me how to shoot a hunting rifle, but I read a book about the history of the flintlock pistol and asked Jonathon to teach me how to shoot. I own an overcoat pistol, but I prefer the longbow or my dagger."

"Why?"

She bit her bottom lip for a moment while she debated about how to answer. "For a few reasons, actually. The first is, the pistol only has one musket ball and takes a few minutes to reload. Secondly, it emanates a loud noise when fired, and produces smoke which makes it easier to detect the origin of the shot. The third reason is that I find the longbow to be more accurate from long distances," Eliza said confidently. "I am deadly accurate till about two hundred meters. Over two hundred meters, I can wound an animal, but the arrow is not strong enough to kill the animal outright."

Benedict's eyebrows went up in response. "That is impressive."

Eliza looked longingly at the box trees that encompassed one side of the stream. They reminded her of the box trees that grew on her uncle's property. "Even though I stalked the red deer, my favorite pastime was to creep up to them and see how close I could get before they caught my scent. At times, I got so close that I could almost reach out and touch the deer." Embarrassed, she glanced at him before saying, "As I mentioned before, I spent a lot of time alone in the forest."

"Where was Lord Beckett?" he frowned.

Sighing, she answered matter-of-factly, "Uncle Charles mainly spent his time in London, but when he came home we would spend hours playing chess and other games. A few months after I moved in, Uncle Charles gave me puzzles that were in different languages, and he taught me how to look for specific patterns to solve them. I loved these puzzles, because it took all my knowledge of philosophy, mathematics, and logic to crack them. One of my favorite puzzles used a fourteen-hundred number system and added meaningless figures to the end of the letters. For a long time, I thought Uncle Charles was trying to keep me busy, but when I found out that I was helping the Crown by deciphering enemy codes, I felt needed. I did not feel like an embarrassment anymore..." Eliza's voice trailed off.

Benedict pulled her into an embrace. "You did nothing wrong. Your mother was cruel to you." Resting her head on his chest, she realized how safe she felt with him. His voice sounded deep when he asked, "Why did you not go live with your father?"

"To avoid scandal." Eliza snuggled a little closer to him while breathing in his masculine scent and found it oddly comforting. "Although, I used to wish that Lady Anne could have been my mother, even though it would have meant I was illegitimate. Lady Anne has always been so kind to me."

"I am sorry you were so lonely at Lord Beckett's estate. Did you ever get to see your brothers and your twin sister?"

"I was able to see them on holidays when I was invited for dinner at the abbey, or at my father's estate, but Luke was at Oxford, and Jonathon was at Eton. Mother forbade me from spending time with Kate, but we started meeting up once a month on our afternoon rides. Even though Kate and I were always escorted by footmen, they would let us sit and talk for hours without ever telling the duchess." Eliza grew sad for a moment. "Kate and I met up for the last time before her wedding to Lord Camden, and she was so dejected by her upcoming nuptials."

"It must have been hard for you having to sneak around to see your sister all the time," Benedict pointed out.

Pulling her head off his chest, Eliza looked him in the eyes. "When I first moved into my uncle's estate, I used to feel sorry for myself, then a quote from *Paradise Lost* came to me. 'The mind is its own place, and in itself can make a heaven of hell, a hell of heaven'." She smiled at him as she explained, "I could choose whether I would be happy or miserable. I could complain and grow bitter which would only hurt myself, or I could choose to be happy with my lot in life. I chose to be happy."

Reaching over, Benedict placed a piece of Eliza's brown hair behind her ear, then he cupped his hand on her cheek. "Well, now I know how you learned to decipher codes and shoot the longbow. How exactly did you become the notorious *Shadow*?"

She let her head rest for a minute on his hand before asking, "Why do you do that?"

"Do what?" He raised his eyebrows.

"Whenever you want me to tell you something, you touch me," Eliza observed.

"I do? Does it work?" Benedict asked.

"Yes, I suppose it does. You make me feel safe and protected." She lowered her head to rest on his chest. "I cannot remember the last time I felt this content."

"Good." He kissed the top of her head.

Chapter Twelve

"So, how did you acquire the code name *Shadow*?"

They had been sitting contentedly for some time without speaking, so Eliza was a bit surprised when he spoke. But she did not mind sharing this part of her story, since it did not make her feel as vulnerable. She removed her head from his chest, and leaned back against the bench.

"When I was seventeen, my father started assigning me to go on diplomatic missions with Jonathon. We traveled all over the world and met the most amazing people. Uncle Charles saw this as a perfect opportunity for me to spy on other countries. As a young girl, I could easily sneak away and find the offices of the dignitaries, or ambassadors. Luckily, I never was caught spying, mainly because I never had to steal any paperwork, since I could wait till we got back to the safety of our ship or townhouse before I would transcribe what I found."

"What would Jonathon do on these diplomatic missions?" Benedict asked curiously.

"He would go to meetings in place of my father. Our role was to charm the leaders of various kingdoms, in hopes that they would continue to side with England against Napoleon. As children of the Duke of Remington, we were welcomed into most countries with open arms."

Benedict arched an eyebrow. "And yet, you spied behind their backs?"

Eliza smirked. "Now you are beginning to understand."

Benedict chuckled.

"It was not until later that I realized Jonathon was sneaking out at night to hand off the papers I copied to other agents. One night in Italy, I decided to follow him. To ensure Jonathon did not see me, I crouched low against the building, and tracked him into an alleyway. He and the other agent started having an intense argument and became too distracted to notice a man was creeping up behind Jonathon with a stiletto. I do not know what happened, but I just reacted and threw my dagger into the man's back." Swallowing nervously, she admitted, "That was my first kill, but I did save Jonathon's life."

"What did Jonathon do?"

"He was furious," she admitted. "He escorted me home before he started ranting and raving about how I could not sneak out in the night, since it was unsafe being an unescorted female in Florence. He threatened to send me back to Uncle Charles' estate."

"I could see Jonathon doing that," Benedict commented.

Eliza's eyes roamed the birch trees for a moment. "That night changed me," she stated firmly but more to herself. "After that, I started following Jonathon every time he went out at night, but I gradually changed my wardrobe. At first, I would wear men's shirts and trousers, but the white shirt and tan trousers were visible at night, so I had my lady's maid dye them black, which made them almost undetectable in the shadows of the buildings. I would also pull my hair up into a black cap and would wear a long, black cloak. Later, I started bringing along my longbow and arrows, which allowed me to stay further away. Most of the time, Jonathon would hand off the papers and nothing would transpire, but it all changed when we arrived in India." She stood and slowly wandered closer to the stream.

Benedict's voice came from behind her as he cautiously pressed, "What happened in India, Eliza?"

Watching the water flow over and around the rocks in the stream for a moment, she then turned around to face him. "Mr. Larson joined us shortly after we left Italy because Uncle Charles assigned him to protect me when I went out at night. I convinced Mr. Larson to take me to the market since it was in a rough section of the city, but I was not overly concerned, as we kept to ourselves. As we were passing by a large tent, we heard a commotion coming from inside, so I peeked in." Eliza leaned down to pick up a pebble and tossed it into the babbling brook. Once the rock settled, she continued, "A light-skinned young woman with scraggly blonde hair, who appeared to be slightly older than me, was dressed in rags and her hands were bound with rope. There was a short, balding Indian man standing next to her, yelling out numbers, and it became apparent that they were auctioning her off. Since I knew these men would not take me seriously if I tried to bid on the girl, I had Mr. Larson buy the young woman."

"What happened to the girl?" Benedict asked with concern.

Eliza placed her hand on a downy birch, while briefly admiring the whiter bark that ran along the tree. "Her name is Martha, and she became my lady's maid. She is from a town an hour north of here and is the daughter of a vicar. When she was sixteen, she fell in love with a man that tricked her into running away with him. She left a note for her parents that told them she was going to be married. Unfortunately, the man took her to your stepbrother and sold her to him. By the time I found Martha in India, she had been violently abused for years. Evidently, the brothel owner grew tired of her lack of enthusiasm with his customers, and he decided to sell her to someone else." She shuddered at that thought.

"That is appalling," Benedict said while shaking his head.

She nodded in agreement. "It took some time, but Martha started to trust me and told me about what happened. She told me that someone named Mr. Wade had bought her and placed her on a ship to India. Martha explained that she, and the other women he bought, were shipped in the cargo hold and were chained down to the floor. When they arrived in India, they were cleaned up and given new dresses, then they were brought up to the top of the ship and men would bid on them."

"I cannot even begin to imagine what horrors those poor girls have had to endure. I never thought Aaron would sink so low as to treat innocent girls like chattel." Benedict clenched his jaw as he looked towards the stream. "I wish I had known what he had gotten himself involved in earlier, and I could have stopped him."

"Your brother tried to stop him, and Mr. Wade killed him for it," she pointed out.

Benedict grimaced. "True, but my brother was not trained as an agent. I would have had no problem taking Aaron out with one shot from my pistol."

Eliza's lips curled into a smile. "Now you are starting to sound like me. I do not think Uncle Charles would approve of my influence over you."

"I find your influence to be quite exemplary," he said teasingly. His eyes danced with amusement as he folded his arms across his broad chest and leaned back against a tree. "If we cannot just kill Aaron, how do you propose stopping him?"

"That is what I have been working on for the past two years," she said in frustration. "I have been able to thwart four of Mr. Wade's shipments, but it has been difficult to build a case against him in the courts. He is a shrewd businessman and is not afraid of turning on his business partners."

Benedict nodded. "I have searched his home on multiple occasions, but I have failed to locate anything that would implicate him in these abductions. Besides, no witnesses to his crimes have come forward. How were you able to stop his shipments?"

Eliza reached down and picked up a wedge-shaped leaf from the ground. "When we finally arrived back in England, I went straight to Uncle Charles, so I could reveal what I learned about a man named Mr. Wade abducting, or buying, women off the streets in England. My uncle did not seem to be surprised that this was happening, and he gave me permission to begin investigating your stepbrother. I started trailing him around town, and I noticed he spent a lot of his time in a run down, wooden building near the docks."

Giving her a disapproving look, Benedict asked, "Did you trail Aaron to the docks by yourself?"

She gave him a smug smile. "Yes, but I had my longbow with me."

He shook his head. "That is not backup, Eliza. Do you have any idea how dangerous it is for a woman…"

"Do not finish that sentence," Eliza warned as she cut him off. "Do I need to remind you that I am a capable spy, and I have no problem trailing a suspect undetected?"

Benedict put his hands up in surrender. "You are right, I have no right to condemn you. What exactly did you discover from trailing

Aaron?"

She dropped the leaf and watched it while it slowly glided to the leaf-covered ground. "One evening, I waited till Mr. Wade left the building and snuck in to see what occupied so much of his time. Inside, I discovered fifteen young women, huddled together on the floor, with their ankles and wrists bound with rope, and they were guarded by two men. Immediately, I went and notified Uncle Charles, who dispatched agents over to rescue the girls, but he told me to go home and he would notify me of what transpired."

Putting his hand to his chin, he said teasingly, "Let me guess, you put men's clothing on and snuck after them?"

Eliza beamed up at him. "What else was I going to do?"

Benedict chuckled. "What else could you do?"

She rested her back against a tree. "Since I was at the building before, I snuck back through an open window and quickly climbed up to the loft that overlooked the interior of the building. Sadly, the three agents showed up at the wrong time, because the girls were being prepared to be relocated to Mr. Wade's ship that had just docked, and now there were four guards. It quickly turned into a kill or be killed battle, and our agents were on the losing end. I did not want to give away my position too soon, but when one of the agents was thrown down while clutching his bleeding arm, with a tall, grimy man looming over him preparing to plunge a knife into his chest, I shot him with an arrow to his heart." Eliza hesitated, lowering her voice while saying, "I ended up killing two men that night."

"You may have killed two men, but you saved three agents and fifteen girls," Benedict countered.

Eliza gave him a grateful smile, then gazed towards a brown, spotted sparrow that had just landed in a nearby tree. "Those three agents started sharing their story about how a man who lurked in the shadows had saved them that night. Uncle Charles decided it was an appropriate time to announce *Shadow* was an agent, and I became a legend overnight."

She wrapped her arms around her waist. "Uncles Charles confirmed that *Shadow* could break any code, sneak into any home, both in England and abroad, all while staying hidden. It provided a way to give the agents a much-needed boost in morale during a time when England seemed to be fighting everyone. Ironically, other countries did not know what stories to believe about *Shadow*, so they just put a price on my head," Eliza huffed.

"Do the stories have some truth in them?" Benedict asked.

"Yes," she laughed. "But the claims are grossly exaggerated, especially the stories in the newspapers. Uncle Charles started leaking information about *Shadow* as an attempt to rally England behind the war with France. It worked splendidly, just like he predicted."

"I do enjoy reading the articles about *Shadow* in the newspaper."

Eliza smiled good-naturedly. "Jonathon will not let me read his newspaper when there is an article about *Shadow*. He says that it will inflate my ego."

"Some of the stories have seemed a little far-fetched, but are quite entertaining." He chuckled, then asked, "Can you really sail a ship?"

Letting out a loud laugh, Eliza threw her hand up to cover the noise. "No, I cannot sail a ship, and I have never joined a band of pirates. Sometimes I think Uncle Charles drinks too much port before he writes those stories."

"Does he print any facts about your missions?"

"He does. He wants the other countries to know that *Shadow* bested them, both now and in the past. Most of the time, he waits awhile before he publishes a factual story, and he leaves out any information that could incriminate me or any Englishman. Besides, no one would ever suspect the daughter of a duke to be a spy."

Benedict nodded his head in agreement then he stayed silent for a moment. "Well, now I know why you hate Aaron as much as I do."

"I did not realize it was a competition," Eliza said as her lips curled up in amusement.

"I did not mean to imply it was a competition," Benedict smiled.

Eliza tucked a loose piece of her hair behind her ear. "My personal mission is to gather enough proof to send your stepbrother to Newgate or the noose because, frankly, I really do not care if he lives or dies," she stated emphatically.

Pushing off from the tree, Benedict took a step closer to her. "You do realize when we rid the world of my delightful stepbrother, that other men will take his place at trafficking women?"

Eliza nodded her head in agreement. "I do, but at least we got rid of Mr. Wade and that makes the world a little safer."

Benedict edged closer until he stood right in front of her. "You are an amazing woman, Eliza," he said, his eyes flickering to her lips.

The whole world seemed to fade away as Eliza realized how desperately she wanted him to kiss her. She was not sure if her heart had ever pounded so fast in her life, and she was afraid he could hear it. His dark blue eyes were filled with an intensity she had never witnessed before, and her breath hitched, as she found herself lost in his passion-filled gaze.

He started to bring his head closer as his hands reached for hers, engulfing them tenderly. She could feel his breath on her face, and she was sure he was going to kiss her. His lips were hovering close to hers, a breath hanging between them, and it was torture. As she nervously licked her lips, she debated about ending this torment by just claiming his lips.

Suddenly, Benedict cleared his throat and took a step back. He slowly turned his head to glance up at the sky. "We should head back. It is getting late."

Eliza sighed inwardly as she realized the moment had passed. She had not realized how long they had lingered in her private haven, but the sun was casting shadows amongst the trees. He reached for her hand and slowly guided them back to their horses, hand in hand.

"Are you familiar with German whist, Eliza?"

"Yes, I am."

"Excellent. Are you up for a game?"

Eliza laughed. "I feel as if I should warn you that I am quite good at whist."

Benedict smiled down on her. "We shall see about that, my dear."

Chapter Thirteen

Much later in the evening, Benedict and Eliza were sitting in her drawing room after he had accepted her offer to dine with her. They were swapping stories of their childhood and now that Eliza had told him about living with Uncle Charles, she did not shy away from stories that included those years.

Benedict was lounging next to her on the sofa, with a gracefully shaped cushioned back, which allowed his arm to perfectly drape over her shoulder. Watching her face as she shared a story of her childhood, he witnessed all range of emotions written there. He was so proud of how much she had accomplished so young and he admired her courage and strength, even when faced with such rejection from her mother. He was still gazing upon Eliza when he noticed that she had stopped talking, and was smiling at him so sweetly.

She yawned and her hand flew up to cover her mouth. "I am truly sorry, Benedict. I did not sleep well last night."

He thought this might be a good time to broach the subject again. "Because of your horrid dreams?"

"Yes, because of..." she started as her eyes grew wide. "Who told you about my dreams?"

"You did."

"I did?"

"Yes, this morning you told me that you had a bad dream last night," Benedict pointed out.

Eliza dismissed his comment with a wave of her hand. "Oh, right. It was just a bad dream." She moved to stand up.

"I heard you are having these bad dreams every night now."

"And who told you that?" she asked suspiciously as she turned to look at him.

Benedict saw no reason to hide the truth. "Jonathon and Mr. Larson."

"They should not have done that." She sounded angry.

Leaning closer, he lowered his voice. "Can you tell me about them?"

"No," she said firmly.

"Why not?" Benedict reached for her hand, but Eliza jumped up off the sofa. She scurried to the fireplace and watched the low flames as they crackled and sparked. He arose and was slowly approaching her when she turned back to face him and put her hands up.

"No, you cannot come over here and hold me, and expect me to tell you what you want to know," she said sternly.

Benedict stopped short. "I hold you because I like to be near you, not because I am trying to trick you into talking to me."

Eliza stared repentantly at him for several seconds, then lowered her gaze to the floor. "I like to be near you, too. I apologize for assuming otherwise."

Resuming his approach, he slowly reached for both of her hands, as he led her back to the sofa. "I am asking you about your dreams, because I find it helps if you talk about them."

"Do you have them, too?" She seemed relieved.

Benedict nodded. "Sometimes."

"My dreams seem so real," she said softly.

"Can you tell me about them?"

"Benedict... No. I cannot," Eliza whimpered as she dropped his hands.

"What are you afraid of, Eliza?" he asked.

Her eyes darted nervously around the room. "I am afraid of... you..." her voice trailed off.

Benedict reared his head back in shock. "You are afraid of me?"

Eliza shook her head vehemently. "No, I would never be afraid of you."

Putting his hand to her cheek, he forced her to look at him. "Then what are you afraid of?"

"I am afraid of what you will think of me after I tell you the truth behind the dreams." Her eyes filled with tears.

"Are your dreams about France?"

"Yes."

Benedict removed his hand from her cheek but stayed close. "Please tell me what happened that night in France, Eliza. I want to help you."

Her tears flowed down her face, as she looked away. He had difficulty hearing her when she said, "No one can help me now."

His lips curled down at what she said. "I do not believe that to be true," he said patiently.

Eliza sighed sadly. "You have to promise me that you will not be disgusted with me after I tell you."

Benedict's heart was filled with sadness for her. What had happened in France that she would be afraid to talk about it? She had already told him about her childhood, which included being abandoned by her mother. What could be worse than that? "I promise," he said honestly.

Eliza's eyes slowly latched onto his, looking young and vulnerable as she started sharing her story. "We knew that Mr. Wade was preparing to unload some merchandise in a small harbor in France near Le Havre, so Jonathon and I had arrived a few days prior and received permission from the French ambassador to board the English ship when it docked." Benedict knew most of this, but he had not known about her involvement until recently.

She licked her lips nervously. "On the morning of the mission, I scouted out a two-level building next to where Mr. Wade's brig was docked, and it allowed me to have a full vantage point of the ship's deck while remaining out of sight. As usual, I would stay on the roof during the mission with Mr. Larson accompanying me to keep anyone from sneaking up behind me." Eliza started slightly shaking. Benedict was still holding her hands, so he squeezed them since he wanted her to know she was not alone. "As you know, the sailors were hiding when you and the other agents boarded." She seemed like she was stalling. "After you walked past the men hiding, they jumped out to ambush you, and it became obvious that they were expecting you."

"Yes, I remember that part," he said, as he subconsciously started rubbing his thigh where he was stabbed.

"Yes... you would remember that. I knew that." Eliza looked flustered. "Then you probably remember that I killed some of the sailors with my arrows."

Benedict gave her an encouraging smile. "You killed five sailors, and you saved all the agents on the mission. Not to mention, you saved those girls that were chained in the cargo hold."

"I killed six men." She grimaced.

He shook his head. "Eliza, you only killed five sailors on the ship."

Her shoulders slumped. "I killed five men on the ship, but I killed another man... on the roof." Eliza started trembling again.

Benedict knew this must be the source of her recurring dreams, and he wanted to encourage her to tell him what happened. He pulled her onto his lap, and she wrapped her hands around his neck, laying her forehead on his shoulder. "Eliza, can you tell me what happened on the roof?" he asked.

For a few minutes, she did not say anything, then her voice shook as she started speaking. "I had just released my last arrow, and I heard a loud thump behind me. I started to turn around, when I heard a thunderous boom, and my left shoulder was on fire. As I grabbed my shoulder, I realized I was bleeding, and I had been shot. I looked around and saw that Mr. Larson was on the ground, but he was bleeding from a wound on his head. I did not know if he was still alive," Eliza admitting as her voice hitched.

She tightened her hold around his neck and it appeared she was attempting to swallow her emotions before she continued. "Before I knew it, a man had shoved me onto my back, leaning over me, and his hands were choking me. My cap must have fallen off, because he relaxed his hold for a moment and forced out, 'You are a girl?' By relaxing his hold on my throat, I had enough room to reach for my dagger tucked into the waistband of my trousers. I pulled the knife out, and with all my might plunged it into the man's right side. Briefly his hands tightened around my neck, and I thought I was going to die. Then his hands relaxed and he just collapsed on top of me."

Eliza stopped speaking for a moment, and Benedict held her. He could feel his white shirt was damp with her tears. "What happened after that?" he prodded.

A few minutes later she continued, "It took me a few minutes to roll him off me, because of the pain in my shoulder. I tried to stand, but kept slipping because the ground was covered in blood. While I was attempting to crawl away, the man grabbed my ankle and pulled me back. He was gurgling blood, but he was trying to tell me something. Since he was dying, I felt that I owed it to him to hear him out, but as I leaned closer to hear what he was saying, I realized he was taunting me. He kept telling me that I would never be safe as long as I lived. He started laughing, which turned into coughing up blood onto my face, and he refused to let go of my leg. I started screaming, 'Let go', over and over. Finally, I could not take it anymore, so I grabbed the knife out of his side, and I slit his throat."

She was trembling again, so Benedict continued to hold her even though he was not sure if there was more to the story. "What else, Eliza?" he asked after a few moments.

Pulling her head back, she met his gaze. "Did you not hear what I said? I said, 'I slit his throat'," she said in a fiery tone.

"I heard you, but I do not understand why you are so upset. You survived someone trying to kill you," he said firmly.

"I killed a dying man, because he was taunting me. I detested him and stole his last few breaths." Eliza dropped her hands from around his neck. "How could I do that? How could I slit his throat? Have you ever slit a man's throat?" She glared at him as if she knew the answer, and Benedict shook his head no. "The blood was everywhere. My hands and clothes were coated in blood." She peered at her hands as if she remembered the blood being there.

Benedict was afraid to point out that Eliza was also bleeding from being shot, which added to the amount of blood. She kept trying to flee out of his arms, so he released her, and she walked to the opposite side of the room. He watched her cautiously as she was wringing her hands together, but he remained seated to avoid upsetting her any more. "Does Jonathon know about what happened on the roof?" He knew the answer, but wanted to ask her anyway.

Eliza shook her head no. "No, of course not. If he did, then he would force me to stop working as an agent."

"Would that be so bad?" he ventured.

She stared at him as if it was the worst idea in the world. "What else would I do with my life?" she shouted as she threw her hands in the air.

Benedict knew that he wanted to spend the rest of his life with Eliza, but he did not want to point that out too soon, since he was afraid that might scare her off. He decided not to answer her question, so he asked her one of his own. "How did you get home without Jonathon knowing you were shot?"

Eliza started pacing. "That was the tricky part. Once I slit... once the man was dead... I checked on Mr. Larson. He had been knocked out, but was waking up. Thankfully, he could walk on his own, because I was in pain and could not carry him. We left the building, and I hired someone to take us to an inn. I did not know who the man was, but he had a horse and carriage, and I offered him a great deal of money to take us away from the docks to a respectable inn. Once we arrived, I asked the proprietor to send for a doctor and paid him for his silence. When the doctor arrived, he examined Mr. Larson's head and my shoulder. I was lucky, since the bullet did not embed into my shoulder. The doctor explained it was basically a deep scratch, and I just had to watch the area for infection. Once he bandaged us up, we snuck back into the rooms we were renting. Jonathon was frantic by the time we got back, but I told him we were being followed, and we were forced to take a longer path home. I knew he did not believe me, but I could not tell him the truth."

Benedict did not understand why Eliza needed to hide the truth from Jonathon. "Why did you lie to your brother?"

She stopped pacing and turned her full attention towards him. "I told you, if he knew I was shot then…"

He interrupted. "No, why did you lie about killing that man on the roof?"

"If I had told him…"

"Do you not think your brother, who was also your partner, had a right to know you almost died that night?" Benedict asked, raising his voice.

"I did not lie to Jonathon. I just did not tell him everything," Eliza shouted defensively.

"He was your partner! Now that I'm your partner, are you going to lie to me, too?" he said with a hint of sarcasm.

Narrowing her eyes, Eliza folded her arms defiantly. "I do not need a partner. I am doing fine on my own."

Benedict rubbed his eyes with his fingers. "Yes, I can see that," he said mockingly.

Her eyes kept darting towards the door, and he knew if she left this room, then she would not come back to this conversation. He quickly arose and walked to the door to stop her retreat. Benedict had no intention of letting her run from this conversation or from him.

After a few minutes of an intense standoff, Eliza's shoulders deflated. "You are right, I am not doing fine on my own." Leaning against the door frame, he waited for her to continue with her explanation. "I killed a man because he was taunting me. I slit his throat to shut him up, and because of that, I am having horrifying dreams every night. I am not doing fine," she said weakly as she slowly sat down on a nearby wingback chair.

Benedict pushed off from the doorframe and started walking towards her, but stopped when Eliza's blazing eyes latched onto him. He did not fully understand why she was so upset. "You did nothing wrong on that roof. That man shot you, then he tried to choke you. He would have killed you if you had not grabbed your knife."

Eliza shook her head. "But I slit..."

"The man would not release you. You warned him. You tried to flee, and your body was in shock. You survived!" he said emphatically.

"Benedict, you do not understand," she hesitated, dropping her gaze from him before continuing, "I have killed so many men." She rested her elbows on her legs and cupped her face. "I have killed hundreds of men. You were correct about me being an assassin." Dropping her hands into her lap, she looked up at him. "The night I slit that man's throat, it changed me. It made me realize how many lives I have taken." Her eyes started to fill with tears. "For the past few years, I have been able to separate my life from the actions of *Shadow*. When I become *Shadow*, I do not think about the consequences of my actions." She winced as she said, "When I have to kill someone, I distance myself from them. I treat them as if I were hunting game in my uncle's forest. I do not even remain after I pull my last arrow, because I know my aim was true, and I always shoot to kill."

Benedict's heart ached for Eliza. He wanted to pull her into his arms, but he did not dare. She was not ready to be comforted by him. "As an agent, you have to distance yourself from the kill. I think that is a necessary skill."

Eliza brought up her tear-streaked face to look at him. "After I killed that man in France, it made me look at everything I have accomplished as a spy. I have killed sixteen men by my own hands, but I have killed hundreds more by decoding enemy messages." Her voice trailed off. "Some of the codes I have broken, or algorithms I have created, have given locations of French warships and American merchant ships. Uncle Charles has confirmed that our warships have engaged these ships and sunk some of them. Do you know how many lives were lost during those skirmishes?" she asked as her voice hitched.

Benedict could not stand by and watch her suffer alone so he knelt in front of her, reaching for her hands. "You have killed those men in defense of your country. You have saved thousands of Englishmen's lives."

Eliza shrugged her shoulders. "That is what I keep telling myself, but it does not work anymore. It does not ease the memories of taking away so many lives."

He thought for a moment. "You are right."

Biting her lower lip, she looked up helplessly at him. "I have been *Shadow* for so long that I am spending less time just being a lady. My spare time at Beaumont Castle normally consists of fencing practice or dagger tossing, and the only time I see my friends are at gatherings that I attend to spy on someone. I do not want to be a full-time agent for the rest of my life, but I cannot quit. Being a spy is all I ever wanted, but I cannot keep killing people," she said with a resigned look in her eyes.

Benedict's heart broke for her as he tightened his hold on her hands. "Would it be so bad if you stopped being an agent?"

Eliza shook her head. "My whole life I have been training to be an agent. What would I even do? It is not possible for me to have a normal life anymore. It is too late for me."

"Why is it too late for you?" he asked, intertwining their fingers.

She stared at their hands. "Sometimes, I view my life as a game

119

with all of its twist and turns, hoping I will be victorious in the end. The problem is, I am tired of playing this game since there can be no winners."

Benedict cupped her face with his hands to force her to look at him. "Do you know what I see, Eliza? I see a beautiful woman that has accomplished much in her young life." She was not trying to move out of his hands, so he proceeded. "I see someone that has endured much pain and rejection in her youth, and yet has managed to make a real difference in the world." He leaned closer. "I know you are carrying the weight of the world on your shoulders, but you do not have to do it alone anymore. I am your partner and your friend."

He wanted to mention that he wanted to be much more, but he decided it would not be an appropriate time to push her, so instead he said, "When you killed that man on the roof, you almost died. That feeling of panic and fear does not go away. I know those feelings well, because I would have died that night in France, if you had not saved me." Eliza locked eyes with him as he continued, "You may have killed a lot of men in the defense of your country, but you are not out murdering innocent men in the street." She gave a slight laugh at his last comment. "You are the daughter of a duke, and a spy, and it is time you stop separating them. It is time to embrace who you really are, because I am quite fond of the real you."

"Who is the real me?" she asked, her eyes searching his.

"The real you is a kind and loving lady who is saving innocent women from the cruelties of this world, by using all your skills and unique talents to make that happen." Benedict smiled lovingly at her. "You charm your way into everyone's lives, including my own, just by being yourself."

"Benedict, it is an act," Eliza said dejectedly. "You see, I have to act a certain way…"

"No, it is not an act," he asserted, shaking his head. "No one can be that good of an actress. The fact that you know how to fence and throw daggers makes you even more fascinating to me," he said tenderly. "Eliza, you need to forgive yourself and move on."

She looked at him in disbelief. "How can I just forgive myself?"

"I do not rightly know, but I know you will," Benedict answered truthfully. "You have done more than survive these past few years. You have thrived."

Her eyes crinkled with worry. "But I have done so many horrible things in my past."

"It is in the past," he said without pause. "You need to let it go, because you have done nothing wrong." While he gazed at her, he noticed small brown flecks in her green eyes and they captivated him.

Eliza smiled through her tears, but it was not a bright smile. Rather, it was a smile of deep gratitude. Since he was already so close, he leaned in and kissed her. Her lips felt so soft on his, and a moment later her lips parted, melting into his own. As much as Benedict wanted to keep kissing her, he broke the kiss and leaned back. He did not want to take advantage of her emotional state.

He helped her to rise, and they slowly walked over to the sofa. As they sat down, Benedict put his arm around her, and Eliza nestled her head against his shoulder. For a long time, neither of them spoke. They were content to simply hold each other.

"That man was right about one thing, though," she hesitated before saying, "eventually someone will figure out who I really am, and I will be hunted."

Benedict kissed the top of her head. "I will keep you safe, Eliza," he said fiercely, knowing he would do everything in his power to protect her.

He was enjoying the feeling of Eliza's head resting on his chest and relaxed against the soft, cushioned sofa. A little later, he became aware that her breathing was deeper and realized she had fallen asleep. While Benedict was debating whether to take her upstairs to lay her down, he heard someone walking into the room. He looked over his shoulder to see Mr. Larson approaching them. Benedict groaned inwardly. He was not in the mood for a lecture on propriety.

Mr. Larson moved to stand in front of them and looked down at Eliza sleeping on Benedict's chest. "Did she tell you?" They both knew what he was asking.

Benedict nodded. "Yes, she told me about France." His answer was given in a hushed tone, because he did not want to disturb her.

Mr. Larson nodded his approval.

"Did you hear any of our conversation?" Benedict asked.

"I only heard bits and pieces of it."

"Did you know she has killed sixteen men?"

Mr. Larson frowned. "I was not aware that she killed that many."

"She blames herself for every death she has caused by deciphering enemy codes, too." Benedict tightened his hold around Eliza's waist. "She cannot keep killing people. It is destroying her."

"I agree with you. After what happened in France, I was worried she might never recover."

"She was shot and strangled. Anyone would have bad dreams after that," Benedict admitted.

"I told her that, too, but she did not seem to believe me. But, I did not try kissing her afterwards," Mr. Larson smirked.

Benedict chose to ignore Mr. Larson's comment. "She believes she is more assassin than agent now."

The older agent's face grew somber again, as he rubbed the back of his neck with his hand. "I had no idea that she felt that way."

Although Benedict enjoyed having Eliza sleeping on him, it was time to take her to bed. He started to shift. "I should carry her up to her bedchamber now."

Mr. Larson put up his hands to stall him. "What if I pull over a chair, so you can put your feet up and sleep down here for the night?"

Assuming he misunderstood Eliza's protector, Benedict looked up in surprise. "You want me to spend the night with Eliza?"

Mr. Larson's eyebrows shot up. "No... No... Do not make it sound so deplorable. I just know that she is very tired, and I do not want to move her. That way, if she has one of her dreams, you can help her tonight."

"How exactly can I help her?"

"Eliza trusts you and you seem to have a knack for calming her down." Mr. Larson shrugged. "Regardless, it is too late for you to travel home unescorted. Highway robbers roam the main roads, looking for easy prey. I could arouse a few guards to escort you home, but dawn will be breaking in a few hours."

Benedict was more than willing to agree to stay the night, because it meant more time with Eliza. Although, he was not sure if he should be offended that Mr. Larson considered him *easy prey*. "If it is permissible, I would prefer to stay with her."

122

Looking relieved, Mr. Larson grabbed an armless chair and brought it over. They both were aware of the impropriety of this situation, and that it would ruin her reputation if word ever got out. However, the whole household staff was loyal to Lady Eliza, and Benedict felt confident that Mr. Larson would ensure it was never spoken of again.

Mr. Larson blew out the candles and started to walk out of the room. He said over his shoulder, "If you make one inappropriate advance towards her tonight, I will kill you."

Benedict smirked. That was the Mr. Larson that he knew and still slightly feared.

Chapter Fourteen

Eliza woke up to the morning sun coming through the windows. She felt rested for the first time in weeks, but noticed rather quickly that her pillow was moving up and down. Fully opening her eyes, she realized she was sleeping on Benedict's chest. She lifted her head and saw that they were still in the drawing room. She must have fallen asleep on him last night. Why was he still here? Why had Mr. Larson not sent him home? While she was coming up with all types of questions, she looked longingly at his handsome face.

Noticing he had dark stubble along his jaw line, Eliza found she desperately wanted to touch it. *Well, he is asleep.* She tentatively reached up, rubbing her hand along his stubble and quietly giggling as the little hairs tickled her hand. Benedict was still asleep, so she grew bolder with her actions. Her finger started tracing the outline of his left ear, then down his neck as she noticed that his white shirt hung open at the top. Her fingers started tracing the top of his muscular chest, as she admired his rugged physique.

Eliza heard his sharp intake of breath, and she quickly stalled her fingers. Slowly, she raised her eyes to look up at his face and confirmed his eyes were still closed. She pushed out the breath she was holding. It would have been mortifying if he had caught her taking such liberties with him. She decided she should go upstairs and change, but first she had to remove his hand from around her waist. Carefully, Eliza started to move.

Benedict suddenly tightened his arm around her waist. "If I pretend I am still asleep, will you keep touching me?" he asked flirtatiously, peeking through one eye.

Eliza gasped. "You were awake?"

He chuckled. "Of course, I was awake. How could I possibly get any sleep when you were lying next to me all night?"

Her face burned with embarrassment. "Does Mr. Larson know you are here?"

Benedict chuckled again. "That is the ironic part. We were up late and you fell asleep on me. Mr. Larson walked in and told me to stay for the night. He even pulled up a chair for me to rest my feet on." Eliza glanced down and noticed the brown, armless chair at his feet. "Although, Mr. Larson did tell me it was my turn to help with your recurring bad dreams."

Astonished, Eliza turned to look at him. "I did not have an episode last night. That is why I feel so rested."

"You cried out a few times, but I just rubbed your arm and told you that you were safe. It seemed to calm you down."

"I am sorry I kept you awake," she said apologetically.

"Your crying out did not keep me up."

"Then what did?"

Benedict smiled down on her with the crooked grin that she had grown to love, while he tightened his grip on her waist and pulled her tight against him. "Hmm… I would have to say that it took all my strength not to kiss you all night long."

Eliza blushed at his implication, but quickly realized she wanted another opportunity to kiss him. "Well, my lord," she flirted, "you did save me from my bad dreams last night, and I believe I owe you a favor for your bravery."

His smile grew broader. "I will accept your favor, my lady."

Her hand went behind Benedict's neck as she tentatively pulled him forward until his lips captured hers. She parted her lips, and he tilted his head to deepen the kiss. Her fingers started weaving through his hair, as he kissed her with a fervor that threatened to consume her. After a few moments, his lips moved towards a sensitive part of her neck below her ear.

"I warned you! Now I am going to have to kill you!" A gruff yell echoed throughout the drawing room. Eliza's head popped up, and she saw Mr. Larson storming into the room with a murderous look on his face.

She quickly disentangled herself from Benedict and jumped up.

She took a moment to adjust her dress, then focused on her protector. "Nothing happened, Mr. Larson. I was thanking Lord Sinclair for helping me with my bad dreams last night."

What she said seemed to curb Mr. Larson's anger. "You still had an episode last night, and more than one?"

Standing up, Benedict faced the older agent. "Not really. She did cry out a couple of times, but I was able to calm her down."

Mr. Larson pointed his finger at Benedict. "You promised you would not take advantage of her. I only left you alone for a few hours."

Eliza put a hand on her hip. "I kissed him."

Directing his glare at her, Mr. Larson asked, "Why did you do that?"

Eliza quickly glanced in Benedict's direction, while putting a hand to her mouth to cover her smile.

Mr. Larson threw his hands up in the air and growled, "Do not answer that!" Then he glared at Benedict. "I still might have to kill you, so do not get comfortable." His eyes kept darting back and forth between them. "I am not going to leave you two alone again." He pointed at Eliza. "You go upstairs." He pointed at Benedict. "You… do not touch anything."

Benedict smiled at Eliza, and she decided it would be a good time to run upstairs and change for the day. Walking quickly out of the room, she could hear her protector lecturing her partner about how disappointed he was in him.

Martha was waiting for her in her bedchamber. She had a pale blue, cotton dress laid out on the bed, and Eliza hastily changed her clothes. Coming behind her, her maid buttoned up the back of her dress, then Eliza sat down at the dressing table. "So, Benedict is still downstairs?" Martha ventured.

Eliza sighed. She had loved waking up in Benedict's arms, but it was nothing less than scandalous. Was Martha shocked by her behavior? She spun around and gripped the back of the chair with her arm. "What you must think of me?" she asked, mortified.

Her lady's maid and friend laid her hands over Eliza's as she smiled down at her. "My opinion of you has not changed, my lady. I thought it was sweet that you fell asleep on him."

"How did you know I fell asleep on him?"

"I woke up in the middle of the night, and I went to check on you. I was worried that I had slept through one of your dreams. I noticed you were not in your bedchamber, so I went downstairs. I saw Mr. Larson leave the drawing room, and I peeked in. It was lovely how Lord Sinclair's arm was draped around you," Martha said sweetly, as she took out Eliza's pins and started brushing her hair.

"I told Lord Sinclair about France last night," Eliza said frankly.

Martha's hand froze. "And?"

"He told me that I survived, and he was proud of me."

"He is right, you know."

"I do believe him. I was so afraid to tell anyone else about what happened on that roof. I still remember the sound of my dagger slicing through his neck." Eliza shuddered.

"That man was trying to kill you," Martha said, still brushing her hair.

"I know that. My mind just could not seem to process what I had done," Eliza said honestly.

"Does it help you to talk to Lord Sinclair?"

Eliza rubbed some rose-scented cream on her hands. "I know I have only just met Lord Sinclair, but I feel like I can trust him with all my burdens. When I look into his eyes, I see trust and love, and when he holds me, I feel safe and protected." She bit her lower lip. "Perhaps I am just lonely?"

Martha started placing hair pins into her hair. "No, that is not it. You have had many gentleman callers over the years, but Lord Sinclair is different. It would appear that you have met your match."

Eliza nodded. "I feel that way as well."

Her maid chuckled. "It probably helps that Lord Sinclair is incredibly handsome."

"Possibly," Eliza smiled.

"And a good kisser?" Martha teased.

Eliza's smile grew. "Perhaps."

Martha pushed the last pin in place. She sensed that Eliza was anxious to get back to Benedict. "Go to him, my lady," she said teasingly. She was still laughing as Eliza walked swiftly out of the room.

Benedict knew he was grinning like a bloody fool, but he could not stop himself. After Mr. Larson rebuked him for daring to touch Eliza, he stormed out of the room. Benedict knew it would ruin Eliza's reputation if anyone found out that he fell asleep at her castle, but since no one knew she owned Beaumont Castle, and the household staff consisted of former agents, he felt confident no one would ever find out.

When he woke up to find Eliza touching him, he was ready to pledge his undying love to her. He would give anything to have her wake up in his arms every morning. He knew it should be impossible, but he was already in love with her.

Mr. Larson stepped into the drawing room. "Wipe that stupid grin off your face." Benedict was confident that Mr. Larson was not a morning person. "Breakfast is ready in the dining room," the older agent stated in a clipped tone, then stormed out.

Benedict knew he eventually needed to go home to change, but he was not ready to leave. As he walked towards the dining room, Eliza descended the stairs. She adorably blushed and adverted her eyes when she saw him. He jogged up the stairs to offer her his arm and assist her into the dining room.

As they slowly made their way, Eliza's dress kept brushing up against his leg, and he was utterly distracted. He just wanted to drag her into the other room and kiss her. As he was looking for an available room, he saw Mr. Larson shooting daggers at him. Benedict wondered if the man could read his thoughts, and since he could not rule out that possibility entirely, he decided to just escort Eliza to the dining room.

Benedict assisted Eliza to her seat, then he quickly grabbed his chair. He moved it closer to Eliza and sat down. She smiled at him, and he found himself unable to look away. He leaned closer to inform her how beautiful she looked, when Mr. Larson loudly cleared his throat. Eliza glanced up at her protector with an amused smile on her face, while she picked up her fork and started eating. Benedict decided he should just focus on the breakfast that was placed before him.

Roger walked into the room and handed Mr. Larson a note with a red seal. Dismissing him, Mr. Larson handed Eliza the note. "Lord Beckett sent over a message, Lady Eliza."

She placed her fork down and wiped her mouth with a napkin from her lap. Taking the note, she broke the seal. Once she finished reading it, she demurely placed it on the table and picked up her fork.

Benedict was curious. "Well?"

Eliza looked at him innocently, as she slowly put her fork down. "Well what?"

He shook his head. The minx was teasing him. "What was in the note?"

Smiling, she said lightly, "Oh, the note." She grabbed her cup and took a sip of tea, then she turned to him. "It appears that your stepbrother has arrived in town and has sent a note of acceptance for a party that Lord Chambers is hosting a few nights from now."

"We should go."

She nodded in agreement. "Jonathon and I received an invitation a few days prior for Lord Chambers' house party, so I will send a reply in the affirmative." Eliza frowned before continuing, "My uncle also informed me that four more girls have been abducted. This time, two of them were abducted from their bedrooms and they were both ladies. The Bow Street Runners have opened an official investigation into the missing girls."

Benedict was preparing to take a bite of his breakfast, but stopped his fork in mid-air. "Why would Aaron take such a risk and abduct titled girls from their bedrooms?"

Eliza seemed to ponder what he had asked. "We are missing something here. Mr. Wade is breaking from his pattern and now he is risking the wrath of the peerage. In addition, the Bow Street Runners are now searching for the girls, which will force him to take extra precautions when abducting and hiding them."

"How did the abductors know which rooms to find the ladies in? There must be a leak in those homes," Benedict pointed out.

"Good point. I will ask Uncle Charles to have the Bow Street Runners follow up with the household staffs and see what they can uncover," Eliza said.

"Does Aaron always abduct girls three to four weeks before his ship departs?"

"It depends," she said. Benedict noticed that Eliza was including Mr. Larson in the conversation. "Either way, the girls will be somewhere near the wharf, so they can be transported discreetly when Mr. Wade's ship docks, alongside the Shadwell Basin. We need to go look at the buildings closest to the docks, and see if we can find the girls. Since eighteen girls have been abducted, they would have to be held in a large space." She paused before continuing, "Your stepbrother's ship is set to depart in less than two and a half weeks. I hope we can find the missing girls before they are forced onto the ship."

"Does Aaron own any buildings near the docks?" Benedict inquired.

Eliza nodded. "One, but that warehouse is currently near the western dock and is being watched by agents. Although, I doubt anything will come of it. Mr. Wade likes to keep his legal business dealings separate from his more lucrative venues," she said, her voice dripping with contempt.

"Did Lord Beckett look into Lord Vernon's real estate holdings?"

"Yes, but his only holding is his manor, and it is entailed. His son's betrothal was a necessary means to an end, since his future daughter-in-law brings in a much-needed dowry."

"Delightful," Benedict said sarcastically. He was aware that members of the aristocracy married for financial status, but it did not mean he had to approve. "What if I just go pay Aaron a visit at his home and convince him to tell me where the girls are?"

Eliza shook her head. "Mr. Wade has been noticeably absent from his townhouse. The fact that he is attending Lord Chambers' house party is a break from his usual pattern."

Benedict pushed away his plate. "I broke into Aaron's townhouse a week ago, but found nothing about any missing girls in his files. Of course, I was not specifically searching for that."

Amused, Eliza's lips curled up into a smile. "When did you break in?"

He put his hand to his chin. "Last Thursday, I believe."

She chuckled. "I was there on Friday, but I did not find anything about the missing girls either. Mr. Wade has never left any documents in his townhouse that could expose him, but I still break in periodically to be certain." Her eyes danced with merriment. "It drives Jonathon crazy."

Benedict chuckled at Eliza's amusement at irritating Jonathon. "From my experience, it does not take much to drive Jonathon crazy."

"True," she said with a broad smile. She pushed away her plate and placed her napkin on the table. "Mr. Larson, can you please call for the carriage?"

Mr. Larson tilted his head. "Yes, Lady Eliza," he said as he exited the room.

Benedict liked Eliza's plan of searching the buildings near the docks, except for one key component. He did not want her anywhere near the foul-smelling docks, since it was no place for a lady. He gave her a charming smile, determined to reason with her. "You must be very tired from staying up so late. Why don't you stay and rest, while Mr. Larson and I go and search for the girls?"

Eliza's eyebrow arched at his comment, and Benedict waited for her reply hoping she would agree with him. She placed her hand over his hand on the table. "I think it is a grand idea that Mr. Larson should go." Benedict nodded, but she was not finished. "But I am going, too." She patted his hand as she stood up. "I should change if we are going to search the docks."

Grabbing her hand, he grinned suggestively. "By change, you mean men's black clothing?"

"Of course not, my lord," Eliza said, flashing him a cheeky smile.

Benedict released her hand, and she started towards the door. When she reached it, she turned and held onto the door frame. "Black clothing would be too obvious during the day. I will be wearing tan trousers, a blue shirt and Hessian boots." Eliza laughed merrily, as she disappeared from the room.

Mr. Larson walked back into the room with a gloating look on his face. "Did you honestly think you could convince Eliza to not go search the docks by telling her she needed rest?" Benedict shrugged his shoulders. The older agent laughed. "You have a lot to learn about women."

Benedict only wanted to learn about one woman in particular. He would have to find another way for her to start listening to him. After all, women could be reasoned with. Could they not?

Chapter Fifteen

$\mathcal{A}$ few hours later, Eliza, Benedict and Mr. Larson were walking along the crowded, dirt-encrusted streets closest to the docks. The smell of human waste and the stench of unwashed bodies, along with the bellowing of various street sellers, were all familiar sights and sounds associated with the docks. Weary-looking women were hustling around the sidewalks, many with laundry on their backs, and some of them wore nothing more than ragged dresses.

Eliza assumed that Mr. Wade had selected a building close to where his ship would be docked, so the plan was to search all the abandoned warehouses and factories alongside the Shadwell Basin. As they were passing by a group of rowdy young men, Benedict was shoved roughly into Eliza, and he quickly grabbed her arm to keep her upright. While they were waiting for the men to pass, he leaned in and whispered teasingly, "I do not know why you insist on wearing trousers, because it is obvious to everyone you are a woman in them."

Curling her lips up into a sassy smile, she said, "Well then, I hope you enjoy the view, my lord." Benedict's eyes widened at her blatant flirting.

Mr. Larson started sputtering. "Lady Eliza, you will refrain from saying such statements," he demanded in a hushed tone. Benedict seemed to recover from his shock and smiled flirtatiously at Eliza, who beamed back at him. Mr. Larson witnessed this exchange and said mockingly, "You are obviously feeling better."

She tilted her head towards him. "I am. Lord Sinclair has been very supportive and has given me some great advice. I just need to stop dwelling on the past and focus on the future."

Mr. Larson nodded. "I thought talking to Lord Sinclair might help." They kept walking down the street trying to avoid getting bumped, but it was difficult due to how many people were on the crowded sidewalks. "Are you going to tell your brother now?" he asked.

"Yes, I suppose so." Eliza stopped at a run-down brick building and peered into a dirty, broken window until she was satisfied that the girls were not being held there. She faced the two men and offered, "I think we should split up."

"No," they said in unison.

Eliza pursed her lips together at their outburst. "Pray tell me, how are we to search all these buildings if we stay together?" she asked while glancing down at all the various sized buildings lining both sides of the street.

"We will walk faster," Benedict suggested and Mr. Larson grunted his approval.

"Fine," Eliza said with a huff as she started walking down the street.

For the next few hours, they searched the abandoned warehouses and structures for any sign of the missing girls. Eliza even searched warehouses that had workers in them, much to Mr. Larson's dismay. Benedict would not permit her go into any building that appeared to be on the verge of collapse, so he would go in alone while she waited with her protector. So far, they found nothing that would indicate eighteen girls were being held captive in this general vicinity, and Eliza was extremely frustrated. Where would the girls be held if they were not near the docks?

As the sun was setting, they decided to call it quits for the day and were making their way back to Benedict's carriage. It started sprinkling as Eliza said, "We still need to search Paul Warner's office. I am hoping as his solicitor, he has some paperwork on your stepbrother that might aid us in our search."

"When would you like to go?" Benedict asked.

"Tomorrow night would be best," Eliza said, pulling her cloth cap down lower on her head, attempting to shield herself from the rain.

Benedict offered her his arm, and she placed her hand in the crook of his elbow. "I have no problem with that."

"Thank you," Eliza said, leaning closer to him.

Mr. Larson cleared his throat. "If I may, why don't I accompany you to Warner's office?"

Eliza furrowed her brows in confusion at his request. "You are welcome to join us, but it will be harder to stay concealed with three people."

"Actually, I thought Lord Sinclair might have the night off," the older agent suggested, glancing over at her.

Eliza stopped a short distance from the carriage and turned to face her protector. "What are you not saying, Mr. Larson?"

The older man rubbed his chin with his hand, and Eliza swore he was stalling. "Nothing. It just makes more sense for you and me to go." She lifted an eyebrow and waited for him to continue. She knew something was going on. Mr. Larson huffed. "Fine, if you must know, I do not want to leave you and Lord Sinclair unaccompanied."

One side of Eliza's mouth lifted in amusement. "Do you not?"

Mr. Larson narrowed his eyes at Benedict before he responded. "Yes, because I have been tasked to keep you safe from any harm."

Eliza frowned as she dropped her arm from Benedict's grasp. "And you think Lord Sinclair would harm me?"

Mr. Larson's gaze landed on Eliza. "Not intentionally, no."

Benedict's jaw was clenched as he stated, "With all due respect, sir, I would guard Lady Eliza with my life." Eliza could tell that he was upset by the insinuation.

The older man's eyes flickered to Benedict, as he placed his hand on her shoulder. "You do realize I am not talking about physical harm."

A blush crept up Eliza's cheeks as she lowered her gaze. "I do now."

Dropping his hand, Mr. Larson gave his full attention to Benedict. "Young man, I want to make something explicitly clear. I do not care a whit about your title. I just want your word that you will show Lady Eliza the respect that she deserves."

"I give you my word," Benedict said, his eyes never wavering from Mr. Larson's intense gaze.

Mr. Larson's lips pressed into a tight line as he continued to stare down the young man. "Fine, but you have been warned." He turned and started walking towards the carriage, leaving them behind.

Benedict offered her his arm as they leisurely went to catch up with Mr. Larson. "Tomorrow night, will you be wearing a dress, by chance?"

"No." Eliza paused and said with a grin, "At night, I wear black clothing."

He gave a slight groan. "What about a black dress?"

Stopping and dropping her hand, she turned her full attention towards Benedict. "Does it really bother you that much that I wear men's clothing?"

Benedict shook his head. "That is not the reason." He diverted his eyes towards the sky as the rain was starting to come down harder. "It is very distracting for me when you wear form-fitting trousers."

It took a moment for Eliza to realize what he was implying, but she found it quite flattering that she could drive him to distraction. Her lips curled up into a smile, as she watched the rain run down his face, and he refused to make eye contact. Benedict appeared to be unsettled by his own admission, and it amused her.

She boldly placed her hand onto his chest, as he lowered his gaze to meet her eyes. She saw desire flicker in his eyes, and she had an overwhelming desire to kiss him. She fisted his white shirt and pulled him down to initiate a quick, but firm kiss.

"Lady Eliza, will you please manage some form of decorum?" Mr. Larson shouted from somewhere near the carriage as soon as their lips touched.

Releasing him, she quickly hopped into the waiting carriage. If the footman who was holding open the carriage door was shocked by her scandalous behavior, he did not show it. She was laughing when she heard Mr. Larson lecture Benedict outside the carriage. "She was not like this before you came. You have ruined my Eliza."

She watched Benedict as the men climbed into the carriage. Benedict sat down next to her, but as he reached for her hand, Mr. Larson cleared his throat and shook his head. Eliza hid a smile as she glanced out the carriage window and noticed the rain was quickly turning into more of a downpour. The torrential rain would make the dirt road near her castle almost impossible to pass, so she would have to wait till tomorrow to return home.

"It appears that I will not be returning to Beaumont Castle tonight. Would you like to join me for dinner at Jonathon's townhouse?" she asked while turning towards Benedict.

He smiled as he ran his fingers through his damp hair. "I would be delighted."

Mr. Larson just let out a grunt to express his disapproval and folded his arms. Once again, Eliza put her hand up to her mouth to hide her smile. Since Benedict had come into her life, she realized she was smiling more often, and sometimes, for no reason at all.

Chapter Sixteen

Eliza could not breathe. Her eyes flew open and she quickly realized a man's hand was covering her mouth. He was leaning over her, and his other hand was pressing a knife tightly against her throat. He whispered menacingly in her ear, "I will move me hand if ye not scream. If ye scream, I will cut yar throat."

She nodded slowly. For a brief second, she panicked, as the thought came that someone finally discovered she was *Shadow.* The man removed his hand from her mouth, but kept the knife in place. She waited for him to give her another command, because she needed to know his intent. Eliza quickly ascertained that if he was sent to kill her, then she would have already been dead, which meant he was trying to abduct her.

The man leaned back from her and sneered. He was ugly and stocky, with a huge, open scar running from his left eye down to his chin, and his greasy, long black hair was tied behind his head. His face was pale, with sunken eyes. He was also missing most of his teeth, which indicated that he was most likely a sailor suffering from scurvy.

He seemed satisfied that Eliza was not going to scream, so he removed the knife from her throat and walked to the open window. Putting his head out the window, he appeared to be giving some type of signal. She took that opportunity to slowly reach for her dagger under the pillow. Gripping it, she slowly slid it up the sleeve of her nightgown until she held the tip of the blade in her hand.

Eliza was certain that this man had no idea she was *Shadow.* The fact that he removed the knife from her throat and walked away from her made her believe that he did not think she was a threat. Which meant she would play along until she could figure out why she was being abducted.

The man walked back over to her and hissed, "Get out of that bed."

He just stood there, sneering at her as she slowly got out of bed. Pretending to be shaking, Eliza tried to bring tears to her eyes. She needed to play the role of a simpering female right now. Once she was off the bed, he grabbed her upper arm and jerked her towards the open window.

Eliza decided now would be a good time to start asking questions. She kept her voice shaky as she asked, "Why are you doing this?"

The man tightened his grip.

"Where are you taking me?"

He stopped her in front of the open window and gazed out. She saw a thick rope was tied to the leg of a table near the window and was dangling over the edge. She knew she needed to find out what was going on, because she was not going out that window. "Please tell me. I'm scared," she pushed out.

The man sneered as he leaned closer to her, and his breath reeked of tobacco and fish. *How did she not smell that before?* "Ye don't know what fear is." He roughly kissed her on the mouth and ran his slimy tongue along her bottom lip. "Thar will be more of that later, I promise. Yar boss lets me'n'th' crew rub ye lasses. We just can't enjoy yar..." he paused to lick his lips vulgarly, "services till later."

Eliza wanted to gag after his kiss, but needed to keep her wits about her. "Who is your boss?"

The man let out a deep chuckle. "Don't ye fret none, lady. Yar boss will take ye on a voyage an' give ye a new purty dress to wear." He put his head out the window and looked down at Jonathon's garden. "Ye climb out this here window. If ye try to run, that man down thar will gut ye like a fish." He jerked his head to indicate the shadowy figure at the bottom of the rope.

It was apparent that she was not going to get any more information out of this man, but it was obvious that she was supposed to join the women that Mr. Wade had abducted. She needed to continue to play along until she could rid him of the knife in his right hand, which was currently pointing towards the ground.

The man let go of his death grip on her arm and indicated he was ready for her to climb out the window. Eliza put her right leg up on the window sill, as she put her left arm on the window frame and the other hand on the bottom sill, pretending she was trying to balance herself. She was trying to get the man to assist her, so he would have to step behind her.

She succeeded, and when the man stepped behind her to help balance her, she threw her right elbow back as hard as she could. The man staggered back and Eliza was rewarded to see blood gushing out of his nose.

He tilted up his head to try to stop the flow of blood. "Ye stupid lass. Yu'll pay for that," he threatened through gritted teeth.

In one fluid motion, she spun around and dropped the dagger down her hand till she gripped the hilt. She went into a defensive stance and raised her hand with the dagger. The man wiped his nose on his grubby work shirt, which took his eyes completely off Eliza, and it gave her a chance to run and plow into his stomach.

As they smashed into her dressing table, the man crumbled into it, but she righted herself and ran towards the opposite side of the room. The noise from the breaking table should have alerted Jonathon's household that something was amiss in Eliza's room. The man slowly stood up and spit out blood onto the Persian floral rug.

"Yu'll die now," he growled as he clutched his knife so tight that Eliza could see his hand was turning white.

Sadly, this man was prepared to fight her to the death. As he started advancing towards her, she pulled her arm back, aimed for his chest and released the dagger.

It hit its mark, plunging deep into the middle of the man's chest. He looked down at the dagger sticking out, then back at her with shock written all over his face. He dropped to his knees and relinquished the knife he was holding. His eyes rolled into the back of his head as he fell face forward onto the rug.

Immediately, Eliza ran to the window to search for the man's partner, and she saw him jump over Jonathon's garden wall. He must have heard the commotion in her room and decided to abandon his partner to his own fate.

Mr. Larson burst into her room, with two of Jonathon's footmen right behind him. His eyes roamed all over Eliza, then fell to the man on the floor. As he looked back up to her, his concern was evident on his face, but she did not have time to ease his worries.

"The man's partner just jumped the garden fence and is heading south," she shouted. Pointing to the two footmen, she yelled, "Go after him!" The footmen immediately responded to her order and raced out of the room.

Walking up to her, Mr. Larson put his hands on her shoulders. "Are you all right, Eliza?"

Her gaze landed on the man that had tried to abduct her, then she slowly brought her head back up to look at her protector. He was waiting for her to say something, but she just nodded her head.

"Did he hurt you?"

She shook her head. "He was trying to abduct me." Eliza's eyes sought out the dead man on the floor again and she could not seem to look away.

"Would you like me to send for Lord Sinclair?" Mr. Larson asked hesitantly.

Her head jerked back. "Why would you call for Lord Sinclair?"

"He could calm you down?" Mr. Larson seemed to look unsure.

Eliza frowned. "I will be fine."

"Are you sure?"

She shook off his hands and wrapped her arms around her waist. She just wanted time to process what had happened. "I will sleep in the yellow guest bedroom on the third floor, since the maids have already prepared it for Lady Hannah," she stated.

"Eliza…" Mr. Larson let the word hang.

She pointed to the man on the floor. "He wanted to abduct me, but I stopped him. He would have killed me, but I killed him first. I had no choice," she said confidently.

Mr. Larson nodded. "I assume that this was Mr. Wade's doing."

"Yes, it was." Eliza turned to leave but stopped when she saw all the damage inflicted on her room. "Can you take care of this mess?"

Mr. Larson walked to the body and turned him over. He retrieved her dagger and wiped it clean with the man's shirt, then handed it to her. "I know you will sleep better with this under your pillow."

She grasped her dagger against her chest and smiled gratefully at him. "We must have a leak in our household, because it appears the men knew which bedchamber was mine. Can you talk to Jonathon's butler and ask if he recently hired anyone new?"

"That is part of my job description." Mr. Larson smiled understandingly at her.

Eliza gave him a tight frown. "It seems to me that you are doing a lot of things outside of your job description these days."

The former agent put his hand on her shoulder. "My job is to protect you at all costs."

Wrapping her hands around his waist, Eliza hugged him. Mr. Larson had been with her for over three years, and he was like a father to her. His hands went around her shoulders, and they remained that way for a few minutes until she felt his arms release her. She gave him a forced smile and went to try to get some sleep.

Chapter Seventeen

Eliza woke up to a commotion outside of her door. She could hear a very agitated Benedict and an equally frustrated Mr. Larson arguing. Slowly, she sat up in bed and pulled the covers up over her chest.

"I just want to make sure she is all right." Yes, that was Benedict's voice.

"Lord Sinclair, you cannot be up here. As I told you in the message I sent over, and countless times today, she is resting," Mr. Larson said in a weary tone.

"I want to make sure myself."

"Lord Sinclair!"

"Please," Benedict said in a defeated tone.

The arguing stopped and the door opened as Benedict rushed into the room. He gently sat down on her bed and reached for her hand. "How are you doing, my love?" He seemed to be searching her face for any sign of injury.

Eliza was puzzled. Did Benedict just declare his love for her? Was it possible for two people to fall in love so fast? No, he must have said the term of endearment without thinking, because he was so worried about her. She realized he was waiting for her to say something. "I am fine," she said unconvincingly.

He scowled as he reached up and tenderly touched her throat. He turned towards Mr. Larson. "Why was there not a footman posted at her door?" he demanded.

Mr. Larson rolled his eyes, which greatly amused Eliza. "Lord Sinclair," the former agent paused as if trying to rein in his temper, "Lord Jonathon's house is secure. The man scaled the wall and came through her window because he was tipped off by a newly hired footman." Looking at her, he continued, "It was one of the footman you sent out to search for the partner, and he did not come back."

Benedict turned back to face her. "You are coming back to my townhouse where I can protect you."

"Absolutely not!" Mr. Larson and Eliza shouted in unison.

Benedict kept his attention on Eliza. "Why not? I will keep you safe," he replied with such determination that she had no doubt he would keep her safe at all costs.

Smiling, she squeezed his hand. "I am safe here. The man came through the window and tried to abduct me, but he had no idea who he was dealing with. He underestimated me and that was his mistake." Eliza hesitated with the word *mistake*, since she knew that mistake cost the man his life.

Benedict put his hand to her cheek, and she rested her head on his hand. Concern etched his brow, and his dark blue eyes swept over her face. Eliza sighed contently into his hand, since it felt wonderful to have him watching out for her. She could not remember a time when someone showed such care for her well-being.

She remembered something as she raised her head, and Benedict dropped his hand. "Last night, the man that tried to abduct me was definitely a sailor by the way he looked and spoke, but he did something odd." Eliza shuddered at the memory. "He kissed me and implied he would do far worse after he bought me."

"What?" the men shouted in unison. Benedict jumped off the bed in outrage, and Mr. Larson stormed closer to the bed.

Amused at their overreaction, Eliza's lips twitched upward for a fleeting moment. "My point is, normally after we rescue girls from the ship, we find that they remain untouched, since we all know innocents are more valuable. This sailor was under the impression that he would be able to molest me once he abducted me." She wrinkled her nose as she took a moment to think about it. "This whole situation feels awry."

Benedict sat back down on the bed. "What are you thinking? This is the second time where you have suspected something is off."

"I definitely think your stepbrother is involved, but I am not sure this is just about abducting girls and selling them. If so, he would not have made such a public spectacle, and he would guarantee the girls he abducted stayed innocent." She started chewing her bottom lip thoughtfully.

Reaching over, Benedict placed an errant piece of hair behind her ear, which caused Eliza to give him a tender smile. As she took a moment to gaze at his handsome face, she noticed the tiniest scar along his chin that she had not noticed before. She boldly lifted her hand and ran her fingers along it and felt an overwhelming desire to discover everything she could about this man. She did not think she could ever tire of learning about him.

Mr. Larson cleared his throat after a few moments, and Eliza dropped her hand. "Lord Sinclair, as you can see Lady Eliza is well. Please think of her reputation, since we are in Lord Jonathon's townhouse and not at Beaumont Castle."

Standing slowly, Benedict smiled lovingly at her. "I will be downstairs in the dining room when you are ready to come down." He walked out of the room with Mr. Larson in tow.

Eliza threw off her covers and jumped out of bed. Her cream, high-waisted dress with a lovely floral design was laying on the upholstered settee at the base of the bed, which meant Jonathon's housekeeper must have brought up the dress early this morning.

She had not planned to stay at Jonathon's townhouse for the evening, so Martha had stayed behind at Beaumont Castle. Fortunately, she always kept extra clothes and necessities at the townhouse in case she had to stay over unexpectedly. Changing quickly, she was grateful that this particular dress did not have any buttons in the back.

Sitting down at the dressing table, she looked at her reflection in the mirror. She gasped as she saw that the knife held to her throat had left a slight puncture wound, and dried blood was caked on her neck. Earlier, Benedict had touched her throat and scowled, but she did not realize the knife had cut into her skin. Eliza stood and reached for the water basin to scrub the wound.

Sitting back down, she attempted to pin her hair up. After a few failed attempts, she pulled it back into a loose bun at the base of her neck, since she did not have Martha's hairdressing skills. As she stared at her reflection in the mirror, she touched the pink puncture wound.

She did not doubt that people would try to kill her if her cover was blown, but this was different. Mr. Wade sent someone to abduct her. He wanted to abduct and sell her into slavery.

Eliza had not thought she could loathe Aaron Wade any more than she previously did, but she was wrong. She was angry, and it was time for her to get back to work.

Benedict was in the dining room staring at the door while his food remained untouched in front of him, but he did not care. He was waiting for Eliza to walk into the room. When he'd received a message this morning from Mr. Larson detailing that she had been attacked but was uninjured, he ignored his valet and threw on his own clothes. He even tied his own cravat as he raced over to Jonathon's townhouse. Luckily, it was early and none of the ton was up to witness his five-block dash.

Benedict had never been so frightened in his life, mainly since he never had so much to live for. Without Eliza by his side, his life seemed meaningless. That knowledge, combined with the fear that he could have lost her, scared him witless.

On the jog over, he decided he was going to convince her to marry him, thus protecting her day and night. Now that he could see her with his own eyes, he realized she only had a flesh wound on her neck. However, he wondered if the abduction had fractured the advances they had made towards helping her put her past behind her.

At that moment, Eliza walked into the room with squared shoulders and a determined stride. *This was a good sign.* Benedict pushed his seat back, standing up almost immediately after she entered and moved to assist her with her chair. A footman placed a generous helping of scones accompanied by strawberry jam in front of her, and she reached for her utensils to begin her morning meal. He decided it was a good time to eat his food, since she was busy eating.

A few minutes later, she put down her fork and turned to face him. "Tonight, we need to break into Mr. Warner's office. I just handed a note to Jonathon's butler to send to my uncle detailing last

146

night's attack."

Benedict could not let her sneak into Mr. Warner's office tonight. She had just been attacked a few hours ago, and he did not want her in any more danger. "I will break into Mr. Warner's office tonight and look around," he said, casually glancing over to Mr. Larson.

Eliza's eyes narrowed. "Without me?"

He decided to state the obvious. "You were just attacked a few hours ago."

"Your point being?"

"I think you need some time to recover," Benedict said as he took a bite.

Eliza arched an eyebrow. "Do you now?"

"I do. You suffered a traumatic event last night and need some down time."

"I am going with you to break into Mr. Warner's office tonight," she said firmly.

He shook his head. "No, you are not."

Eliza stood so fast that she knocked her chair over. Benedict noticed that Mr. Larson was at the door observing them, but had just discreetly removed the footmen from the room. "You do not get to dictate what I do, Lord Sinclair," she drawled out.

She was angry. She was back to calling him Lord Sinclair. Benedict tried to reach for her hand as she stepped back. "No, we have been over this. You do not get to just hold my hand or kiss me and then expect me to do your bidding," Eliza said while shaking her head. "It is not going to work."

"I am not trying to do that," Benedict said patiently. He noticed that Mr. Larson was in the process of staring daggers at him. Obviously, the older man did not like what Eliza just revealed.

"Yes, you are." She folded her arms over her chest.

"I am trying to protect you."

"You do not need to protect me," she countered.

"Yes, I do. That is exactly what a partner should do," Benedict said defensively.

"Would you tell Jonathon he should not go somewhere?"

"No, but I also have not kissed Jonathon," Benedict said with a crooked smile. He was hoping to disarm her by making her laugh.

Instead, Eliza threw her hands up in the air. "What does that have to do with anything?"

"Everything," Benedict raised his voice. "I care for you, Eliza. I do not want you to get hurt."

She was not showing any signs of calming down. "There is an obvious solution," she said simply. "We need to stop kissing, so you will stop worrying about me getting hurt."

Benedict did not like this solution and threw his napkin down on the table. "That is stupid."

Eliza's eyes widened. "Now I am stupid?"

His eyebrows shot up. "What? No, I said your solution is stupid. You are definitely not stupid." Why was she acting so irrationally?

"Lord Sinclair..." Eliza started to say.

"Benedict." He did not want to go back to Lord Sinclair with her.

She shook her head. "I will not have you dictate my every move. I have lived two and twenty years without *you* telling me what to do. For the past four years, I have been on my own. I have travelled all over the world, and I go where I want and when I want!" She placed both hands on her hips while she was speaking and her cheeks were fiery red.

He spoke very carefully this time. "I am not trying to dictate your every move. I only recommended you not accompany me to Warner's office."

"Oh, it was just a recommendation," Eliza said deliberately. She paused and tapped her finger against her lips. "I am ignoring your recommendation, and I am going with you." She smiled triumphantly.

Benedict noticed that Mr. Larson was still in the corner, and he seemed to be looking at him with pity. Obviously, he must agree with him. "Even Mr. Larson thinks you should stay behind tonight," Benedict offered up.

Eliza whipped her head around to her protector. "Is that right?"

Mr. Larson shot Benedict a scowl, but his face softened as he directed his gaze back towards her. "Lady Eliza, you did have a traumatic night," he said trying to be diplomatic. "What if I go with Lord Sinclair, and you stay home and rest?"

Scoffing at his response, she turned back to Benedict. "I am beginning to understand the problem."

Benedict took a deep breath and exhaled. Finally, she was beginning to see reason.

"You think I am a weak woman, and I need to be coddled," she said frankly.

"What?" he asked, confused.

"I trusted you, Benedict. I confided in you, and now you think I cannot handle being an agent," Eliza said defensively.

Benedict started shaking his head. "No, that is not what I think."

"It is. You think I am broken. You told me yourself that I was a survivor, yet you do not think I can handle breaking into someone's office," she said in disbelief.

"Eliza, you are blowing this out of proportion," he was exasperated.

"No, I am not."

"Yes, you are," Benedict said while raising his voice.

"Do I need to remind you that you do not own me?" she exclaimed as she walked towards the window, keeping her back to him.

Benedict sat there stunned for a few moments before he dared to continue. "Eliza, I know I do not own you, nor do I want to dictate your every move. I care about you and want you to be safe. Do you believe me?" Her spine was rigid as she stared out the window. "Please believe that I would never try to control you or break your spirit," he said.

"I am going to make this very simple for you." Eliza's voice was firm as she turned to face him. "I am going with or without you."

He shook his head. "Well, you most assuredly are not going alone."

"Then you can come with me," she said stubbornly.

Benedict stood and walked slowly to her. "Fine. We will both go tonight to break into Mr. Warner's office."

"Thank you," Eliza said sarcastically.

Furrowing his brows in concern, he gazed at her. "Please believe me when I say that I just want to keep you safe."

Eliza's green eyes reflected a fierceness that he had not seen before as she stated, "This is who I am. I am an agent for the Crown, just like you and Jonathon. Sometimes I find myself in dangerous situations, but I am well trained. You need to trust me, Benedict. I know what I am doing."

"I do trust you, Eliza. I know you can take care of yourself, but why do you refuse to let other people take care of you every now and then?"

"I am used to being on my own. It is safer that way," she said with a resigned look in her eye.

"That is not a good way to live." Benedict reached for her hand and was pleased that she did not pull away. "Why are you so afraid that I am trying to control you?" he asked curiously.

She stared at him for a moment before answering, and he could see doubt flicker in her eyes. "Men always try to control women." She looked down at their hands. "I will not be controlled," she said firmly as she swiftly removed her hand from his. "That is why I never want to get married."

Benedict considered her for a moment and knew he needed to proceed with caution. He could tell Eliza believed what she was saying. "You once told me that you would get married if you fell in love," he reminded her.

"I did say that," she sighed, "but I fear that love may not be enough."

Stepping closer so that no distance was left between them, he gently placed his hands on her forearms. Eliza hesitantly met his gaze, and he just wanted to wipe away any doubt that she had concerning his feelings towards her. Slowly, he lowered his head, giving her ample opportunity to resist if she felt so inclined, but he was met with no resistance. As his lips captured hers, he could feel her lips melting into his own. He broke the kiss and softly said, "It is if you marry the right person."

Tenderly, he kissed her again, and felt the moment she surrendered into his arms. She brought her hands up his chest and around his neck. He tilted his head, while deepening the kiss as he pulled her tightly against him.

Then, he remembered that he was still in Jonathon's dining room. As much as he wanted to continue, he reluctantly broke the kiss, and she laid her head against his chest. He marveled how it felt like the most natural thing in the world to have Eliza in his arms.

After a few moments, Benedict looked out the window. "We have to wait till it gets dark enough to sneak into Warner's office." He rested his cheek on top of her head. "We could keep holding each other the whole day, or we could play chess?"

Eliza tightened her hold on him. "I vote we stay like this all day."

Someone cleared his throat very loudly on the other side of the dining room, and Benedict did not even have to guess who it was.

"My love, I am afraid Mr. Larson will shoot me if we keep carrying on like this." He removed Eliza's hands from his neck and offered his arm to her. "We should go play chess."

She laughed. "I fear I should warn you that I am very talented at chess."

Benedict smirked playfully at her. "You said something similar about German whist, and I believe I held my own against you."

She put her finger to her mouth. "Did you now? I seem to remember beating you rather soundly."

"You beat me by one game," he laughed.

Eliza's face lit up in amusement. "Whether I beat you by one game or twenty, I still won."

Shaking his head good naturedly, Benedict escorted her towards the drawing room.

Chapter Eighteen

Eliza was snuggled up next to Benedict as they rode in comfortable silence in Jonathon's carriage towards Mr. Warner's office. A few hours ago, Uncle Charles had sent a messenger over with the address, and it was only a short carriage ride across town.

Today has been a perfect day, she thought, as she relished being in Benedict's arms. After breakfast, they retired to the drawing room where they spent hours playing chess, and it became apparent that she had met her match at the game.

When Benedict pulled ahead by one game, he insisted they take a break and go on a ride through Hyde Park. It pleasantly surprised her when he handed her the reins, and patiently taught her how to drive the curricle. As a lady, she had never been given the opportunity to drive a curricle, and always secretly wanted to learn.

She loved spending time with Benedict, especially since he seemed to value her opinion. Most gentlemen of the ton felt certain topics were off-limits to ladies due to their delicate constitutions, yet he did not shy away from controversial subjects such as religion and politics with her. Eliza rejoiced that they could openly discuss their past missions with each other. She felt safe and cherished in his presence, and she also knew, without a doubt, that she had fallen in love with Lord Benedict Sinclair.

However, everything would change if they got married. *Isn't that what happened in marriages?* Benedict might love her for a few years, but eventually he would tire of her. After his heir was born, she would become meaningless, and he would lock her up in an estate, to be forgotten again. Eliza predicted it would only be a matter of time until he was unfaithful, since all gentlemen have mistresses, even the supposedly happily married ones.

Eliza groaned inwardly, as she realized what a fool she was for starting to believe she could get married, and live the sheltered life of a pampered aristocrat. She had no desire to lounge around an estate, ignoring the social injustices being committed around the world. After they got married, Benedict would refuse to let her do anything remotely dangerous, which meant he would make her stop working as an agent.

She had been trained as an agent, and she refused to change who she was to be with Benedict. Furthermore, she would not lose control of her life, so getting married was inconceivable right now. No one was going to force her to stop working as an agent!

"Why do you look so sad?" he asked, placing his hand on her knee, his voice filled with concern.

She swallowed the lump in her throat. He was being so kind. Perhaps she should just overlook the fact that everything would change for her if they continued down this path? No, she could never do that.

Benedict put his finger under her chin and forced her to look at him. "What is wrong, Eliza?"

She did not want to have this conversation right now. It would break her heart, so she had to think of something fast to appease his concern. "I just miss Jonathon."

"No, that is not it," he said without missing a beat.

She should have known he would not have fallen for that. Eliza decided to just blurt out her greatest fear, mainly to gauge his reaction. "I was wondering if we got married how long it would take before you took a mistress."

Benedict jerked back as if she struck him. "What?"

"I said, 'I wonder how long it would take for you to take a mistress'," Eliza repeated deliberately, as her eyes searched his for some type of truth.

She had come to greatly respect and admire Benedict, and desperately hoped he was not like the other vain, titled men who felt their positions permitted them to engage in indiscretions.

"What did you say before that?" he asked, his eyes betraying nothing.

Thinking back to what she said, Eliza closed her eyes in overwhelming embarrassment. She should not even presume that he wanted to marry her. "I fail to recall," she mumbled, because she did not want to repeat what she just said.

"I believe you said, 'if we got married'," he said, never taking his gaze off her.

"Yes, but…"

Her words were cut off by Benedict's lips crushing into hers. Eliza could not believe that he was really kissing her, and not just his usual gentle kiss, but a passionate, consuming kiss that seemed to demonstrate how much he truly cared for her. His lips were firm and insistent, as his hands roamed up and down her back, pulling her tight against him.

She twisted in the carriage, as she moved her hands up his chest and around his neck. His hands circled her waist, then he effortlessly pulled her onto his lap. His lips guided her mouth open and he deepened the kiss. Just when she was convinced that his kisses could not get any closer to perfection, he placed a kiss below her ear and trailed passionate kisses down her neck.

Oh, how she craved Benedict's touch and did not think it was possible to ever get enough. She cradled his face with her hands and forced his mouth to come back to hers. His kisses were all-consuming, and Eliza realized the barriers around her heart were rapidly thawing. In his arms, she felt like she was infinitely precious to him, and together they were truly whole.

Benedict broke the kiss and rested his forehead on hers. "Not *if* we get married, Eliza." His voice was breathless. "*When* we get married." His mouth claimed hers, as he slowly and gently taught Eliza how to truly kiss.

The carriage rolled to a stop, and Eliza broke the kiss. "We stopped. We need to get…"

Benedict's mouth claimed hers again, and he was not satisfied with a quick kiss either. His hands rested on her hips, as her fingers started weaving through his hair. She was thoroughly enjoying this moment and decided they did not need to get out of the carriage right away, or ever.

There was a knock at the carriage door indicating the footman

154

wanted to open the door for them. Benedict reluctantly broke the kiss and leaned against her, breathing hard.

"Give me a moment," he growled at the door.

Eliza laughed in amusement at his reaction to the footman. "It is not his fault we have arrived at our destination."

His face filled with love as his eyes latched onto hers. "We will finish this conversation later."

Eliza raised an eyebrow. "I do not recall having a conversation," she said teasingly.

Benedict had a crooked grin on his face. "Have I kissed you so thoroughly that I caused you to forget what we were talking about before we kissed?"

Eliza's eyes grew wide. "Oh." She remembered that Benedict had told her that he wanted to marry her.

Mimicking her, he said, "Oh." He chuckled as he gently removed her from his lap, and turned to open the carriage door. "We have to walk the last block on foot to avoid detection."

They both hopped out of the carriage and started walking cautiously towards Mr. Warner's building. Eliza needed to find a way to avoid the subject of marriage. She loved him and might agree to marry him, especially if he kept kissing her like he did in the carriage. The problem was, she did not want to give up her freedom as an agent, nor did she believe that men could forego mistresses.

Shaking her head, she realized she needed to focus on the task at hand. They needed to break into Paul Warner's office and see if they could find any incriminating evidence against Aaron Wade. After all, the sooner they finished this mission, the sooner Mr. Wade would be in Newgate, and the sooner the abducted girls would be returned home.

Although, the sooner the mission was over, the sooner she would lose Benedict as a partner. Eliza sighed as she realized she did not want to lose him as a partner, but knew it would be for the best. After all, that is what she wanted, was it not?

Benedict was deliriously happy. Eliza had said she wanted to marry him. Well, not really, but she had implied they would get married. He was pleased that she was even thinking of the possibility. He should have paid more attention to what she was saying, but he got distracted when he heard the word *marry* escape her lips.

Although, he did hear her mention something about him taking a mistress. Why she thought he would take a mistress was beyond him. She seemed to state it as a fact that he would take on a mistress at some point. He would have to clear that up and let her know that he would never take a mistress, or be unfaithful. He was not the type of man to break his vows.

He wanted to hold Eliza's hand, but she was wearing men's clothing, and that would draw attention to them. Benedict smiled to himself as the thought of broaching the subject with her about not wearing men's clothing after they were married. After all, when she was the Marchioness of Lansdowne, she could not dress in men's clothes around their household staff and tenants.

Benedict chuckled, because he knew she would continue to do as she pleased regardless of what other people thought of her. Yes, he would definitely enjoy being married to Eliza.

He knew that she would bring excitement and joy into his life. His future as a marquess was filled with reviewing ledgers, meetings with account managers, touring his lands, and keeping his estates profitable, but it had seemed so dreary until Eliza entered his life.

With her by his side, he would enjoy meeting with his tenants and improving their lots in life. He knew she would love the tenants and would be fiercely protective of them. Eventually, she would have their children and they would be spitfires, like their mother. Benedict was finally happy with the way his life was going, but he just needed to convince her that he was worth the risk.

Eliza ducked into the compact alleyway between a pair of three-story brick buildings. The alley was narrow and filled with discarded waste, but it was empty of any potential witnesses to what they were about to do. She grabbed his arm and leaned close to his ear. "I am going to see if I can scale the side of this building and look for an open window on the second floor." Releasing him, she went to find a foothold on the brick to start the ascent.

Laura Beers

Benedict kept watch as she started scaling up the side of the building with remarkable skill. When she reached the second story, she stopped at the first window she came to and pulled on it, but it did not budge. She slowly started to edge her way towards the next window on her right. When she stood in front of that window, she reached out and pulled on it. The window squeaked open and Eliza climbed through. Looking down at him, she waved triumphantly.

Scaling the brick building, he pulled himself into the open window. Once inside, he closed the window and pulled his pistol out of the waistband of his trousers in case they encountered anyone in the building. Being vigilant, he preceded her as he ascertained there was no one on the second floor and indicated she should proceed.

Eliza found the stained wooden door that had *Paul Warner, Solicitor* labeled on it. Benedict tried to open the door, but it was locked. Before he could think of the next step, she was on her knees with two pins from her hair, jamming them into the lock, moving them back and forth until it clicked. With Benedict keeping watch, she opened the door and stepped into Paul Warner's office.

Chapter Nineteen

Eliza quickly scanned the office, because she did not want Mr. Warner to notice that anything had been disturbed. She headed to the large oak desk that was located towards the back of the modest one-room office. Upon arriving at the front of the desk, she quickly lit a candle, then turned to close the window drapes.

Turning back to the desk, Eliza noticed the large drawers had locks on them, so she pulled out some pins from her hair and crouched down. Once the first drawer was unlocked, she pulled it open and started sorting through the documents, but saw none that were related to Aaron Wade, or his ships. She returned the files and relocked the drawer. After she unlocked the second drawer, she started rifling through the files till something flagged her attention. She pulled the dossier out and spread the papers on the desk.

She noticed that Benedict was vigilantly keeping watch at the door, and she turned her attention back to the papers. Luckily, the candle illuminated the room enough to read them. Eliza was absorbing the pages as she was reading, and she discovered that this dossier held the contract for the *Deceiver*. It listed Mr. Aaron Wade, Lord Vernon, and Mr. Timothy Saxton as owners of the brig. As she perused the contract, she realized that Lord Camden had recently sold his shares of the ship to Mr. Saxton.

Eliza gasped, and Benedict looked over at her with concern. "What is wrong?"

"Your stepbrother is only part owner of the *Deceiver*. It appears that Lord Vernon and Mr. Saxton are co-owners as well," she stated. "Lord Camden sold his shares of the *Deceiver* a few months ago to Mr. Saxton." She hesitated before adding, "Lord Matthew Camden is my brother-in-law."

Benedict took a deep breath and released it, but as he turned towards her he had a smile on his face. "Great, now we both have horrible relations."

Stifling a laugh, Eliza threw her hand up to cover her mouth. After a moment, she said, "I have only conversed with Lord Camden a few times, but it has been enough. He is a cruel man, and I do not like him. I wonder if Uncle Charles is aware that Lord Camden used to be in business with Mr. Wade."

Benedict shrugged. "Perhaps Lord Camden sold his shares, after he realized Aaron was using illegal means to make money?"

Eliza shook her head. "No, they are cut from the same cloth."

A short time later, she had finished absorbing all the documents in the dossier and started organizing the papers. He noticed that she had stopped reading and asked, "What did you discover?"

Pausing in her organization of the papers, she turned her attention to Benedict. "It appears from this paperwork that your stepbrother is only a partial owner of three brigs now, since he had to sell off two of his other ships. He makes his money as a merchant as we knew, but it appears that he has lost the majority of his fortune." Eliza held up papers to show bank loans that were past due. "Mr. Wade has not paid the remaining three ships off yet, and the banks are threatening to foreclose on them. It appears that by taking on investors for the *Deceiver*, he has been able to make a partial payment to the bank."

Benedict's brow rose. "That does not make sense. When my brother Henry first hired a Bow Street Runner, we were told he was wealthy."

"A few years ago, he was wealthy, but look at the ledgers of the ships." Eliza handed the documents over to him as he came closer to the desk. "Last month, we raided one of Mr. Wade's ships, the *Commander* in France, rescuing fourteen girls, and the ledgers show that they lost thousands of pounds on that voyage."

Frowning, Benedict continued reading the documents. "I cannot believe Aaron would have made thousands from selling those girls."

Eliza shook her head. "No, he would only make a few hundred pounds on the girls."

"I am shocked that Aaron could be so heartless for such a small amount," he said in disgust, as he threw the pages onto the desk.

She reached for the pages and placed them back in order. "When we got permission to board the English ship in French waters, we made an agreement with the French that would allow them to tax Mr. Wade's ships heavily for their goods. If he refused to pay the additional taxes, then the ship would be confiscated. It would appear that he paid the taxes."

"Who came up with the idea to approach the French government to make such a lucrative arrangement?"

"Me," Eliza stated as she continued with her explanation of the pages in front of her. "We have raided Mr. Wade's ships four times, but only three times in France. One ship, the *Defiance*, was raided on the docks before it left England, and the authorities confiscated it. Mr. Wade is still fighting with the courts to get the ship back, but he has already spent thousands on solicitor's fees."

Eliza knew that her missions had taken a huge financial toll on Mr. Wade, but she saw that it was not enough by reading these files. "Even though we have rescued a total of fifty-seven girls from these voyages, it clearly shows in these ledgers that Mr. Wade was still able to sell hundreds of girls at different ports around the world," she said in frustration.

"How can you tell?" Benedict asked intrigued.

"The ledgers have a number as a line item like we saw on Lord Vernon's list. For example, the *Commander*'s ledger has a line item of fourteen and we rescued fourteen girls on that mission," Eliza explained while pointing to the line item fourteen.

"Do not fret about those girls right now. We need to focus on those that are missing and ensure Aaron will never have an opportunity to sell another girl," he asserted.

Eliza nodded since she knew he was right. "We need to get this dossier over to Uncle Charles. I do not want to risk these ledgers disappearing."

Benedict hesitated. "If we take these ledgers, then Mr. Warner is going to know that someone broke into his office and will notify Aaron."

"With these documents, we have enough proof to send your

stepbrother to Newgate permanently." She smiled up at him. "They clearly state that Mr. Wade smuggled goods to the French and has abducted and sold hundreds of English girls into slavery. Besides, smuggling is punishable by death," she said with a smug smile.

Placing all the papers back in the portfolio, she handed them to Benedict, then she closed the bottom desk drawer and locked it. Even though she knew Mr. Warner would eventually discover the files were missing, she did not want to leave an obvious trail. Slowly they crept out of the office, careful not to disturb anything, then locked the door. As they left the building by the alley door, they walked silently towards the carriage because they both recognized the importance of the portfolio in Benedict's hands.

When the footman saw them approach, he hopped down from the carriage and opened the door. Once it started to roll away, Eliza turned to Benedict and said apologetically, "I am sorry that we have not found anything that will tie your stepbrother to Henry's death. We will keep looking."

Benedict shrugged. "I knew we would not find anything in Mr. Warner's office. Aaron is smart and calculating, but I doubt he wrote anything down about Henry's murder." He smiled down at her. "I am relieved to know that Aaron will finally receive his just deserts for all his villainy."

Satisfied with his response, Eliza leaned back against the plush seats. After a few moments, she said, "I wonder how Jonathon's mission is going. He has not returned home yet with Lady Hannah. I hope everything is all right."

Benedict reached for her hand. "Jonathon is a great agent. I know he has everything under control." She squeezed his hand and rested her head on his shoulder. A few moments later, he asked, "How do you suppose Aaron was able to trade with the French, being an English merchant?"

"Mr. Wade passed himself off as a French merchant, complete with forged documents, which is why he was granted access at their ports. By informing the French ambassador of his deceit, the French could increase the tax on his ship profoundly," Eliza stated.

"I am curious how you convinced the French government to allow English agents access to their docks when we are at war?"

Her lips curled downward for a moment. "I used to believe that men were inherently good and would choose to do the right thing when given the chance. I appealed to the French ambassador's sense of humanity, as I explained the plight of Martha and so many other defenseless women. It took some convincing, but when I proved to Monsieur LeBlanc that the French government would make a generous profit, they granted permission on a case by case basis."

"Why did you say you *used* to believe that men are inherently good?" Benedict asked curiously.

"The longer I work as an agent, the more I am starting to question if there is any good in the world," Eliza said sadly.

Benedict leaned closer. "Do not let men like Aaron take away your ability to see the good that is all around you. They do not deserve that power over you."

Considering what he said, Eliza bit her lower lip. For the past couple of years, she had intermittently lost faith in mankind. She wanted to go back to believing the best in people, regardless of what she had experienced on her past missions. Gazing at Benedict, her heart filled with gratitude towards him. With him by her side, she knew she could become the lady she desperately hoped to be.

Chapter Twenty

If Benedict was not in love with Eliza before, then he most certainly would have been tonight. He had arrived at Jonathon's townhouse to escort her to Lord Chambers' house party, and was rendered speechless as he saw her descending the stairs.

Eliza was dressed in a sheer, off-the-shoulder, pink muslin ball gown with a low neckline. Her glorious, chestnut brown hair was piled up high on top of her head, with petite white flowers spaced evenly throughout, and soft curls hung around her face and along her back. A wide, diamond-encrusted choker partly covered her elegant neck, presumably to hide the knife wound. Benedict was mesmerized as she stood in front of him.

"Benedict?" her voice broke through his stunned silence.

He kissed her gloved hand. "You look beautiful, Eliza."

Her hand went to her choker. "I'm wearing one of my grandmother's necklaces to hide the puncture wound. Is it too much?"

"No, my dear, it is perfect," Benedict stated, as his fingers itched to touch her bare shoulders. "You are perfect," he amended his statement.

"Thank you," Eliza said with a coy smile. Tentatively, she raised a hand and brushed his hair off his forehead, her fingers lingering on his skin.

He relished her touch as he locked eyes with her, and realized he would do everything in his power to make Eliza his wife, his partner in life. He was humbled to realize that he had never needed anyone before, but he needed this woman now. He needed her strength, her friendship, and her love.

Benedict opened his mouth to declare his feelings, but stopped when he noticed Jonathon's staff observing them. Instead, he offered his arm and together they strolled towards his carriage.

Once they were inside, Eliza smoothed out the fullness of her dress as Benedict turned and faced her. "You truly look stunning. When you walked down the stairs, I just wanted to pull you into a corner and devour you with kisses," he confessed as his hands gently touched her shoulders.

"I would not have complained." She smiled.

Benedict groaned. "You cannot say things like that, Eliza."

"I cannot speak the truth?"

"No, you must always speak the truth to me, but you must not encourage me to ruin your reputation," he said teasingly.

Raising an eyebrow, she asked, "Even if I want to be kissed in the corner?"

Benedict's warm smile turned into a mischievous one. "Especially if you want to be kissed in a corner."

Eliza laughed and he rejoiced, because the more time he spent with her, the more she seemed to let go of her burdens from the past. He placed his finger under her chin, and leaned in to claim a kiss. As he released her lips and started to lean back, she followed him and proceeded to kiss him in return.

After a few minutes of enjoying her sensual kisses, Benedict rested his forehead on hers. "We have two options," he said hoarsely. "We could turn this carriage around and race to Gretna Greens, which would ensure we could do more than just kissing in the corner tonight."

Eliza's face turned bright red, and she cleared her throat. "Um… what is the second option?"

Benedict chuckled at her response. "Or we stop kissing, so we do not ruin your lovely hair and proceed to Lord Chambers' gathering as planned, hoping that my stepbrother is in attendance."

"I think the second choice is the better option," Eliza said calmly, even though her cheeks were still rosy pink. He pulled back from her forehead and stole one more kiss. She started fanning her face and Benedict chuckled under his breath at her obvious embarrassment of his mentioning the wedding night.

After a few moments, Eliza put her fan away and sought out his gaze. "We need to track Mr. Wade's movements to see who he talks to, and hopefully we can discover a clue to indicate where the girls are being held."

"And if that does not work, then I will trail him tonight after the house party to see if he leads us to them," Benedict stated.

"Are you sure you do not want me to join you?"

He chuckled. "I am confident that even Aaron would notice a lady in a ball gown trailing him."

"Good point." Eliza hesitated before asking, "When was the last time you saw your stepbrother?"

Benedict thought deeply for a moment. "I guess it has been over three years now."

Putting her hand on his arm, her eyes betrayed her concern. "Will you be all right seeing him tonight?"

"Let us hope that I do not kill him," he said half-heartedly, shrugging his shoulders.

Eliza smiled, but he noticed it did not reach her eyes. She appeared anxious by his response. "Would you like me to hold your pistol in my reticule?"

He tapped her nose playfully, hoping to charm her again. "That will not be necessary. I will avoid killing him tonight, unless he gives me cause."

Her face softened into a big smile. "I can agree to that," she said playfully, as she wrapped her arm around his. "Oh, I sent a messenger over to my uncle's office with the dossier, and a letter updating him with the status of the mission. Furthermore, I asked my uncle to investigate Mr. Saxton's real estate holdings to see if he owns any buildings down by the docks."

Giving her a crooked smile, he asked, "Did you put in the letter that you rather enjoy kissing me?"

Eliza laughed loudly. "Of course, my lord. I wrote 'Lord Sinclair is a wonderful kisser. Please let my father, the Duke of Remington, know, so he can challenge Lord Sinclair to a duel'."

Benedict countered with, "Or you could have written, 'I find that Lord Sinclair is so dashingly handsome that I cannot remember what our mission was supposed to be'."

They laughed all the way to Lord Chambers' house, as they traded their opinions about what Eliza should have written in the letter to Lord Beckett.

Eliza's arm was on top of Benedict's as they stood in Lord Chambers' ballroom. She was impressed by the crush in the rectangular ballroom with intricate artwork dominating the domed ceiling. The flickering lights emanating from the two large, ornate gold chandeliers, transformed the ballroom into a truly romantic setting. She watched as dancers twirled by in orchestrated dance moves, and the laughter surrounding her confirmed the tone of the house party.

They stayed in the crowded ballroom, rather than searching the card rooms for Mr. Wade. They did not want him to have any indication that he was being watched, since they wanted to discreetly see who he conversed with.

"Lady Eliza, I did not expect to see you here." Eliza's concentration was broken by a feminine voice behind her.

Dropping her hand from Benedict's, she spun around when she recognized the voice. "Lady Rachel," she exclaimed, pulling her into an embrace.

She had become fast friends with Lady Rachel three Seasons ago when she found her in the library reading *Gulliver's Travels* during Mrs. Turner's house party. Immediately, they had discovered they were both bluestockings and bonded over their love of books. Lady Rachel was a beautiful girl of average height with hair the color of wheat. She had brilliant blue eyes that flickered with an astounding intellect. She was also the only child of the Earl of Exeter, a prominent member of the Whig party.

Eliza provided the introductions. "Lord Sinclair, may I present my good friend, Lady Rachel."

Lady Rachel curtsied, while offering him her gloved hand. Benedict gave a polite bow and kissed her proffered hand. "I am delighted to meet you, Lady Rachel."

She smiled up at him. "It is a pleasure to meet you, Lord

Sinclair." She glanced between Benedict and Eliza and smiled knowingly.

Eliza glanced around to see who had accompanied her friend. "Is your mother in attendance?"

"Yes, she is coming this way," Lady Rachel replied. "When I saw you from across the ballroom, I had to hurry to come over and say hello."

Lady Exeter, who was a charming and attractive older version of her daughter, glided up to the group. "Rachel, if you insist on acting like a hoyden, then no gentlemen of importance will ask you to dance," she said sternly, but her eyes did not hold the same censure.

Lady Rachel did not appear to be chastised by her mother's rebuke by the way her lips twitched in amusement. "Yes, mother. I will strive to act less hoydenish."

Lady Exeter gave her daughter an exasperated look and turned towards Eliza. "How are you, my dear?" her voice filled with compassion.

Smiling, Eliza responded by saying, "I am well, thank you."

Rachel's mother was the exact opposite of Duchess Diana. Where her own mother criticized and berated her, Rachel's mother showered her daughter with praise and encouragement. Whenever Eliza called on her friend, she would marvel at the kindness they bestowed on each other. More than once, she witnessed Lord Exeter greet his wife with a kiss on the mouth and she would feel a twinge of jealously that their home was filled with love, whereas her home had been filled with bitterness.

Eliza placed her hand on Benedict's arm. "Lady Exeter, I would like to introduce you to Lord Sinclair."

Lady Exeter's face grew pensive as she watched Benedict bow. "I am dear friends with your stepmother and I am sorry to hear about the loss of your brother."

Benedict swallowed hard, obviously attempting to control his emotions. "It has been a hard transition."

"As well it should. Losing a brother is akin to losing a best friend, in my opinion," Lady Exeter said sympathetically.

"I agree wholeheartedly," Benedict said, his voice holding a hint of emotion.

Lady Exeter turned towards her daughter, "I must go see Lady Pierce. Will you be all right if I leave you for a few moments with Eliza and Lord Sinclair?"

Smiling, Lady Rachel said dramatically, "I believe I will manage."

After Lady Exeter murmured her good-byes, Rachel's eyes sparkled with mischief as she observed them. "Pray tell, how long as this been going on?" she asked, motioning between them.

Eliza's eyes grew wide. She could not believe how boldly her friend was behaving. "I do not know what you are referring to."

Her friend let out the most unladylike huff. "Do not insult me. I have known you for years and I can tell you are both besotted with each other."

Benedict chuckled quietly as he leaned closer to her. "I like her."

Eliza ignored his comments and focused on Rachel. "We are just friends," she lied, hoping her friend would drop the interrogation.

Rachel gave her a look of disbelief. "Can I inquire how you two were introduced?"

Benedict gave Eliza a crooked smile. "We met at Lord Vernon's ball, where she fell into my arms."

Laughing, Lady Rachel's hand covered her mouth. "Is that so?" she asked, amused, while glancing at Eliza.

"Good heavens, Lord Sinclair. Please do not exaggerate," Eliza admonished in a hushed tone. She turned to her friend and explained. "We met at Lord Vernon's ball where Jonathon introduced us. They were roommates at Oxford."

Benedict's eyes held a gleam of amusement as he continued with his version of the story. "Lord Vernon's ballroom was overly warm so I left the main hall and Eliza came barreling around the corner." His smile grew mischievous. "She almost knocked me over, but I was able to recover quickly and prevent us from falling. I had to pry her arms off my person."

Eliza's mouth gaped open. "That is not remotely what happened."

Rachel started giggling as Benedict leaned closer to her. "You are easy to provoke."

"I am not provoked. I just prefer to stay on the side of honesty," Eliza murmured, attempting to hide her irritation.

"Did you know that whenever you get frustrated, your eyebrows pull down so they slope inwards?" Benedict pointed out.

Eliza looked up at him in surprise. To her knowledge, no one had been able to read her so perfectly before. As she met his amused gaze, she found herself returning his smile, even though she felt a little silly for her behavior.

Due to the loud music in the ballroom, and their close proximity, Eliza had hoped that their conversation went unnoticed, but Lady Rachel was observing them and her lips were twitching. It appeared that she was holding back a smile, and Eliza was mortified when she realized that her friend had overheard them.

Lady Rachel leaned closer to her and talked only loudly enough for her to hear over the music. "I am truly happy for you. It appears you've met your match, and a handsome one at that." She leaned back and smiled approvingly at Benedict. "Lord Sinclair, are you a lover of books as much as Eliza and I?"

"I am. My townhouse boasts a magnificent library. You are welcome to peruse my library and borrow any book you would like," he informed her.

Lady Rachel's eyes lit up at his generous offer. "I would like that very much. Thank you."

As Eliza scanned the room, she noticed Mr. Wade walking towards them through the crush. Benedict and Rachel were conversing politely, so she tilted her head towards his stepbrother. She hoped to catch his attention when it became apparent that Mr. Wade was on a direct path to approach them.

Mr. Aaron Wade was a tall, muscular man and was extremely attractive, especially when dressed in a black superfine dress coat, form-fitting pantaloons, white vest and a nicely tied black cravat. He had dark blond, curly hair and kept it fashionably short, and he was most definitely a dandy. Wade reminded Eliza of the Greek demigod Perseus, if only he did not have a heart that was as black as Hades.

He stopped short in front of them and said curtly, "Dear brother, I was hoping to run into you this evening."

Benedict's jaw clenched. "I see that you are still delusional as ever, since it would appear that you forgot you are in fact my *step*brother."

Aaron Wade scoffed at this response before his predatory eyes shifted to Eliza, and he slowly perused the entire length of her body in a lewd fashion. Immediately, Benedict placed a protective arm around Eliza's waist and gently pulled her close to him. "Are you not going to introduce me to these lovely ladies?" Mr. Wade asked politely as his eyes kept darting to Eliza's exposed bosom.

Benedict growled out an introduction. "Lady Elizabeth and Lady Rachel, this is my stepbrother Mr. Aaron Wade."

Eliza tipped her head towards Aaron, since Benedict refused to loosen his grip on her waist. Rachel dipped into a curtsy as Aaron bowed to them, but he kept his focus on Eliza. "Lady Elizabeth, I was not aware that you were friends with Lady Rachel."

Eliza raised an eyebrow. "Who I am friends with is none of your concern, Mr. Wade."

Briefly narrowing his eyes, Mr. Wade then plastered on a smile. "Of course not, my lady. I did not mean to imply otherwise." He extended his hand towards her. "May I have the pleasure of your company for this dance?"

Benedict stepped in front of her and shielded her from Aaron's view. "No, you will not dance with Lady Elizabeth. Not now, not ever," he said firmly.

Aaron Wade seemed to take note of his stepbrother and raised his voice. "And why not, Lord Sinclair?" He was intentionally talking loudly to attract attention. "Does Lady Elizabeth not dance with untitled men?"

"Go away, Aaron," Benedict growled. "Go back to the gutter that you crawled out from."

Mr. Wade leveled a hostile glare at his stepbrother. "I understand that you are a fancy earl now that Henry is dead, and soon you will be a marquess when your father finally kicks the bucket." He smirked. "That must be nice for you."

Benedict took a step towards his stepbrother and Eliza grabbed the back of his jacket to stop him. Nothing would be accomplished if Benedict lost his temper and physically beat the loathsome man in this public setting.

Pursing his lips for a moment, Mr. Wade stated, "Although, it really is a shame that Henry was not as good a rider as he claimed to be."

Stiffening at his words, Benedict's hands balled into fists. "I suggest we take this outside," he said in a commanding voice.

"I would be a fool to engage in a fight with you," Mr. Wade replied, placing his hands up in front of him.

Benedict stepped closer to Aaron. "No? Are you afraid of a fair fight?" His eyes narrowed in anger, and he said mockingly, "Or is beating defenseless women more your style?"

Mr. Wade stiffened, his eyes blazing with fury. "You will pay for that comment."

It was apparent that they were starting to create a scene by the way people were turning to watch their interaction, so Eliza came out from behind Benedict. "I will dance with you, Mr. Wade, but then I must insist you refrain from speaking to us again this evening, or ever."

Benedict gently grabbed her forearm and whispered, "You do not have to dance with him."

Eliza turned towards him. "I know, but I feel that he is up to something."

Benedict was shooting daggers at his stepbrother, as Eliza extended her hand towards Mr. Wade, who escorted her to the dance floor. Luckily, it was the cotillion and not the waltz, so there was not much time to talk. Although, she felt Mr. Wade's intense gaze on her throughout the entire set.

After the dance ended, Mr. Wade offered his arm, and Eliza accepted it, as polite society dictated. He started veering her towards the lighted patio and not back towards Benedict. "Mr. Wade, I would appreciate an escort back to Lord Sinclair," she said as she looked for her partner, but he was nowhere to be found.

Mr. Wade dropped his arm and tightly gripped her forearm. "I insist that we spend a few minutes alone discussing things," he whispered menacingly.

Eliza decided to allow Aaron to lead her to the patio instead of creating another scene in the ballroom. There were hundreds of people at the gathering, and he would not try anything with so many witnesses. What harm could it do?

Chapter Twenty-One

As Mr. Wade led Eliza into the courtyard, he veered left towards a darkened corner and out of view of the ballroom. He forced her to face him, then he threw her back against the wall. Her head hit the uneven stone exterior and blackness threatened to overtake her.

Before she collapsed, Aaron Wade grabbed both of her upper arms tightly, and shoved her against the stone. "You stupid chit." He started shaking her as he said angrily, "Why did you feel the need to interfere in my business? Do you know how much you have cost me?"

She was not sure which Mr. Wade she should answer, since she was currently seeing three of him. She decided to focus on the one in the middle. "I am not sure what you are referring to…" Eliza broke off.

"Do not insult me, Lady Elizabeth. I have waited for a long time to get you alone and have a nice chat," Mr. Wade said with contempt.

Her head was throbbing, but she managed to lock eyes with him. "Then talk."

He chuckled. "My dear, you do not have to put on such a brave front." He leaned closer to appear as if they were in a lover's embrace. "How did you get Monsieur LeBlanc to convince the French to tax my ships?"

Eliza stiffened. How did Mr. Wade know about the meetings with Monsieur LeBlanc?

"You did not think I knew about those meetings, did you?" He took one of his hands off her arms and started caressing her cheek. "Pray tell me, who is *Shadow*, Eliza?"

"I have no idea."

Laura Beers

Taking his right hand off her cheek, he slapped her hard across the face. "Do you think me to be a fool? Is it just a grand coincidence that *Shadow* shows up to rid me of my precious cargo after you meet with the French? It only stands to reason you are acquainted with *Shadow*." Mr. Wade leaned in and whispered into her ear, "*Shadow* has become a thorn in my side and needs to be stopped."

Even though Eliza's face throbbed from the slap, she refused to cower. "I think it is you who needs to be stopped. You abduct girls and sell them to a fate worse than death." He leaned back, his nostrils flaring with rage by her declaration. "You are a pitiful man. You abuse women and think you will get away with it."

Mr. Aaron Wade started laughing, but there was no humor in it. He slapped her hard across her cheek again. "I always get away with it. You may run to your Monsieur LeBlanc, and I may get taxed, but it only slows me down. There are always men willing to sell their women for next to nothing." He rested his hand on the wall behind her, while leaning in, and she could feel his breath on her cheek. "And there are always men willing to buy women. I am just a businessman."

"No, you are vile man. I will personally cheer when you have a noose around your neck," she said defiantly.

Without warning or hesitation, Mr. Wade punched her in the stomach as he dropped his hands from her. Stepping back, he started tsking at her. "I see you have a lot to learn about showing respect."

Eliza collapsed to her knees and struggled for air. While she was gasping for breath, she tried to reach for her dagger, but she could not get to it. She should have created a slit in her dress that would allow easier access to her dagger. Where was Benedict? How did no one else notice she was being assaulted on the patio?

"Eliza! Eliza!" Benedict's voice could be heard over the music in the ballroom.

Mr. Wade must have heard it, too, because he crouched down next to her. "It appears that our little interlude has come to an end." He put his hand under her chin and roughly forced her to look at him. "I do not rightly know how you escaped that night, but I will come for you again. I will own you, and trust me when I say I look forward to taming you, my dear." He kissed her on the lips and dropped her chin as she jerked back. Jogging towards the garden wall,

173

he hopped over it.

Staying on her knees, she started sucking air back into her lungs. Her damn corset made it nearly impossible to take a deep breath. A few moments later, Benedict's black dress shoes appeared in front of her.

"Eliza, what happened?" he asked as he crouched down next to her. When Benedict saw her face, he let out an expletive. He carefully touched her cheek, but she winced, so he dropped his hand.

"I am sorry, Eliza. After the set ended, people were milling about and I did not see where Aaron led you after the dance. Lady Rachel and I have been searching all over the ballroom looking for you, which has been quite difficult, considering how many people are in there." Benedict put his hand on the back of her head. "You are bleeding," he informed her as he wiped his hand on his jacket. "Can you tell me what happened?"

Eliza told him what had transpired. By the end, Benedict was furious. "I will kill him with my bare hands." He whipped his head towards the garden fence and went to stand up.

"No, Benedict. I am sure Mr. Wade is long gone now. Please do not leave me alone." Eliza sounded pathetic to even herself, but she did not care, because she needed him right now.

Turning back to her, he reassured her, "I will never leave you." Eliza felt in her heart that he was referring to more than just leaving her right now. "First, we need to get you out of here without being seen."

Benedict immediately stood and helped her rise, then carried her to a bench. After she was situated, he went and found a way to get her back to his carriage without being noticed. He removed his black coat and placed it around her shoulders before he scooped her up. As they made their way towards the line of carriages, he whispered, "Put my coat over your head."

Eliza assumed he did not want any of the footmen to see her swollen face, or the dried blood on the back of her head, and start gossiping. As soon as the carriage door closed, Benedict turned towards her with a mixture of sorrow and anger etched on his face. "I should have never allowed you to dance with Aaron. I had no idea he would assault you with so many people around."

Her head and face ached, and she could barely concentrate on anything else right now, but she knew he blamed himself for her injuries. "Benedict, please, you shoulder no blame for this. I did not think Mr. Wade would hurt me either, or else I would not have let him escort me out onto the patio."

Benedict's hand tenderly touched her bruised cheek again, and she winced. "He really hurt you," he said as his hand slowly combed through the back of her hair to look for more injuries. "I am going to kill him," he muttered under his breath.

Eliza rested her head on his chest. "You must not, at least not yet anyway. We do not know where the missing girls are yet."

"But he hurt you..."

She closed her eyes. "Please, I just want to sleep." She did not feel like discussing Wade, and Benedict kept trying to keep her awake.

"We need to get you home, and I will call for a doctor," Benedict said, his voice filled with anguish and regret.

Eliza nodded, as she kept her eyes closed and let the sleep overcome her.

A short time later, they pulled up in front of Jonathon's townhouse. Benedict jumped out of the carriage before it came to a complete stop and reached back in to scoop up Eliza. As he cradled her in his arms, he ran towards the door while a footman proceeded to open the main door.

When Benedict saw Jonathon's butler, Mr. Wilde, in the entryway, he commanded, "I need a doctor for Lady Elizabeth, now!" Without waiting for a reply, he strolled into the drawing room and laid her down gently on the dark blue velvet sofa.

As he was leaning over her, Mr. Larson and Jonathon stormed into the room. Jonathon ran up and pushed Benedict out of the way. "What happened to my sister?" he shouted as he knelt in front of Eliza and observed her face.

"My stepbrother happened," Benedict said without emotion.

"Wade did this to her?" Jonathon went to touch her cheek but thought better of it and withdrew his hand. Immediately he arose, and he turned to face Benedict. "And where were you when he was beating my sister?"

Benedict looked up to meet his friend's anger. "After the set, I lost track of Eliza and Aaron in the crush of dancers. Lady Rachel and I frantically started searching for Eliza, but she had disappeared. When I ran outside, I found her hunched over in the corner." He glanced down at Eliza, his voice pitched with remorse. "I had not considered the possibility that Aaron would attack her around so many people."

"Of course it was a possibility. He abuses women all the time," Jonathon growled through gritted teeth.

"I wanted to go after him and kill him with my bare hands, but I needed to get help for Eliza first." Benedict crossed over to a chair in the corner and sat down. He put his elbows on his knees and let his hands cradle his head. "You have no idea how sorry I am. It was all my fault." He knew Eliza lying injured on the sofa was his responsibility, because he did not protect her. He had failed to keep her safe.

Eliza's voice broke his thoughts. "No, it was my fault," she said adamantly as she tried to sit up, but winced and laid her head back onto the sofa. "I went outside willingly with Mr. Wade. I did not think he was going to assault me. It was a calculated risk. I wanted to see what I could get him to reveal."

Jonathon knelt by the sofa. "That was pure folly. There are other ways to make people talk."

"I know, but I saw it as the perfect opportunity. Unfortunately, I did not anticipate he would attack me so suddenly and without provocation."

"He could have killed you, Eliza," Jonathon huffed.

"No, he had no intention of killing me. Mr. Wade is angry at me for getting involved in his business and wanted to know who *Shadow* was. Somehow, he has made the connection between *Shadow* and me." Eliza put her hands to her head. "He even knew about the meetings with Monsieur LeBlanc."

Jonathon reared back. "Impossible. No one knew about those meetings."

"Mr. Wade did," she confirmed.

Benedict sat up in the chair. "Who else knew about the meetings with Monsieur LeBlanc?"

"Eliza, myself, and Uncle Charles," Jonathon replied over his shoulder.

"I knew, too," Mr. Larson said as he walked closer to Eliza. As he was studying her face, Benedict could see the older agent furrow his brow and he appeared extremely concerned over her injuries.

Benedict knew that Mr. Larson and Lord Charles Beckett were not traitors, so it must have been someone in France. "What about the French? Who knew about the meetings?"

Jonathon shrugged. "Very few. In case you have forgotten, France and England are at war," he said sarcastically. "Eliza approached Monsieur LeBlanc, who is the French ambassador, at his cousin's party in Manchester. She explained the situation about the women, and pleaded for his help. Monsieur LeBlanc agreed to help, but only because he is in love with her." He shook his head, adding, "I cannot imagine it went over well with his superiors, but France is helping us rescue innocent women. In addition, France gets a small fortune from the taxes that they place on Wade's ships, so I am confident that they would not pass information on to him."

"He is in love with Eliza?" Benedict asked curiously.

Jonathon gave him a look of disbelief. "Yes, let us focus on the most important piece of information," he said mockingly. Frowning, he rubbed his chin absently. "I wonder how Wade learned of your involvement."

"I do not know," Eliza said, her face scrunched in pain.

Benedict walked over to her and knelt beside Jonathon, gently reaching for her hand. "How are you feeling, my dear?"

"My cheek throbs, and my head feels like it is going to explode," she informed him. She brought up her hand and rested it on her forehead.

Mr. Wilde strode into the room with the doctor. Jonathon and Benedict both arose and stepped back while they waited for the doctor to begin his examination. Mr. Larson approached them and spoke discreetly. "My lords, may I recommend that you step out while the doctor examines Lady Elizabeth?"

Tilting his head, Jonathon indicated that Benedict should follow him. A few minutes later, they were in the library sipping brandy from snifters. After a few sips, Benedict lowered his glass to sit on the armrest of the deep, buttoned, brown leather sofa. "How is your mission going?"

Jonathon shared the sofa with Benedict, but they were at opposite ends and both staring ahead at the richly carved alabaster fireplace, which contained a low burning fire. "I have been unable to locate Lady Hannah. I have searched everywhere."

"Do you think she was abducted?"

Jonathon huffed out a frustrated breath. "Possibly. Her housekeeper told me that she took her horse on a morning ride and did not come back. I went and spoke with the magistrate, but it was a dead end. Although, I have a suspicion that the steward knows more than he is letting on."

"What does Lord Beckett make of it?" Benedict asked, taking a quick glance over at his friend.

Jonathon shrugged. "He ordered me to keep looking for her. Lord Pembrooke sent out a note to his daughter, giving her instructions to seek out Uncle Charles. I am hoping she is in hiding until the danger passes. I just came home to get a change of clothes, and Mr. Larson and I have been talking."

Benedict took a sip of his brandy. "Has he filled you in on what we have discovered?"

"Yes, he has. I still cannot believe that Lord Camden is involved. I mean, I knew he was a bad person, but I had no idea he had business dealings with Mr. Wade," Jonathon said, leaning back further into the sofa.

"If he was such a bad person, then why did your father agree to the marriage between your sister and him?" Benedict questioned, again glancing at Jonathon.

"Well, he is an earl, and a wealthy one at that," Jonathon paused and swirled his brandy, "but my mother was the one that arranged the marriage. I knew that Father was opposed to it, but he relented when Mother insisted."

"Did Kate not have any objections to marrying Lord Camden?"

Jonathon scoffed. "She did, but she has always been a very obedient daughter."

"Eliza told me that she is not close with Kate since she got married."

"Kate has always idolized her sister, but Mother would not let Kate be around her. Now, Matthew refuses to let her interact with our family," Jonathon said, taking a sip of his brandy.

Benedict was curious about one thing. "Are they very much alike?"

Jonathon let out a loud, amused laugh. "No, they are opposites in every way. Eliza is tall, with brown hair, and Kate is petite, with blonde hair. Eliza is outgoing and strong-willed, whereas Kate is shy and a peacemaker. Apparently, Eliza took after Father's side and Kate took after our mother's."

"Eliza told me that she used to sneak around to see Kate. Why would your mother forbid them from seeing each other?"

"Mother has hated Eliza since she was a little girl," Jonathon shrugged. "She remembers Mother kicking her out of the house at ten, but Mother was cruel to her for years before that. In fact, my sisters never shared a room in the nursery. Kate slept in my mother's adjoining room."

"Why did the duchess hate her own daughter?" Benedict inquired.

Jonathon ran his fingers through his hair. "To be honest, I do not know. Mother resented Eliza because she was so smart, and it took some of the attention away from Kate. But living with Uncle Charles was the best thing that ever happened to her."

"Eliza told me that she would have rather lived with the duke and Lady Anne."

"Impossible. That would have ruined her reputation. My father is not the easiest man to get along with, but he loves his children, and he especially adores Eliza. That is why he made that marriage agreement with her." Jonathon raised his snifter at Benedict whose eyebrows went up.

"What is the marriage agreement?"

Jonathon lowered his glass. "I thought Eliza might have told you. It is not a secret or anything. Father agreed to let her pick her husband. He told her that she could marry for love, which was an opportunity he never was afforded."

"But he did not give Kate the same opportunity?" Benedict asked surprised.

"No, because Mother had her married off right after she came out."

Benedict was anxious to check on Eliza, but tried to distract himself from his frantic state. "I was curious as to why Eliza was not married yet."

A smile tugged at the corners of Jonathon's lips as he lifted the snifter to his mouth, taking a long sip. "It is not a lack of suitors, if that was your concern."

"She's had offers?" Benedict asked as he glanced over his shoulder to look at the door. *Why has the doctor not finished with the examination yet?*

Jonathon grinned wryly. "Yes, twenty-two."

Benedict jerked his head around to face Jonathon. "She has been offered marriage twenty-two times?"

"She is the daughter of the Duke of Remington," Jonathon reminded him, "but to answer your question, she was only verbally offered marriage a few times. Most of her suitors went directly to my father to negotiate for Eliza's hand, and they did not shy away from showing extreme interest in her dowry and lands that she inherited from our grandmother."

"Idiots," Benedict mumbled. "What did your father say to them?"

Jonathon waved his hand in front of him. "He dismissed them. He assumed if Eliza wanted to marry one of them, then she would approach him."

Swirling his brandy in his glass, Benedict decided to broach a subject that Eliza had brought up previously. "Eliza asked me how long it would be before I took a mistress after we got married."

Choking on a sip of his brandy, Jonathon started coughing. "She asked you what?"

Shrugging, Benedict repeated himself. "She asked me how long it would be before I took a mistress after we wed."

"What was the answer?" Jonathon asked directly.

Benedict narrowed his eyes. "If I can convince your stubborn sister to marry me, then I would never take a mistress. How can you even ask that question?"

"Calm down. I just had to ask." Jonathon savored a sip of his brandy then turned towards his friend. "Eliza and I seem to only witness unhappy unions. After all, our parents are a fine example of marriage," he said sarcastically. "It appears that most of her friends that are married were arranged marriages."

"Are any of them happy?"

"I'm sure some of them are, but Eliza only seems to hear from her friends that are miserable." Jonathon sighed. "And we both know that Kate is trapped in an unhappy marriage."

Benedict was beginning to understand Eliza's reluctance to marry. "Do you know why she is so adamant that I would take a mistress, or be unfaithful?"

Jonathon arose and refilled his glass. He went back to the sofa and plopped down. "That would be the curse of being an agent." Benedict hoped that his friend would elaborate, and he did not have to wait long. "Eliza has searched hundreds of studies and offices over the years. She witnesses the public faces of devoted husbands, then she reads their private correspondences. Most of the time, she finds letters or bills from women, or from those types of establishments. I think she has just come to accept it as a fact that men cannot be faithful."

Benedict started to respond when Mr. Wilde opened the study door. "The doctor has finished his examination, my lords."

"About time," Benedict muttered.

They put their snifters down on the metal tray and swiftly walked back to the drawing room. Eliza was sitting up on the sofa, but she appeared worn out. Her face was pale, minus the red, swollen cheek.

Benedict quickly claimed the seat next to her. "How are you feeling?"

She shrugged. "I will live."

Tearing his gaze away from her, he found Jonathon and the doctor observing them. Once the doctor realized he had their attention, he gave his diagnosis. "Lady Elizabeth hit her head hard, and I am worried about possible swelling of the brain. Her face will be bruised for about a week, but it is more superficial. I am recommending that she stay in bed and not lift a finger for the next

181

week, possibly two if she can handle it. The longer she stays down, the better it will be for her in the long run."

The doctor tipped his head to the men and smiled kindly at his patient. "Lady Elizabeth, you need lots of rest. It will help you feel better. I have left some laudanum to help you sleep, but use sparingly. I will leave directions for your lady's maid to follow." He exited the room followed by Mr. Wilde.

Jumping up from the sofa, Benedict scooped Eliza in his arms. "We need to get you to bed."

Jonathon stepped in front of him with his hands extended. "I will take her, Benedict."

"I have her, Jonathon. Just allow me to take her to her bedchamber."

Benedict saw Eliza roll her eyes when her brother refused to move. Finally, Jonathon dropped his hands and stepped out of the way. "Fine, but you will lay her on the bed, then leave immediately."

Nodding, Benedict carried her up the stairs. Jonathon preceded them into the room, and they found Martha pulling down Eliza's white linens. Benedict carefully laid her down on the bed, but as he started to pull the sheets up over her legs, Jonathon cleared his throat loudly. Giving her a tender smile, Benedict said, "I will see you tomorrow, my love."

As he began to turn away, Eliza grabbed his hand. "Please, do not go."

He knew what she was asking, but he had to go and make this right. "I have to." As they locked eyes, they each pleaded for the other person to understand what was in their hearts. They were at an impasse, and neither one wanted to yield.

"Eliza, do I need to remind you that it is not proper for Benedict to stay in your room?" Jonathon asked after a few moments, glancing between the two.

Her eyes flickered to her brother. "I am not asking him to stay in my room, Jonathon," she drawled out. "I am asking him not to go to Mr. Wade's townhouse and seek revenge."

While Benedict turned to face Eliza, he encompassed her hand into his own. "I have to. Aaron could have killed you tonight, and I must not let that go answered."

"Have you considered that Aaron might expect you to seek retribution and has planned a trap for you?" she asked.

He shrugged. He had considered the possibility that this was a trap, but it did not sway him. "First, he killed my brother, and then he attacked you at a party. He has to be stopped, and it is my responsibility to finish this."

"It is *your* responsibility?" Eliza asked incredulously.

"He is my stepbrother," Benedict reminded her.

"So, your plan is just to kill him?" she asked calmly, withholding any judgement in her voice.

His gaze guiltily dropped to the floor. "I have not figured that out yet."

Putting her feet over her bed, she started to stand up. "Well, I am coming with you then."

Benedict's head shot up. "Absolutely not, Eliza."

As she stood, she wobbled momentarily and dropped his hand. "I am your partner, and I am not letting you go into Wade's den without backup."

Martha gasped. "My lady, you cannot be serious," she exclaimed, edging closer to the group.

If Eliza was not so dead serious about joining him, then Benedict would have laughed at the situation. "I will take Jonathon or Mr. Larson with me," he offered.

Jonathon walked closer to the bed and pointed a finger at Eliza. "You will stay in bed. Do I make myself clear?" His voice brooked no room for disagreement.

She opened her mouth to argue, but stopped when Benedict placed his hands on her shoulders and gently sat her back down on the bed. The fact that she did not fight back was a testament to how weak she was at the moment. "Eliza, you need to stay in bed. You were attacked tonight, and your body needs time to heal," he said, crouching down while reaching for her hands.

She arched an eyebrow. "I cannot rest knowing that you are putting your life in danger."

Benedict's lips curled up into a slow smile. "What if I promise not to kill him? Will you rest then?"

Jonathon piped up. "I hate to say this, but I agree with Eliza. If you go after Wade tonight, it could jeopardize the entire mission. If you kill Wade, or just arrest him, he would not tell us where the missing girls are being held. I suggest we proceed as planned, since the brig does not arrive for two more weeks."

Dropping his head, Benedict let out a deep sigh. "I see your point, but I do not have to like it. Sometimes, I really hate doing the honorable thing."

Eliza's hand touched his cheek, and he raised his gaze. "I understand your need for vengeance, I really do, but there is a time and a place for it." Her lips curled into an intimate smile just for him. "Now that I know you will listen to reason, I really would like to get some sleep. After all, I just got attacked today by *your* relations."

Benedict removed her hand off his cheek and kissed her knuckles. "My father and Jane will be a lot more accommodating when you meet them," he said with a chuckle.

"I hope so." She put her head on her pillow. "Thank you, Benedict."

He gave her a puzzled look. "For what?"

Eliza's eyes drooped down. "For making me feel special."

He remained crouched for a few minutes until he heard her breathing become deep. Standing, he turned to see Jonathon observing him. "Would it be permissible for me to come back tomorrow morning to check on her?"

"Of course, you are always welcome here," his friend nodded, then smirked. "I should clarify that statement. You are always welcome in my home, but never in Eliza's bedchamber."

Benedict stifled a laugh. "Thank you for the clarification. I will see myself out," he said as he walked out.

Even though Benedict knew Eliza would be well taken care of, he was already counting the hours till he could be the one to take care of her day and night.

Chapter Twenty-Two

Benedict arrived late morning at Jonathon's townhouse and was escorted into the dining room where his friend was eating. A footman held out his chair for him, and another brought him a plate of food. After a few bites, Benedict decided he should attempt to be social with Jonathon. "How is Eliza?"

Jonathon swallowed the food in his mouth. "I checked in on her this morning. Her face is still swollen, but the bruises are setting in." He reached for his cup of tea and took a sip. "She is also complaining of a headache."

Benedict assumed Eliza would have a headache for a few days. "I am sorry that I failed to protect her," he said, getting straight to the point.

Putting his fork down, Jonathon gave Benedict his full attention. "And I am sorry that I yelled at you last night. I know that you have grown to care for Eliza..."

Benedict interrupted, "I love your sister."

"I know, and it is about time," Jonathon smirked.

"What do you mean about time? We were just introduced over a week ago."

"Benedict, I have known you for over ten years, and I know what type of person you are. I planned to introduce you to Eliza years ago, but the timing was off. After what happened in France, and what happened to your brother Henry, I knew it was time to try to bring you two together." Jonathon gave Benedict a smug smile. "And it worked perfectly. Even Uncle Charles was in on it."

Benedict stared at him dumbfounded, then his face broke out into a wide smile. "Well, then I thank you for your assistance," he said honestly.

Jonathon raised his tea cup. "You are welcome." He took a sip of the tea, then placed the cup carefully back in its saucer. "Just so you know, it was revolting watching you two last night," he stated, feigning disgust.

Benedict shook his head good naturedly at Jonathon's jest and took a moment to finish his breakfast. As he pushed his plate away, he said somberly, "I thought you should know that Eliza told me what happened in France."

Jonathon indicated that his butler should clear the room. "Tell me."

"That night in France, she killed six men."

"Six? We only saw five dead men on the ship."

Benedict nodded in agreement. "There was a man that tracked Eliza on the roof, and he knocked out Mr. Larson before he shot her. After he shot her, he then started choking her, but hesitated when he realized she was a woman, which gave her enough time to slit his throat." Benedict did not tell Jonathon the whole story. He was sure if she wanted to share all the details with her brother, one day she would.

Jonathon started drumming his fingers on the table. "Wade must have anticipated agents would board his ship, and *Shadow* would provide support from nearby."

"That would make sense, since the crew ambushed us."

"Poor Eliza. I cannot believe she was shot."

"How did you not notice that she was injured when you checked on her?"

Jonathon frowned. "She told me she had to retire to her room for her problematic femaleness."

Both Benedict and Jonathon shifted uncomfortably in their chairs. No man wanted to discuss female personal matters. Benedict cleared his throat. "I understand now."

"I wonder why she would not tell me what happened."

Benedict sat back in his chair. "She was afraid you would make her stop being an agent."

"Of course, I would have," Jonathon confirmed. "She made a promise to stop working in the field the moment it got too dangerous

186

for her."

Before Benedict could reply, Eliza shuffled into the room dressed in an ivory lace, high-waisted gown. Benedict immediately jumped up from his chair and closed the distance between them. He stopped in front of her, while reaching for her hands and bringing them to his lips. "Why are you not resting in bed?"

She smiled weakly. "I heard you had arrived, and I wanted to see you." Her eyes flickered to Jonathon and she lowered her voice. "I felt certain Jonathon would not let you go upstairs to my room so I came down to you."

Benedict smiled tenderly at her. "And how are you feeling?"

"My face does not throb anymore, but I have a slight headache," Eliza confessed.

He kissed her hands again and marveled at how lovely she looked, even when half of her face was starting to bruise. Eliza blushed adorably, as they proceeded to gaze at each other, ignoring everything around them.

"Have a care, Benedict. Can you stop staring at my sister so she can have breakfast?" Jonathon said in an amused voice.

Benedict escorted Eliza to a chair next to his, as a footman suddenly appeared and placed a plate of food in front of her. She picked up her fork and ate a few bites before she put it down. She did not seem to have much of an appetite. "I think it would be best if I went back to Beaumont Castle while I recover."

"Would it be all right if I accompanied you to ensure you arrived home safely?" Benedict asked hopefully.

She smiled gratefully at Benedict. "You are my partner. I would appreciate if you came along and protected me."

Thinking this might be a trick, he decided to say something tactful. "I know you can protect yourself Eliza," he ventured.

She smiled, her eyes lit up with understanding, as she reached for his hand on the table. "Mr. Wade threatened me last night by saying he would try to abduct me again, and I fear I could not defend myself right now in my condition." Eliza squeezed his hand. "With you by my side, I would feel safer."

Jonathon arched an eyebrow. "I assume you mean he is by your side only during the day."

"Of course, Jonathon," she replied, never taking her eyes off Benedict.

"I do not mind also taking night duty," Benedict said with a hopeful grin.

Jonathon practically growled, "I am still in the room, Benedict."

She picked up her fork and started pushing her food around for a few moments, which prompted Benedict to lean over and quietly ask, "Is something wrong, Eliza?"

Putting her fork down, she looked at him in the eye. "Do you think I am weak?" she asked in a hushed tone. Benedict started shaking his head in response to her question, and she put up her hand to stop him. "No, I mean from the time you have come into my life, I have cried more than I have in my whole lifetime. I have never been this emotional."

Benedict glanced over at Jonathon who just shrugged back at him before he took a sip of tea. Leaning closer, Benedict answered, "I know how strong you are. I am grateful that you trust me enough to be vulnerable around me."

Eliza seemed to ponder that for a moment, then gave him a tentative smile before she rose from the table. "I should be ready to depart within the hour, Benedict." With a final glance at him, she walked out of the room to prepare for their departure.

Jonathon raised his cup. "Well done."

Benedict's eyes were still on the door Eliza had just passed through. He really needed to convince her that he was worth the risk and marry him soon, because he loved her more every day.

"Did you know my mother used to punish Eliza if she cried?" Jonathon put his cup down. "She said crying is a sign of weakness."

Benedict snorted in disgust over the duchess's treatment of her children. "It is amazing that any of you turned out normal with your mother being around."

Jonathon chuckled. "We were mostly raised by nursemaids and governesses, but Mother would come around every so often to make sure we were scolded enough." He wiped his mouth with a napkin. "Although, Mother picked on Eliza more than anyone else."

"She told me that she did not have any friends that were her age growing up," Benedict stated.

"That is accurate. Eliza was close with Uncle Charles' household staff and Mr. Morton."

Benedict sat back in his chair. "She seemed so happy and full of life when you would read her letters at Oxford, yet she must have been so lonely."

Jonathon pushed away his plate. "I used to think that Eliza had an unbreakable spirit. Whenever I would complain about someone, she would smile and quote Socrates. 'Be kind, for everyone you meet is fighting a hard battle'." He sighed and grew silent for a moment. "Now, at times she just seems... so broken."

"I think I know why." Benedict glanced around the room to ensure they were alone. "Did you know she has killed seventeen men?"

Jonathon's eyebrows shot up. "She has killed seventeen men?"

Leaning forward, Benedict placed his elbows on the table and intertwined his fingers. "It was only sixteen until that man tried to abduct her, but she also blames herself for the ships that were sunk by our navy since she broke the codes and ascertained their locations." Benedict's eyes locked with Jonathon's. "Eliza told me she now feels more like an assassin than an agent."

Jonathon jumped up and placed his hands behind his head before he started pacing the small dining room. After a few moments, he stilled and let out a slow, agonized sigh as he dropped his hands.

"I should have known. I just never took the time to count her kills," Jonathon said with a crestfallen expression. "We have to get her to stop being an agent."

"I agree, but we cannot just tell her to stop being an agent. It did not go well when I told her not to do something." Benedict shuddered at that memory.

"Yes, Eliza does have her own ideas about control," Jonathon laughed.

"We got into an argument in which she stated that no man would ever control her," Benedict informed him.

"Mr. Larson filled me in on that." Jonathon rested his hands on the back of his chair and leaned in. "She is very keen on never losing control of her life."

"Do you think I would try to dictate her life?" Benedict asked, annoyed in spite of himself.

Jonathon put up his hands to ward off his comment. "No, but Eliza was raised with no choice about her life, which is not uncommon for ladies. Although, ever since she started going in the field as an agent, she has embraced her freedom. The moment she gets married, everything she has worked for is gone. Her husband will control where she goes, what she does, and how much pin allowance she is given. Beaumont Castle, and all her holdings that she had retained prior to the marriage, resort back to her husband."

"When I marry Eliza," Benedict paused to see if Jonathon would object, "I will not control her. I love her just the way she is."

Jonathon nodded. "Would you force her to retire as an agent?"

Benedict shook his head. "No, I would not. If she wanted to continue working as an agent, then I would stay on as her partner regardless of Lord Beckett's approval."

"I see." Jonathon appeared to be disappointed by his announcement. "I wish you luck with that."

"You do not agree?" Benedict leaned back in his chair. He did not really care a whit if Jonathon disapproved of his plan, because his main concern was Eliza's happiness.

Coming around the table, Jonathon leaned up against it near Benedict. "I wish we could demand that Eliza stop being *Shadow* at this precise moment, but we both know she would never stop working as an agent if we played that hand."

"She implied that she might be open to quitting the spy business when she told me about France. It is a moot point until we send Aaron to Newgate, since she wants justice almost as much as I do."

Jonathon rubbed his hand over the back of his neck. "Maybe she will stop working as a field agent when you two get married? After all, she will be immediately responsible for a large household staff as the Countess of Sinclair."

"Perhaps, but I want it to be her choice."

Jonathon gave a slight chuckle. "Oh, how the mighty have fallen."

"What?" Benedict asked while lifting an eyebrow.

"I am referencing the fact that you have fallen hard for Eliza.

Before you were assigned to partner with her, you wanted us to force her to stop working as an agent. Now you are on her side," Jonathon said with a lopsided grin.

Benedict crossed his hands over his chest. "Thanks, Jonathon," he said sarcastically. "Can you be at all useful and tell me how I can convince Eliza to marry me?"

Jonathon seemed to give him a pity look. "Her love needs to be stronger than her fears."

"And how will I accomplish that?" Benedict pressed.

"Maybe you could ask Mr. Larson," he said jokingly. Jonathon walked by and slapped him on the shoulder. "From what I have seen, she loves you. You just need to give her time."

Benedict stayed sitting in his chair long after Jonathon left the room. He needed to come up with a plan to show Eliza how much he loved her.

Chapter Twenty-Three

Eliza was resting her head against the window pane in the second story library, watching the deer frolicking around the fields surrounding her castle. It had been a week since Aaron Wade attacked her, forcing her to recover at Beaumont Castle, and she was anxious to resume the search for the missing girls. This morning, Uncle Charles had sent over a messenger with a note stating that her hunch was correct and Mr. Saxton did own a warehouse about a quarter of a mile from the docks, but he forbade her from going to search the building.

She sighed into the window. She knew Uncle Charles was wise in not letting her return to the field just yet. Even though her headaches were less intense, and the bruising on her face was almost gone, she was not fully healed. The only good that came out of her injury was that she could now spend every day from dawn till dusk with Benedict, and she found herself more and more in love with him.

Although, anytime he would attempt to broach the subject of marriage, Eliza would change the subject, hoping to buy herself more time, so she could unravel her complicated feelings. She loved him, but the fear of being abandoned by him was stronger just now.

She heard someone walk into the room, but she did not want to move her head from the window pane.

"Eliza, are you well?" Mr. Larson asked with concern.

"I am."

She heard him walk further in the room till he was standing next to her. "Are you waiting for Lord Sinclair to arrive?"

"Yes," Eliza said, as she continued to watch the deer outside the window.

"I cannot help but notice that you seem a little distracted this morning."

Lifting her head off the glass, she sighed and turned her attention towards Mr. Larson. "What do you think of Lord Sinclair?"

Glancing out the window, Mr. Larson had a tight smile on his lips. "He is a good man."

"Did you know he wants to marry me?"

Her protector turned his gaze towards her. "I suspected as much." He stopped and observed her for a moment. "And yet, you do not seem happy about that."

Eliza bit her lower lip while debating how to answer. "I do love Benedict, but I do not know about marriage."

"Ah, so you trust Lord Sinclair with your secrets, but you cannot trust him with your heart."

"It is not that simple," Eliza said, shaking her head. "I worry that one day I will say or do something that will make him change his mind about me."

Mr. Larson did not respond for a few moments, then he sat down on the window seat next to her. "Why did you buy Beaumont Castle, Eliza?"

She thought this was a strange question. "When I found out Beaumont Castle was for sale, I thought it would be a nice place to restore and would be easily defended."

"True, but we could have protected you at Jonathon's townhouse," Mr. Larson pointed out. "I believe you moved to Beaumont Castle to safeguard your heart from rejection."

Eliza's eyebrows went up. "What? That is a ridiculous notion."

He explained, "You bought Beaumont Castle to be your haven from the world. For these past few years, you have avoided any type of relationship where you felt you might be betrayed. For example, two years ago, your friends started getting married and you felt abandoned by them, so you retreated to Beaumont Castle and focused solely on being a better agent."

Eliza's lips curled downwards. "No, that is not accurate. I had to write a code for the war office and that took some time."

Mr. Larson smiled knowingly. "Have you ever discussed with your friends about how cruel your mother is to you?"

"No, I never have," Eliza briefly frowned.

"And why not? That helped define the lady you are today."

She shrugged. "It has never come up in our conversations."

"I believe the reason you have not confided in your friends is because you fear their pitying looks and possible rejection," Mr. Larson reasoned.

Eliza's lips pressed into a tight line. "Explaining to my friends that my own mother hates me and kicked me out of the abbey at ten is not an easy thing to discuss over tea."

Mr. Larson nodded, smiling his understanding. "All right, another example then. Gentlemen have tried to court you, but you have never really attempted to get to know them. Instead, you would run back to Beaumont Castle, determined to keep your independence."

Her eyes widened at his accusation. "That is not fair. I knew those gentlemen were not for me."

"What about Lord Washburn? He was a suitable candidate for your affections, and if I was not mistaken, you were quite smitten with him."

One side of Eliza's lips curled up when she thought about Lord Washburn. He was a devastatingly handsome earl, and she had enjoyed his company immensely last Season. He had proposed to her, but she politely turned him down since she was not in love with him. Although, she was curious why Mr. Larson approved of him. She narrowed her eyes suspiciously.

"And how would you know that he was a suitable candidate for me?"

Mr. Larson leaned back on the bench. "Because I personally had him investigated."

Eliza grinned at his admission. "Why am I not surprised?"

"You still have not answered my question about Lord Washburn," he pointed out.

"I was not in love with him, though I tried." She sighed. "He was kind, attentive, and witty, and everything I thought I was looking for in a husband."

"But?"

"We had lovely outings, but I found myself unable to bare my soul to him. It was as if something was holding me back."

Mr. Larson smiled encouragingly at her. "What do you suppose was holding you back?

Eliza bit her lip for a moment while she thought about it. "My instinct told me not to trust him with my secrets. I do not believe he would have taken kindly to the fact that I was a spy," she finally revealed.

Nodding, Mr. Larson seemed satisfied. "What does your instinct tell you about Lord Sinclair?"

Turning her head towards the window again, she pondered for a moment. "My instinct tells me to trust Benedict with my heart," she said softly. "But if I am going to be honest, I am afraid that when someone gets to know the real me, they will not like what they see."

Her protector looked at her with a puzzled expression. "Why would anyone not love the real you?"

Eliza's eyes brimmed with tears. "My own mother did not."

Mr. Larson turned towards her. "Eliza, you are a remarkable woman, and I am not just referring to your abilities as an agent. When I was hit over the head on that roof in France, your first reaction was to help me, even though you had been shot. You are a kind, compassionate woman that has spent her life serving other people."

Smiling gratefully, she wiped the tears from her eyes with her hand. "Thank you, but I fear you may be a trifle partial."

Clearing his throat, he said, "I have worked with you for over three years now, and I am very proud of you. If I had ever been blessed with a daughter, I would have hoped she would be half as remarkable as you are."

Eliza slid over, placing her head on Mr. Larson's shoulder, and looping her hand through his arm. She relished being near a man she respected and loved dearly. She was grateful that he was in her life, because he was the one constant that she could always rely on, always trust.

After a few moments, he cleared his throat slightly, and Eliza released him and leaned back. "You might be surprised to know that when I was a young agent, I fell in love with a local girl, and we were engaged to be married. Due to the conflict with France, I was assigned to go deep undercover for a few years. By the time I returned home, my intended had married and had a child with my best friend. I did not blame her, because she thought I was dead, since I was unable to correspond with her." Mr. Larson's eyes were filled with sadness and Eliza swore she saw him blinking away tears. "I wish I could go back and choose love, because we will always be at war with some country."

Her heart stirring with compassion, she embraced him. "I am sorry."

Mr. Larson released her, but watched her closely. "And what will you choose? You were groomed to become an agent, but is this the life you want?"

Eliza leveled her gaze to the floor. *Did she want to walk away from being an agent?* She slowly brought her head up to make eye contact with him. "In my innocence, I used to believe that being a spy would be a grand adventure, but it seems to have brought an excess of regret and grief into my life. On the other hand, I have helped save thousands of Englishmen's lives and hundreds of women from the hands of evil perpetrators."

"So, what will you choose?" he prodded gently.

Eliza huffed. "What would I even do if I was not an agent?"

"For starters, you could be a marchioness," Mr. Larson chuckled, then added, "and a beloved wife with a bushel of children."

Shaking her head, sadness reflected in her eyes. "No, it is too late for me. I do not deserve to have a normal, happy life."

"Fiddlesticks. Who told you that?" he exclaimed.

"I have killed too many men and have done too many horrible..." Eliza started.

Mr. Larson gently grabbed her shoulders and bore his gaze into her eyes. "Listen to me, Eliza Beckett. You will stop this foolish talk. If what you say is true, then no agent should be allowed an ounce of happiness. In essence, you do not think Lord Sinclair deserves to be happy, but instead is destined to have a life full of regret and sorrow? Is that what you truly believe?"

She lowered her eyes. "No, of course not," she said, suddenly ashamed.

"Look at me, Eliza." She hesitantly brought her eyes back up and could see Mr. Larson's eyes flicker with compassion towards her. "Do you love Lord Sinclair enough to trust him with your heart and surrender the past?"

She bit her lower lip. "I love Benedict, but I am scared. I think my heart would break if he abandoned me."

"Can you tell me what you love about him?" Mr. Larson asked as he dropped his hands.

Eliza tapped her finger to her mouth for a moment. "I love how safe I feel in his arms. I love how he makes me laugh and how he cherishes me. I love that I can be completely honest with him and he seems to have accepted my past with no judgement. Most importantly, Benedict makes me remember that the world is full of good and decent people."

"Anything else?" Mr. Larson teased, as his face relaxed into a smile. "Lord Sinclair is a good man, Eliza. Do not let your fears take away the joy from your life." He looked out the window. "Regardless of what you decide about Lord Sinclair, I owe him a debt of gratitude for bringing back the sparkle in your eyes."

She scrunched her forehead in confusion. "My sparkle?"

He grinned broadly at her, as if he was letting her in on a secret. "Yes, the sparkle in your eyes is what makes you so unique. You are brilliant, there is no denying that, but it is your outlook on life that brings joy to everyone around you. It has pained me this past month, to watch the sparkle dim from your eyes."

She had been so wrapped up in her own grief, she had not realized how she had impacted other people's lives. "I am sorry I have been such a burden this past month," she said apologetically.

Mr. Larson placed a hand on her shoulder. "You, my dear, have never been, nor ever will be, a burden to me." He glanced out the window when a movement caught his eye. "Well, it appears that Lord Sinclair has arrived for the day. Why don't you go and greet him, then follow what your heart tells you to do?" He arose and assisted Eliza from her seat on the bench. "Within reason," he said, amending his previous statement.

Eliza glanced out the window and saw Benedict riding towards Beaumont Castle, and her heart skipped a beat, like it always did when she saw him. As she was about to walk out of the room, she spun around and asked, "Did you also investigate Lord Sinclair?"

Mr. Larson's lips curled up in obvious amusement. "No, I did not. You are not the only one that relies on instinct. From the moment I met him, I knew he was a stalwart young man and that he could be trusted." Eliza smiled gratefully and started to leave when he continued. "You should know, Lord Sinclair is one of the finest agents that I have come across, and is widely respected among the other agents."

Eliza lifted an eyebrow. "I thought you said you did not investigate him?"

"I may have asked around a little," Mr. Larson said, shrugging nonchalantly.

Giving him a bright smile, she made her way to the front door. As soon as Benedict dismounted and handed off his black horse to the waiting groom, she cautiously approached him. The closer she got to him, the faster her legs started moving, and soon she was running. Benedict held out his arms and she jumped into them.

He chuckled and spun her around, as Eliza held onto his neck. Once her feet were back on the ground, Benedict said, "That is the best reception I have ever received."

Leaning back from the embrace, she pulled his head down to initiate a kiss. She poured all the love she felt for Benedict into that kiss, and he rewarded her by returning it with the same passion. After a few long moments, she released his lips. "I love you."

Benedict's face broke out into a huge smile. "I love you too, Eliza." He picked her up and swung her around as they both laughed. Once he lowered her feet back to the ground, he smiled tenderly at her. "You have no idea how happy you have made me."

Eliza put her hand on his cheek. "I am sorry it took me so long to trust you with my heart."

"I would have waited for you, even if it meant we were old and grey. I would have never stopped trying to earn your love," Benedict said tenderly.

After that declaration, any hesitation that Eliza felt just melted away, and she knew that he would safeguard her heart. She dropped her hand from his cheek. "Let us go inside and talk about the mission."

Benedict did not drop his hands from her waist, but instead gave her a crooked smile. "Unfortunately, I have compromised you, my love, and I am afraid we will need to marry in haste. We can be at Gretna Greens by nightfall if we hurry," he said teasingly, pulling her closer to him.

Eliza laughed. "We do not have time to go to Gretna Greens right now, since we have a lead on the missing girls." She fisted Benedict's lapels on his waistcoat and pulled him down for a kiss. After she released him, one side of her lips curled upwards. "Besides, I do not mind being compromised, perhaps you can compromise me some more after we discuss the mission?"

Dropping his hands from her waist, Benedict reached for her hand. "It would be my pleasure," he said flirtatiously while escorting her back inside Beaumont Castle.

Chapter Twenty-four

Much later, a very happy Benedict sat in his post-chaise outside of Jonathon's townhouse, waiting for his friend to join him on a mission to search Mr. Saxton's building for the missing girls. Since he had a moment alone, he started reminiscing about spending the morning in Eliza's arms, discussing anything that came to their minds. The more he learned about her, the more he loved her, and was amazed that he had won her love.

After a few hours, their conversation had gravitated back towards the missing girls and his stepbrother. Eliza showed him the note from Lord Beckett, and together they strategized the best course of action. It was decided that Jonathon would join Benedict on the search for the missing girls, and a messenger was dispatched to see if he had returned from his search for Lady Hannah. Luckily, he arrived earlier that morning and sent word back that he would join Benedict at nightfall.

The carriage door squeaked open and dipped as Jonathon hopped in and sat across from him. His hair was greasy and tossed about, and it was apparent by the stubble on his face that he had not bothered shaving in the last couple of days. His faded blue shirt and trousers were covered in dirt and grime. Lastly, his black boots were heavily scratched, and a small hole was forming along the top.

Benedict raised an eyebrow. "Did you hire a new valet?"

"No, I dressed myself tonight." Jonathon gave him a lopsided grin.

Even though his appearance shocked Benedict, it was the smell that gave him a cause for concern. "What is that smell?"

"I decided to wear my slum clothes, in case we need to go into a tavern," Jonathon shrugged.

Benedict still was not satisfied. "And the smell?"

Taking a whiff of his shirt, Jonathon smiled. "This is what the slums smell like, rotten fish and sweat." Reaching over to the carriage window, Benedict opened it to allow for fresh air to circulate. His friend laughed. "Have you not gone into the slums before?"

Benedict gave him a look of disbelief. "Of course, I have gone into the slums. I just avoid wearing the slums out with me."

Leaning back into the velvet carriage seats, Jonathon nodded. "Note taken."

Benedict kept his face close to the window, and his thoughts kept trailing back to Eliza. He was wondering what she was doing right now and wished he could be with her.

"Why are you grinning like a bloody fool?" Jonathon asked, breaking through his thoughts.

"I was thinking of Eliza."

"I thought as much."

"She told me she loved me today." Benedict's smile was wry.

Jonathon's eyebrows shot up. "Wow. That is a big step for her. You must be doing something right."

Benedict nodded in agreement, as the carriage turned onto a bumpy road that led into the shadier sections of town. A pungent smell of animal dung began to infiltrate the carriage and Benedict reached up to close the window. It always astonished him to realize that within a few miles of his luxurious townhouse, people lived in such abject poverty that they lacked the basic necessities of life.

He watched as filthy urchins, some dressed in rags, were darting through the streets laughing, without the fear of being trampled by the oncoming horses and carriages. The streets were lined with discarded barrels and waste, as rough-looking young men were leaning up against the buildings, probably assessing the risk of robbing the carriages that were passing by.

A few minutes later, they pulled up to the address that Lord Beckett provided them, and Benedict noted an oversized one-story wooden building that appeared to be abandoned. It was in disarray, with evidence of dry rot all over the wood, and some parts of the exterior wall had collapsed inward. He shook his head at the condition of the building, almost hoping that the missing girls were not subjected to such filth.

They hopped out of the carriage and started searching for a way in. As they approached a side door, they noticed that the deteriorated door was locked with a chain that showed no trace of rust. Benedict pointed at the chain and whispered, "It appears that someone has been here recently."

Nodding in the affirmative, Jonathon crouched down and produced a small pistol from the back of his trousers. Benedict retrieved his own pistol, then taking a step back, he kicked the door until it collapsed in on itself. It only took a few kicks, because the wood was in such a pathetic state of dry rot.

Jonathon rushed in, with Benedict close behind, and they quickly prepared for an attack. Instead, they were met with eerie silence. It took their eyes a few moments to adjust to the dark interior as they cautiously walked around the building. Benedict focused on the center of the room where he noticed small lengths of rope discarded in a pile.

As he crouched down to analyze the twine, there was barely enough light to make out dried blood caked onto the thin rope. "Jonathon," Benedict said while motioning him to come over. "These ropes were used to tie someone up." He placed his pistol on the ground, as he started counting the pieces of discarded twine. "There are twenty-five ropes here, and I suspect I know who they belong to," he said in disgust, as he threw the twine down. "Most likely, these ropes were used to bind their feet together."

Jonathon reached down to inspect one of the ropes. "Those poor girls."

"Where do you suppose Aaron moved them?" Benedict asked, as his eyes roamed the empty building looking for anything they might have missed.

Frowning, Jonathon tucked his pistol in the front of his trousers. "We know his ship has not docked yet. Which means he must have been tipped off that we were coming."

Picking up his pistol, Benedict straightened up. "Most likely, Aaron's solicitor informed him of the missing documents, and he knew we would eventually connect Mr. Saxton's building to him."

Jonathon looked towards the broken door for a moment, then turned back around. "Well, I know of a tavern nearby, and maybe someone has heard something about the missing girls."

Benedict nodded his head in agreement. "It is worth a shot."

The tavern ended up being a short walk through the roughest section of town that Benedict had ever seen. The side-by-side rickety, blackened buildings seemed to be rotten from the chimney to cellar, and the stench of stale and rotting food, along with smell of unwashed human bodies, produced a monstrous odor. Without speaking, they made their way along a narrow, muddy street, skirting pools of filthy liquid and the occasional carcass.

Outside a run-down shack, Jonathon turned to Benedict. "This is *The Boar Tavern*. Do not eat anything in here, no matter how good it smells," he said with a shudder.

Benedict was not sure if he should be insulted. "I have been in a tavern before."

Jonathon spoke over his shoulder. "Not like this one. Just be alert and keep your pistol close." He threw open the shabby door of the tavern and started strutting into the room.

Waiting outside for a moment, he tucked the pistol into his trousers and followed his friend in, but intentionally steered towards the opposite side of the room. *The Boar Tavern* boasted five long, wooden tables that looked sturdy enough, albeit a bit filthy, and Benedict looked around the room for someone that caught his interest. Towards one corner, a man with greasy, thinning brown hair sat alone, hunched over and appeared to be in one's cup.

Benedict approached and sat across from the man, reaching into his pocket to retrieve a few shillings. Slowly, he slid them across the table to the hunched man. He waited for a few minutes, but the man only gave a cursory glance at the coins before he went back to his drink. Benedict slammed his fist down on the table, and the man's glazed-over eyes glanced up at him.

"What ya want?" The man's mouth was barely visible over the rim of his mug.

"I am looking for some information."

"It will cost ye more blunt," the man said, taking a drink.

Benedict pulled out two guineas and slid them across the table.

"My sister left a note that she ran off to get married, but I just saw her supposed fiancé working on the docks. After some persuasion, he told me that she decided to go work for an Aaron Wade. Where can I find him?"

The man took another gulp of his drink, presumably watered-down ale, while his eyes nervously skirted around the room before they landed on the pile of coins Benedict was offering. "I can't help ya." Benedict slowly reached to reclaim the coins, but the man placed his hand on top of them first. "See that man over there with that wench?" The man tilted his head to indicate a tall, plump man who was in the process of staring at the overflowing cleavage of a barmaid's dress. "Name is Stubby. He does works on da *Deceiver*. Go talk to him." The man snatched up the coins and made a hasty retreat.

Benedict waited for a moment, arising while simultaneously scanning the room for Jonathon, noting that he was in the corner in a heated discussion with a shifty man with a long mustache. He focused on the man named Stubby, and slowly approached his table. He sat across the table from him and spoke discreetly. "I need information, and I will reward you handsomely."

The tall, plump man guzzled his ale and slammed the glass onto the table. "Go away," he said, dismissing him.

Benedict's eyes took in the man, noticing the long scar marks across his face and some stubs where some of his fingers should have been. It was plain to see that this man had spent his life in manual labor, and based on the visible wounds, was not successful at keeping himself out of harm's way. Ignoring the man's warning, he ventured forward by saying, "I am looking for some missing girls, and I was told to talk to you."

"Leave me in peace," the man growled, while some spit escaped his mouth and landed on Benedict's face. The man picked up his mug and shouted, "Wench, get me some more ale."

Wiping his face with the sleeve of his shirt, Benedict stood up, and came around the table. He straddled the bench near Stubby, while pulling his pistol from his trousers and shoving it into the man's gut. He leaned closer. "I apologize if I did not make my intentions clear. I am seeking information on twenty-five missing girls," he said through gritted teeth.

Stubby glanced nervously at Benedict. "Say goodbye to da girls. Ye will not get them back alive."

"Where can I find them?"

The barmaid placed a mug in front of Stubby, and only gave Benedict a cursory glance. Once she walked away, Stubby said, "Ye can't. Da boss is crazy... but don't ye worry none. He just takes whores and gives them a better way to make money."

Benedict narrowed his eyes. "These girls are not whores."

The fat man kept darting his eyes around the room, and the sweat was rolling down his face. "No, I don't mean they was whores, sorry guv'. Our boss keeps moving the wenches around. I don't know where they at."

"Who would know their location?" Benedict asked, shoving his pistol further into the man's gut.

The pudgy man licked his lips nervously. "Two sailors went to move da wenches, but never came back home. Rumor is da boss man killed them."

Benedict twisted the pistol in the man's gut and was satisfied by hearing him grunt in pain. "Can you tell me anything that would help convince me not to kill you?"

The fat man's eyes grew wide, but he picked up his mug with shaky hands and took a long sip. Once he returned the mug to the table, he fumbled out, "Um... they can't find a real Lady. Da boss, he wants her real bad, but can't find her nowhere."

Benedict was certain he knew who Aaron was searching for, but he wanted to ask. "Do you have a name?"

"Um... no, but she is royalty, a daughter of a duke she is, and da pot is a hundred pounds if we find her."

Benedict knew Eliza was safe at Beaumont Castle, and was protected by Mr. Larson and a group of well-trained former agents. He leaned in closer towards Stubby, taking in the smell of rotten fish and body stench.

"If I see you again, I will kill you."

He waited for the man to nod, then he reached into his pocket and pulled out a few guineas. He threw them on the table, as he quickly arose and walked out the door. As soon as the door of the tavern was closed, Benedict started sprinting towards a nearby alley, knowing full well that he just made a new enemy that might decide to try his hand at retribution.

After jogging around town for twenty minutes, he arrived at the carriage and notified the footmen of a possible attack. Benedict was pleased to see the footmen arming themselves with pistols and staying alert for any signs of danger. He jumped into the carriage and sat back in the plush seats, waiting for Jonathon's arrival. About thirty minutes later, his friend hopped in, and the carriage rolled rapidly away from the discarded buildings.

Jonathon ran his hand through his hair. "I hate my hair this long, but it makes me blend in more."

"I thought you blended in because of the smell?" Benedict laughed.

"That too. Did you learn anything interesting?"

Benedict took a few moments and told him everything that he learned. When he was done he asked, "What did you learn?"

Shrugging, Jonathon answered, "About the same as you. Wade seems to keep moving the girls around to avoid anyone locating them, and he is furious that he has not abducted Eliza yet."

Benedict shook his head. "Going after Eliza seems so personal. Why would he take that risk?"

"He knows that she has helped thwart his business of selling girls and wants to be certain she can't stop him again. Furthermore, he believes she knows the identity of *Shadow*." Jonathon leaned forward and ran his hand over his mouth. "Regardless of Wade's intentions, we need to keep Eliza at Beaumont Castle and keep the guards on high alert."

Benedict agreed with that assessment. "I will continue riding out to Beaumont Castle to guard her."

"Yes, I am sure that is a hard assignment for you." Jonathon laughed wholeheartedly.

Benedict's lips curved upward at his friend's jesting, but then folded his arms over his chest. "I am starting to agree with Eliza, that Aaron should just disappear."

"That is a tempting thought," Jonathon said, rubbing his eyes.

"I will tell Eliza and Mr. Larson when I arrive at Beaumont Castle tomorrow. Will you send over a message to Lord Beckett?"

"I will go and talk to Uncle Charles first thing tomorrow."

Benedict watched out the carriage window as they left the slums behind. "I am not sure if we will find the girls before they are moved to the ship. We just need to have patience and hope that we can still rescue them. Although, I wonder when Lord Beckett plans on arresting Aaron, since he has all those documents proving his guilt."

Jonathon let out a frustrated sigh. "I do not understand why Uncle Charles has not arrested Wade yet, then we could force him to tell us where he stashed the girls." He glanced out the window. "Although, my uncle always has a reason for his decisions."

A few moments later, they pulled up to Jonathon's townhouse, and Benedict watched him hop out of his carriage. When he started to close the carriage door, he stopped and leaned in. "Keep my sister safe."

Nodding his head in agreement, Benedict watched his friend run up the few steps and disappear into his townhouse. He leaned his head back against the seat and knew he would do everything in his power to keep Eliza safe.

Chapter Twenty-Five

Benedict glanced over his shoulder to see Eliza gaining on him as they raced their horses through the fields near her castle. It had been almost two weeks since Aaron attacked her at Lord Chambers' estate, and she seemed to be fully recovered. He could not seem to stop himself from turning back to admire her in her dark green riding habit, as her hair kept breaking free from the confines of the hair pins. He could hear her laugh dance merrily through the wind, and the sound warmed his heart.

Benedict arrived at the cluster of birch trees first, reined in his horse, then effortlessly dismounted. He hurried over to help Eliza dismount, giving him the perfect opportunity to sneak in a kiss before he escorted her to the bench by the stream. Once they were both seated comfortably, he put his arm around her shoulder. They sat quietly for a few minutes listening to the babbling brook. He was still curious about one thing. "I have a question."

Snuggling closer to him, she grinned. "Just one?"

"Did you really save the prince regent's life?"

Laughing loudly, she threw her hand up to cover her mouth. "Yes, but Prinny has grossly exaggerated what happened."

"I heard that *Shadow* scaled the wall of the palace, then fought off three assassins that were in his room, using only a small kitchen knife," Benedict said dramatically.

Eliza's continued laughter was like music to his ears. Even when she stopped laughing, she held an amused look on her face. "It was nothing so dramatic," she said, as she started rubbing her fingers along his draped arm. "The prince regent was at the abbey for my parent's annual house party a few years ago. As I was sneaking down towards the library to escape my mother's scrutiny, I heard two men speaking German, and they indicated that the plan was in place. They noticed me and stopped speaking, so I smiled at them and asked them where the retiring room was."

"Smart move," Benedict confirmed.

"Since the majority of English ladies do not speak German, they just assumed I did not understand them. Furthermore, it did not take a genius to figure out what their plan was. I notified Prinny's guards of the impending threat, and went to speak to the prince regent myself." Eliza's eyes danced, and her face lit up with merriment. "I announced to him I was going to sleep in his room that night."

Benedict started laughing. "You did what?"

Her smile grew wide as she shook her head up and down. "After I explained I would be hiding behind the curtains while a lump of pillows would be disguised as him in the bed, he was amendable to the plan. Prinny and his mistress, Maria Fitzherbert, discreetly moved to my room, and only his guards knew of his new location."

"So, you could technically say that the prince regent has warmed your bed before?" Benedict teased.

Her cheeks flamed pink as she huffed. "No, I would definitely not say that."

Benedict loved making her blush, but he was curious about what happened next. "Please continue. I will stop teasing you."

Eliza's lips slowly curled up into a smile, suggesting she did not believe he would stop his teasing so easily. After eyeing him for a few moments as if she was daring him to interrupt her, she continued.

"Early the next morning, a German man climbed through the window of the guest bedroom that the prince regent was supposed to be sleeping in, and discharged his pistol into the pile of pillows. As soon as the pistol went off, I flung away the drapes and leveled my pistol at him. Within minutes, his guards had the man in custody."

"How did the assassin know which room Prinny was in?"

"A scullery maid went missing the night of the party, and we concluded she was the informant. The German man never revealed any of his accomplices, even when he was tortured, and he was hung a few days later."

"Well, I think what you did was heroic," Benedict said proudly, as he kissed the top of her head.

Eliza beamed up at him. "So did Prinny. My Uncle Charles confided in him that I was *Shadow*, and the prince regent decided that I needed to be rewarded for my valiant service. He addressed both Houses of Parliament, and testified how *Shadow* saved his life and was a true hero. Through the joint session of Parliament, *Shadow* was awarded fifty thousand pounds for saving the prince regent's life." Her smile grew. "By Parliament awarding *Shadow* money, it made the legend of *Shadow* grow even more."

"I see that you are quite the heiress," Benedict said in jest.

Eliza tilted her head. "I am. I have received multiple lump sums from the House of Lords for various missions, but I have given Jonathon half of the money. It is only fair, since he was my partner."

"That was very kind of you."

She shrugged one shoulder. "I love my brother, and he is the reason I became a field agent." A comfortable silence followed, and he was content holding Eliza while listening to the birds chirp from the trees. "Benedict?"

"Hmm?" he murmured, as he closed his eyes and relaxed against the bench.

"I thought perhaps you were going to ask a different question," she commented quietly.

"And what question would that be?"

"Well, you have not brought up the subject of marriage in over a week, and I was wondering if your position had changed," she fumbled.

Benedict opened his eyes, while smiling at Eliza's question, as he quickly removed his arm from her shoulder and turned his full attention to her. "Are you sure you are ready for that question?"

"Yes, Benedict, I think I am," she said, as she hesitantly met his gaze.

"Do you trust me enough to know that I would never take a mistress, or be unfaithful to you?" he gazed lovingly into her eyes, pleading for her to understand how much she meant to him.

Eliza glanced down at her hands in her lap. "I do. I am scared that you might lose interest in me, but I trust you enough to know that you would never intentionally try to hurt me."

He tenderly cupped her face with his hands, so she would look at him. "How could I ever lose interest in you?" he asked incredulously. "You are a stubborn, beautiful hoyden who is completely unpredictable, yet somehow you have firmly captured my heart and soul. You cannot even begin to comprehend how much joy you have brought back into my life."

She sighed into his hands, and Benedict leaned in for a kiss. It quickly turned into a passionate, all-encompassing kiss, as he relished that Eliza truly wanted him. After a few moments, he broke away, but kept his lips hovering above hers and whispered, "I give you my word that I will treasure you till I take my last breath."

He quickly went down on one knee before her, and reached for her hands. She smiled encouragingly down at him, and her eyes welled with tears. "Lady Elizabeth Beckett, I love you..." he started.

They were interrupted by the sound of a horse approaching fast. Benedict quickly rose to shield Eliza from the rider's view and reached for his pistol, but he relaxed when he saw that Mr. Larson was the rider. As he drew closer, he shouted at them, "Lady Eliza, your father is at Beaumont Castle, awaiting your return." Without waiting for a reply, he reared his horse around and raced back the way he'd come.

Eliza's mouth hung open in shock, as she stared at Mr. Larson's retreating figure. "I thought you said the duke did not know about your castle," Benedict said confused.

"I thought so, too," she said still in shock.

They quickly mounted their horses and raced back to Beaumont Castle. As they walked in, Benedict offered Eliza his arm, and together they walked to the drawing room, where he would finally meet her father, the Duke of Remington.

As they entered, they noticed that the Duke of Remington was resting his hands on the mantle of the ornate stone fireplace. Eliza could practically see the tension radiating off his stiffened shoulders. She scanned the room and saw Uncle Charles, Jonathon, and Mr. Larson were all seated, but her brother was focusing on the ground with a perplexed look on his face.

All the men stood when she fully entered the room, and she sent Jonathon a questioning look, to which he just shook his head. Her father turned from the mantle and smiled tenderly at her, as she released Benedict's arm. She quickly walked over and gave him a kiss on the cheek.

Eliza turned and put her hand out towards Benedict. "Father, may I present Lord Sinclair."

Benedict performed a slight bow. "Your Grace."

The Duke of Remington acknowledged him with a small nod. He then turned back to Eliza with a clenched jaw. "I have something to tell you," he hesitated for a moment, "and I know it will not be easy for you to hear. I just want to tell you beforehand that I am sorry for all the deceit, and trust me when I say I did it to safeguard your future."

Eliza studied her father's well defined, handsome face and noticed that his usual smile had drawn into a hard line. His strong hands were clasped behind his back, as he held her attention. The duke's usual commanding presence had been replaced with a side of vulnerability that she had never witnessed before.

"Very well," she said, as she sat on the sofa, while her father remained standing near the fireplace.

Clearing his throat, he brought his hands to his side. "I just told Jonathon everything that I am about to tell you, but I wanted to tell you separately, since it affects you differently." He looked towards his son, who was staring at the floor and frowned, then turned back to Eliza. "Charles believes it is time to reveal the truth, so please do not interrupt me until I have finished."

Eliza nodded as she straightened her back and clasped her hands in her lap before he began. "I have been in love with Lady Anne most of my life. Her parents had a neighboring estate, and we grew up together. I do not know when we both started falling in love, but we did, and I planned to marry her as soon as I came of age. Unfortunately, I was not told till I was eighteen that my parents had a betrothal contract between myself and the Duke of Windcom's eldest daughter, Lady Diana."

Eliza watched as her father turned towards the fireplace and placed both hands on the mantle. He seemed deep in thought, as she waited for him to proceed. A few moments later, her father turned back to face her.

"I fought the contract, but Lady Anne and I both knew it was in vain. My father got his way, and I eventually married Diana when I turned twenty-four. We tried to make a go of it, but we were two vastly different people. In fact, we started resenting each other openly by the time Luke was born. After your mother got pregnant with Jonathon, we agreed to live at separate estates permanently. She resided at the abbey, and I moved to our country home. It was around that time I ran into Lady Anne at a ball. We were both still very much in love, and she agreed to be my mistress."

"A few years later, Lady Anne became pregnant." His voice wrought with emotion. "As it turns out, your mother was also pregnant, but she refused to identify the father. I was furious, and threatened her with a divorce." The duke rested his back against the wall and crossed his arms. "I know I was a hypocrite, but I did not want to raise her by-blow."

He took a deep breath and pushed it out. "So, your mother and I came to an arrangement of sorts. I would recognize her child, and she would raise my child as her own. We would raise the children as twins. Even though you were born a few weeks after Kate, it did not matter because she was such a small baby. To keep the household staff quiet, we generously paid them off, and made them sign contracts to ensure their silence."

Eliza did not know what to say, and she glanced over to Benedict to see how he was taking the news that she was actually illegitimate. Would this affect his feelings towards her? Instead of sensing any judgement on his face, he walked over and sat down next to her, reaching for her hand in a show of support. She gratefully smiled up at him.

Her father looked down at Benedict and Eliza holding hands, and she saw his face soften. "Your mother, let us call her Diana for right now to avoid confusion, tried to like you, or at least that is what she told me. After she realized what a peculiar mind you had, she wanted nothing to do with you. She insisted that I send you away to boarding school, but I refused. It was at that stalemate that we reached a new agreement. I would send you to Charles' estate and would see to your education, finishing, and would have the ultimate say on everything that applied to you. Diana would have full control of her daughter Kate, even who she married. That is why I allowed Kate to marry Lord Camden, because Diana demanded it."

Her father looked so defeated in that moment, but she had a lot of questions. She started to speak up when her father put out his hand to stop her. "There is more, Eliza."

"How can there be more?" she asked in disbelief.

He rubbed the back of his neck with his hand. "It gets worse." He looked up at the ceiling and let out a deep breath. "About three years ago, Diana started to come over to my estate unannounced every few months. She would pretend she had to see me to discuss her pin money and would wait in my study. Most of the time, I was out of the house on appointments or touring the estate. A few times I was home, I would walk into my study to find her standing over my desk. I began locking my correspondences in the desk drawer, but I would notice that they would be disturbed. At first, I thought she was just reading my personal letters, then I realized the papers from sessions of Parliament were also disturbed. It bothered me enough that I went to see Charles and told him about my concerns about Diana." Her father looked over at his brother sitting in a chair. "Charles started having her watched, and we discovered Mr. Wade visited her every couple of months."

Uncle Charles cleared his throat and spoke up, "I will take it from here." He leveled his gaze at Eliza. "The reason I did not want you to kill Mr. Wade is because he is working with someone who is a traitor to England. Lord Camden, your brother in law, has been supplying information to the French for years. He has used his position as an earl to pass on confidential information to the French, and we have been investigating him. We cannot arrest Lord Camden till we have irrefutable proof, because no court would find an earl guilty of treason with only circumstantial evidence."

Eliza's father interjected, "I know that you are *Shadow*, and I am very proud of you." The duke smiled fondly at her. "Charles has kept me up to date on all of your assignments and secret missions. He has sent me monthly status reports on what you and Jonathon have been working on."

"You knew I worked as a spy?" Her eyes widened in surprise.

The duke looked lovingly towards her and pushed off the wall. "I knew you were destined for greatness when I would find you in the library reading Socrates at age six. Who do you think arranged for your tutors? I wanted to provide you with the finest education." He leaned forward and softly said, "Your real mother, Anne, has a similar mind. That is why I knew what you were capable of."

Giving her father a tentative smile, Eliza's eyes filled with tears. For so long, she felt that she never belonged, and now she discovered that she had a mother with the same abilities.

Charles spoke up again. "We are confident in our assessment that Duchess Diana has used her position as the Duchess of Remington to gather information from her husband and relay it to Lord Camden through Mr. Wade. We also are in agreement, that Duchess Diana has passed information to Aaron Wade about who *Shadow's* real identity is."

"How would that be possible? Did you ever specifically mention my code name?" Eliza asked in surprise, glancing between Uncle Charles and her father.

Charles leaned back in his chair and crossed his leg. "Never, but I corresponded with your father about your meetings with Monsieur LeBlanc, and I gave him specific details of your missions over the years. Furthermore, we exchanged many letters about your last mission in France." Charles glanced hastily at her father after that admission.

Mr. Larson spoke up from the opposite side of the room. "I believe that Duchess Diana has not discovered that Eliza is *Shadow*. However, with the information she has fed to Mr. Wade, I believe he could reasonably assume that either Jonathon or Eliza was *Shadow*."

Eliza bit her lip for a moment. "Mr. Wade did not know at the time he ordered my abduction that I was *Shadow*, or he would have ordered the man to kill me, rather than abduct me." She put her finger to her lip. "It was also apparent that he had no idea that I was *Shadow* when he attacked me on the patio, because he specifically asked me to reveal *Shadow's* identity."

"My stepbrother blames Eliza and *Shadow* for ruining his

business," Benedict brought up. "Aaron knows *Shadow* is helping the agents retrieve the girls he is trying to sell. More importantly, as the man on the roof in France demonstrates, Aaron is also hunting *Shadow*.

"When Wade discovers that they are the same person, he is not going to hesitate to kill her," Jonathon warned.

Charles spoke up. "True, but we do not know for sure that Mr. Wade has discovered *Shadow's* true identity yet."

Turning to Uncle Charles, Eliza asked, "Let us assume that Mr. Wade knows now who I really am. How would he draw me out?"

Mr. Larson stood up, walking closer to the window. "No one has come close to Beaumont Castle, which means Mr. Wade must not know of its existence."

Eliza leaned forward in her seat. "What if the twenty-five missing girls was a scheme to get me and *Shadow* out of the way permanently? Mr. Wade knows that I have been meeting with Monsieur LeBlanc, and I have cost him tens of thousands of pounds in lost revenues. He also knows that *Shadow* participates in these types of missions. What if he is using this shipment as a way to rid himself of the two people he blames most for costing him his fortune?"

Benedict squeezed her hand. "You were supposed to be one of those abducted girls. My stepbrother was going to use you as bait for *Shadow*."

"What is this?" the duke roared at Charles. "Wade dared to lay a hand on my daughter, then he tried to abduct her and sell her into slavery? Why in the blazes have you not killed him, Charles?"

"Thank you! I have been saying that for over two years now." Eliza beamed at her father.

Benedict turned towards Lord Beckett. "I would be happy to take on that assignment, sir."

Clearing his throat, Uncle Charles answered, "Mr. Wade has served his intended purpose. I will issue a warrant for his arrest, and all his business associates immediately. We will need to extract as much information out of him as possible before he hangs."

Eliza nodded her head in agreement, since she knew her uncle was politely saying that Mr. Wade would be tortured as soon as he was in custody. They needed to turn their focus back to extracting the missing girls. "I cannot fathom why Mr. Wade would abduct high-ranking women, knowing that the Crown and the Bow Street Runners would investigate the abductions?"

"My stepbrother loathes the nobility, and this is a way to prove that he outsmarted them," Benedict pointed out. "Besides, all the news coverage would guarantee that *Shadow* was aware of these abducted ladies."

"The *Deceiver* is set to depart three days from now," Jonathon reminded the group.

Eliza turned towards him. "Has the *Deceiver* docked yet?"

"Yes. It docked yesterday," he confirmed.

"Mr. Wade would need to move the girls to the ship at night to avoid detection. Since he kept them away from the docks, it will be harder for him to transfer the girls onto the ship without someone noticing," Eliza said while biting her bottom lip.

"What are you thinking, Eliza?" Benedict asked.

"My instinct tells me that Mr. Wade is expecting us to follow our normal pattern of raiding the ship late at night. Normally, we have waited till the eve of the ship is setting sail, but I believe we should strike earlier and take the crew by surprise."

"You want to raid the ship during the middle of the day?" Jonathon seemed skeptical.

Eliza shook her head. "No, I think we should raid the ship tomorrow at dusk. The streets around the docks will have thinned out, and the sailors will not be expecting the attack till the next day." She turned to her uncle and asked, "How many agents can you give us?"

"I can give you six agents, and I can get some Bow Street Runners to assist with the mission," Uncle Charles offered.

"That should be enough," Eliza said. She turned towards Jonathon and Mr. Larson. "Are you two in?" They both nodded affirmatively. "Excellent. Now we just need to come up with a plan to rescue the girls, and avoid having anyone die."

Benedict squeezed her hand. "Maybe you should sit this mission out? Aaron will kill you if he sees you."

"No, I am going," she said determinately. "Your stepbrother has planned this whole elaborate trap to get me to come to him. Why would I disappoint him? Besides, if we are lucky, he should be making himself comfortable at Newgate before we even raid the ship."

"You cannot stay in the background this time. We know Aaron wants *Shadow* dead, and he probably has guards hunting you," Benedict pointed out.

She smiled at him. "Precisely. I think it is time for *Shadow* to come out of hiding."

For the next few hours, they brainstormed the best way to board the ship and rescue the girls. Eliza felt good about the plan they put into place. There were a lot of risks involved, but she did not mind the risks, if they could rescue those girls.

Chapter Twenty-Six

"Explain to me again why Jonathon, Mr. Larson, and I all had to wear black clothes again?" Benedict asked good-naturedly as he crouched down next to Eliza.

"If I am the only one wearing black clothing, then the other agents could reasonably assume that I am *Shadow*," she said in a hushed tone.

"I think the agents would notice a few other things before they even thought about *Shadow*," Benedict teased, as he perused her figure. "Although, I must admit, you wearing trousers is definitely growing on me." His lips slowly curled into a seductive smile.

"Will you please be serious, Benedict?" Eliza said, willing herself not to smile back at his playful banter, even though he was extremely difficult to resist. "We do not want to draw anyone's attention up here," she said, attempting to chastise him, but failing miserably.

Eliza watched from their vantage point on the rooftop of a building overlooking Aaron's brig, the *Deceiver*. His ship was over one-hundred-fifty feet long, with two square-rigged masts, and she counted twelve cannons on the ship, six on each side. She was aware that a merchant ship had to be prepared to defend itself in open water, and it appeared that Mr. Wade took that role very seriously.

Over the course of a day, they had strategized this raid and coordinated with the Bow Street Runners. Fellow agents confirmed that the girls were moved onto the brig last night, and it boasted a crew of fifteen men, plus the captain. As luck would have it, an agent was able to confirm that the crew held a nightly meeting with the captain just before supper in the galley on the tween deck. Eliza and Benedict determined this would be the best time to strike and ambush the crew.

Currently, they were on the rooftop waiting for the sun to set, and for the crowds of workers near the docks to start thinning out. When Eliza gave the signal, all the agents would descend out of their hiding spots and take out the three guards posted along the gangway. They needed to surprise the guards, or they might warn the rest of the crew.

"Are you sure you do not want me to go with you into the cargo hold?" Benedict asked.

"Yes, I'm positive. As we discussed, you will need to be above deck to lead the charge of the ambush and supervise the sailors going into custody." It was hoped the agents would take the crew by surprise, and they would surrender rather than fight. Eliza's assignment was to clear the cargo hold of guards and retrieve the girls.

"What if there are more than two guards in the cargo hold?"

"Then I will take them out just as fast," she countered. She could see the worry in his eyes, so she tried to reassure him by saying, "I doubt there are more than two guards watching chained up ladies."

"Will you at least take Mr. Larson with you?"

Releasing an exasperated sigh, she replied, "No, we need as many agents as possible above deck to ambush the crew and avoid causalities."

"Please be safe, my love," he said, his voice betraying his concern.

Turning towards him, she cupped his cheek with her hand. "I love you, Benedict. I love that you are worried about me, but I will be fine. I want you to focus on keeping yourself alive, because I am quite fond of you." She leaned in and kissed him.

"Will you two please stop being so affectionate all the time? It is quite exhausting to watch," Jonathon said from behind them.

Eliza broke the kiss and smiled back at him. Her brother tried to appear upset, but she could see his lips curled at the ends trying to stifle a smile. She looked towards the horizon. "It is time. Is everyone ready?"

The group murmured their consent and she arose, nocking an arrow into her bow and pulling back. She released the bowstring, and it struck inches away from one of the guard's right boot on the lengthy, wooden gangway. In rapid precision, Eliza released two more arrows, and they landed in front of the other two guards' boots. The guards had bewildered expressions on their faces, as the agents converged around them with their pistols raised.

The guards immediately put their hands up in surrender, and were led towards the awaiting Bow Street Runners. It was decided that the Runners would board the brig the moment Benedict gave them the signal, or if there was any sign of trouble.

Eliza, Jonathon, Benedict, and Mr. Larson quickly left the safety of the building and cautiously moved towards the gangway. Benedict acknowledged the six agents waiting to board the brig and valiantly led them up the narrow ramp, with his pistol drawn. Eliza had her longbow out, covering the agents as they boarded the brig, then she quickly ascended to the ship.

The *Deceiver* was a three-decker sailing ship, and the cargo hold was located below the tween deck. An informant told Eliza that there were two sets of stairs that descended to that level. One set of stairs was towards the bow of the brig, leading down to the galley where the meeting was being held, so Benedict and the other agents took that route. The other set of stairs was near the stern, leading to the living quarters.

Eliza kept her longbow in her hand for easy retrieval if necessary, as she walked cautiously down the stairs near the stern and searched for the hatch of the cargo hold.

Finding the large hatch, she pulled it up quietly until it rested on the ground. She cautiously descended the stairs with her longbow set with an arrow, as she quickly surveyed the cargo hold looking for any posted guards. Instantly, the stale, musty air greeted her, along with the scent of freshly oiled wood. As Eliza dropped down onto the last step, a squirming heap of black, chattering rats scattered in various directions, while some scurried past her up the stairs to take advantage of the open hatch.

The cargo hold spanned the length of the ship and had three evenly spaced spout candle lamps glowing on each side. They allowed just enough light for Eliza to see a large group of women clustered together in the middle of the cargo hold. She also took note of the various-sized barrels stacked together around the perimeter, and noticed the large, wooden poles that framed the hold. Even though the edges were cloaked in darkness, Eliza lowered her longbow, since she was certain there were no guards posted.

She did not take the time to count the girls, but was positive that these were all the missing girls. Some of the girls were in nightgowns, while some were in half and full dress, but all of their clothing was filthy and torn. As she approached them, she saw that they were covered in dirt and grime, and most of them had tear streaks down their faces.

As she came closer, she heard one of the girls exclaim, "Eliza, is that you?"

She glanced towards the girl who called her name and recognized Lady Rachel. Dropping to her knees in front of her friend, she saw that Rachel was wearing her nightgown, and her blonde hair was crusted to her face.

"Yes, it is me. We are going to get you out of here," Eliza assured her, as she ran her eyes over the other girls.

Just then the roar of multiple pistol shots was heard, followed by men stomping on the deck above them, and lots of muffled shouting. Eliza had no idea what was going on up there, but she needed to rescue the girls. She put down her longbow and grabbed the chains that were around Rachel's wrist. She noticed these chains were anchored to the floor.

"Rachel, do you know where the keys are?" Eliza asked hopefully.

Rachel shook her head. "No, I do not. Mr. Wade carries them with him. He does not trust anyone else with the key."

Eliza pulled her pins out of her hair, and started working on unlocking Lady Rachel's shackles. "When were you abducted?"

"The night after Lord Chambers' party. I was abducted from my bedroom. Mr. Wade told me to thank you, because I was not originally on the list. Do you know what he was referring to?"

"Yes, I do, and I am sorry. I will explain all of this later to you, but first we need to get you out of here," she said determinedly.

Eliza had just unlocked Lady Rachel's chains around her wrist, when someone started stomping down the stairs. She looked up to see the silhouette of a tall, muscular man descending the stairs into the cargo hold. She watched as the man stopped and turned to close the hatch behind him and bolted it from the inside. She was puzzled why a lock was installed on the inside of the cargo hold, but she would deal with that later, since this man appeared to be up to no good.

"Lady Eliza, where are you?" the man called out, and she immediately recognized the voice. It was Mr. Aaron Wade. "Eliza, come on out," he said, as he crept closer to the cluster of abducted young women. "Eliza…" Aaron's voice trailed off as he stopped his approach.

Lady Rachel stiffened. "Mr. Wade is here," she said as a sob escaped her lips.

Eliza was surprised to see Mr. Wade, since Uncle Charles had informed her that he was sending agents to arrest him this morning. "It will be all right," she said as she arose, throwing off her cap and reaching for her longbow. She nocked the arrow on the string, and drew back the bow while aiming for Aaron's cold, black heart. "Here I am," she announced.

She could see Aaron squint his eyes, as he resumed his approach. He stopped a short distance away. He was close enough to the light that she could discern his facial features. "Ah. We finally meet again, my dear." He tilted his head and said approvingly, "I think I prefer you in trousers, because they show off more of your assets."

"I did not dress to impress you, Mr. Wade," Eliza informed him.

"What a pity," he said mockingly. She could see that he was dressed in a dark waistcoat, tan pantaloons, and knee-high black boots. "You may as well put away your longbow, because I know you will not shoot an unarmed man. *Shadow* would never kill a man who meant you no harm," he said with a plastered smile on his face.

Eliza's chest started heaving with fury. "No harm? All you do is harm people. You ruin people's lives, and you do it for a profit." She thought about shooting the arrow into Aaron's chest and just be done with this ridiculous conversation.

Aaron shrugged nonchalantly. "I am a merchant. That is what I do."

"No, you are a traitor! You have been passing on information to Lord Camden, who in return, forwards it to the French," Eliza challenged.

"Like I said, I am a merchant first, and an Englishman second. Lord Camden pays me well for keeping him supplied with secrets," Aaron said smugly.

Eliza shook her head slightly in disgust. "And how exactly did you convince my mother to spy for you?"

Aaron licked his lips suggestively. "Let me say, I was more than welcome in her bed. I guess the duke failed to satisfy his own wife." His eyes lewdly roamed up and down her body. "You should feel honored to know that I had briefly considered you for my wife." Aaron's eyes landed on her chest. "I could have kept you so busy that you would not have wanted to leave our bed."

Nearly gagging at his implication, Eliza hissed, "My father would have never allowed me to marry you."

Aaron's face quickly filled with rage at the mention of her father. "I was not even allowed entry into the Duke of Remington's home to discuss courting you," he growled, then seemed to take a moment to compose himself and straightened his waistcoat. "Put down the longbow, Eliza."

She laughed at his request. "You are lucky I have not already shot you with an arrow."

"You could shoot me, but I know you won't," Aaron said confidently. "I've learned a lot about you, Eliza. When I figured out that you were *Shadow*, I was furious that I had not seen it earlier. It finally made sense to me why *Shadow* was so interested in rescuing those girls."

He glanced at the girls chained to the floor. "I still have no idea how you convinced Monsieur LeBlanc to help your cause, but he will be dealt with soon enough." Some of the girls started sobbing as Aaron walked over to a barrel near them and leaned up against it. "I am surprised that your mother ratted you out to me. I would feel bad for you, but I do not give a damn about your feelings."

Eliza heard more muffled shouting above her, and she hoped her team was all right. She knew Mr. Wade was baiting her, but she refused to take the bait, so Aaron continued his one-sided rant. "I picked a bad time to come and check on my brig. I should have turned around when I saw no one was guarding the gangway, but I wanted to make sure none of these whores escaped. My guards were supposed to be locked in the cargo hold with these girls, but the appeal of supper in the galley was too great for them to refuse," he said bitterly.

Eliza did not relax her bow, since she suspected that Aaron was trying to get her to drop her guard by talking to her. She may as well take advantage of his loose tongue. "You should have been in Newgate by now. How did you escape?"

Aaron glanced towards the cargo hold hatch. "Yes, I heard that some agents went to my home to bring me in. They were easy to evade." Turning his attention back towards Eliza, he smirked. "I always get away."

"Did you inform Lord Camden that I was *Shadow*?"

He shook his head. "No, he does not know. For the last couple of weeks, I have been under the assumption that your brother was *Shadow*."

"How did you discover that I was *Shadow*?"

Folding his arms, he continued to lean against the barrel. "After our conversation on the patio two weeks ago, you just disappeared. I searched everywhere for you, but no one knew where you went, so I decided to pay a visit to your dear mother. She was more than happy to talk about you and divulge that you like to hunt game with the longbow. You should know that the duchess was quite disgusted that you were so proficient at hunting," Aaron said in mock reprimand.

Eliza was amazed that Diana even remembered she went hunting on her uncle's land. "I am surprised you did not reveal my code name to Lord Camden. After all, I thought *you* worked for him," she pressed. If her brother-in-law knew she was *Shadow*, then they would have to bring him in immediately, or kill him, to avoid passing along the information to the French.

Aaron's face twisted with rage. "Lord Camden is a bloody fool. When I went to him this morning for assistance, he told me I was on my own. After everything I have done for him!" Aaron started pacing back and forth. "Did you know that I asked Lord Camden to talk to the French about the taxes they were putting on my ships, and he refused? In fact, it was all his fault, since his forged documents verifying I was a French merchant were useless. He told me that my business was my own affair, and not to bother him with it anymore.

He even sold his shares to my ship!"

Shrugging casually at his venomous tone, Eliza remarked, "None of that will matter when you have a noose around your neck."

Mr. Wade stopped pacing and leered at her. "I did not tell Lord Camden who you were, because I wanted the reward for bringing in *Shadow*. Many countries are willing to pay a small fortune to have *Shadow*, dead or alive. Although, the reward for having you alive would have been much larger." Aaron threw his hands in the air in obvious frustration. "Hence, this elaborate trap was set for you, but when I planned this trap, I had not anticipated that the daughter of the Duke of Remington was *Shadow*. That complicated my plan, but it did not unravel it. Yet somehow, you managed to completely ruin the ambush I have been laying down for months." He glared at Eliza and shouted, "You were not supposed to arrive till tomorrow night. Mercenaries were going to be set on every rooftop waiting for *Shadow*. You stupid chit! You ruined everything!"

"I am sorry to disappoint you," Eliza smirked.

Giving her a murderous stare, Aaron quickly drew a small pistol from behind him, which must have been in the waistband of his pantaloons. He leveled it at Eliza. "Put your bow down!"

"And why would I do that?" she asked in disbelief.

"Put down the bow, or I will kill her," he said slowly, pointing the pistol at a brown-haired young girl wearing a nightgown, lying in a fetal position.

Eliza did not even flinch. "Do not be ridiculous. You only have one shot from that pistol, and as soon as you shoot the girl, I will kill you." The girl in question began sobbing loudly.

"You are right. I do only have one shot." In one fluid motion, Aaron changed his aim and fired at Eliza just as she released her arrow towards him.

Chapter Twenty-Seven

Benedict stood at the quarterdeck's railing overlooking the subdued crew members on their knees while the Bow Street Runners were preparing to relocate them to Newgate. When the agents had boarded the ship, they swiftly made their way to the stairs that led to the tween deck that housed the galley.

The agents stormed down the stairs and attacked the surprised crew members, which allowed for no lives to be lost. Sadly, as the sailors were filing up the stairs, the captain decided to pull out his pistol and shoot a nearby agent. The captain made it a few feet before Jonathon killed him, which ensured the cooperation of the remaining crew members.

When the pistols went off, the Bow Street Runners stormed the brig, assuming their assistance was required. Since they were already there, they took control of the prisoners, as Benedict supervised. The injured agent had been removed from the ship and was on his way to see a doctor.

Benedict leaned his hands on the railing and hoped that Eliza was making quick work of releasing the girls. A few minutes ago, Jonathon had gone down to assist her while the other agents were mulling around on the main deck. To protect her identity, they were limiting her exposure to the other agents. Once the girls were released, the agents would take their statements and assist them home, and Jonathon would covertly take Eliza off the ship.

"Excuse me, sir?" an average-sized, weathered man came to stand by him.

"Yes."

"I heard you were the one in charge?"

"You heard correctly. What can I do for you?" Benedict asked, without taking his focus off the main deck.

The man was quiet for a moment. "Are you *Shadow*?"

Tilting his head towards the man, he answered, "No, I am not."

"Oh, I just assumed with your black clothing and all," the man said, placing his hands in his pockets.

Benedict chuckled under his breath. As usual, Eliza's suspicions were correct about the black clothing. "Sorry to disappoint you, but I am not *Shadow*."

"The other Runners saw a lone agent board the ship with a longbow in his hand. Is *Shadow* running this operation?"

"What is your purpose, sir?" Benedict asked through gritted teeth. He was getting frustrated with this man's fascination with *Shadow*.

"Have you worked with *Shadow* before?"

He sighed. "I have."

"What is *Shadow* like?"

Benedict pushed off the railing. "*Shadow* is... magnificent. Now what do you want?"

This seemed to appease the man. "Sir, the reason I am up here is because I saw a man board the brig before you raided the galley, but he is not with the other prisoners."

Now the man had his full attention. "What did he look like?"

"He was a dandy, for sure. He had a blue waistcoat, tan pantaloons, and knee-high boots. He had short, blond, curly hair, and was a tall, built man," he rattled off.

"Why did you not come forward with this information before?" Benedict roared.

The man's eyes were filled with uncertainty as he took a step back. "I... um... that is..."

"Why was he allowed to board the brig in the first place?" Benedict shouted.

He was now looming over the cowering man. He realized the description matched his stepbrother, but Aaron should not have been anywhere near his brig. Lord Beckett had sent agents over to arrest him this morning. Perhaps it was just a coincidence.

While Benedict was glowering down at the Bow Street Runner,

Jonathon charged up the stairs to the quarterdeck. "The cargo hold hatch is locked from the inside," he exclaimed frantically. "I tried pounding on it, but no one opened up the hatch."

Benedict clenched his jaw. "This man just told me that someone matching Aaron's description boarded the ship right after we raided the galley."

Jonathon started to respond when a muffled booming noise was heard. It sounded like a pistol being discharged, coming from the interior of the ship. Both men sprinted down towards the cargo hold, and Mr. Larson appeared right behind them. When they reached the hatch, they all started banging on it, and looking for a way to open it, but to no avail.

"Why is it locked from the inside?" Benedict asked.

"I heard a crew member mention that the guards spent a lot of time alone with the girls in there. The guards must lock the hatch to make sure they are not disturbed by the crew," Mr. Larson reasoned.

"Do you think Wade is down there with her?" Jonathon exclaimed.

"Well, I am not waiting to find out. I am going to find an ax and break Eliza out of there," Benedict announced determinedly, as he went to search the boat.

Eliza felt searing hot pain in her left shoulder and dropped her bow involuntarily, as her right hand shot up to cover the wound. She pulled back her hand and saw that it was covered in blood. Glancing up, she witnessed Aaron pulling the arrow out of his left shoulder as he roared in pain. Then he doubled over.

She heard banging on the cargo hold hatch, and Benedict's muffled voice, but she knew it was bolted. There was no way she could get around Mr. Wade to unbolt it. Although her uncle wanted Wade alive to extract information out of him, it was looking less likely now. She reached for the dagger on her right thigh and pulled it out. At least her right hand was working.

Aaron straightened up, and Eliza saw a knife in his hand. "You bloody whore. You shot me with an arrow," he snarled.

"You shot me with a pistol," she countered.

He ran and slashed his knife at her. She did not move back fast enough, and the knife sliced her stomach. Eliza screamed, doubling over in pain. She tried to stand to defend herself against the pending attack, but staggered back.

She did not have enough time to move before she saw Aaron stepping forward to slash at her with the knife again. Bracing herself for the attack, she was surprised when suddenly he collapsed face first onto the floor, his knife sliding away.

It took everything Eliza had to rise, keeping pressure on her stomach as she staggered away from him. She felt the blood dripping down her left shoulder, and her black shirt was quickly becoming saturated. She was grateful for the flowy shirt when Mr. Wade attacked, because he only managed to inflict a flesh wound. She knew that surviving a deep knife wound to the stomach was rare.

She quickly shuffled to the bow side of the cargo hold and made her way to a large barrel at the back of the ship. She leaned her back against the curved part of the ship and used the barrel to cradle her left elbow. Eliza winced as she saw Aaron kick Lady Rachel in the face and she crumbled to the floor. Eliza assumed Rachel had tripped him, which had saved her life.

Searching in the direction she had run, he shouted, "Why did you feel the need to get involved in my business?"

Luckily, the edges of the cargo hold were cloaked in darkness, since the candles were located towards the middle, and Eliza took advantage of that while she calmed her breathing.

Aaron had his hand on his shoulder where he had pulled out the arrow, and his voice indicated he was in pain, too. "Why would you care about what happened to these women? They are nothing to you!"

Eliza clenched her jaw, as the pain in her stomach quickly became unbearable. "No one else seemed to care, so I made it my mission," she hissed through gritted teeth.

Latching his eyes in the direction of her voice, he roared, "Your mission was to destroy me?"

She laughed but there was no humor in it. "No, my mission was to rescue the defenseless girls. Ruining you in the process was just for fun."

Aaron's voice shook with rage. "I had everything before you got involved. I had unbelievable wealth and power. I was going to be richer than my stepfather."

"You should have had different goals," Eliza quipped.

"Did my brother tell you that his family turned my mother against me? She turned her back on her own son!" he screamed, his voice echoing throughout the cargo hold.

Eliza tried to push harder on her stomach with her left arm to stop the blood flow, but it was not working. She was getting weaker, but she felt compelled to ask one more question. "Is that why you killed Henry?"

She could make out Aaron shrugging, as if killing his stepbrother was nothing.

"I hated Henry. He had the nerve to hire someone to investigate my business. Throwing Henry off his horse and trampling him to death, was easier than I thought," he said with an eerie, calm voice. "He should never have gotten involved in my business." He took a step in the direction of her voice. "Neither should you."

"I am warning you, put down your knife and surrender, or I will be forced to kill you." Eliza gripped her dagger tightly. The threat might have been more effective, if she was not so breathless.

Aaron laughed loudly. "How are you going to kill me? You are injured."

"Do not underestimate me." Her voice held a dire warning.

They heard pounding from the cargo hold hatch, and it sounded like someone was trying to break it down. They both looked towards the noise, and Eliza knew they were coming for her. Aaron turned his heated gaze back towards her. "I do not care what happens up there, but I will kill you." He took another step towards her. "Then, I will sell *Shadow's* body to the highest bidder and recoup some of my fortune."

"I'm afraid I cannot let that happen." Eliza did not take her eyes off Aaron, even though she could feel her left shoulder and stomach throbbing.

He smirked at her like she was a fool. "*Shadow's* weapon is the longbow, and you already dropped that." Aaron kicked her bow further away. "You probably do not even know how to use that knife."

She took a deep breath before answering, "What, you mean this sharp pointed thing?" She lifted her trusted jeweled dagger. "Yes, I know how to use it."

Aaron came charging towards her, and with a surge of adrenaline, Eliza squared her shoulders, took a step forward, aiming for his chest, and released her dagger. He stopped his charge as the dagger plunged deep into his heart and he slowly dropped to his knees. Staring at her in shock for a moment, his eyes finally rolled into the back of his head and he toppled to the floor.

"I told you I knew how to use it," mumbling to herself, she pushed off the ship. "I have been waiting to do that for years." Carefully, she staggered out of the darkness, keeping herself doubled over. Everything throbbed, and she was light-headed due to loss of blood. She needed to open the hatch, but first she had to stop to catch her breath.

Just then a loud scrape resonated throughout the cargo hold, as Lady Rachel unbolted the hatch. When it was thrown opened, Eliza could see Benedict, Jonathon, and Mr. Larson storming down the stairs. They slowed to a stop when they saw Aaron Wade sprawled out near her feet.

Jonathon looked down at Wade then back up to her. "Uncle Charles wanted him alive to testify against Lord Camden," he said hesitantly.

Shrugging with her right shoulder, she quipped, "You should have arrived earlier." She realized she was swaying back and forth and put her hand on a barrel to steady herself.

Benedict came rushing over to her, and she could see his eyes roaming all over her body, probably looking for injuries. She desperately wanted to let him know she was all right, but as soon as he reached for her, she let the darkness take over.

Chapter Twenty-Eight

Eliza awoke to a commotion outside her door. She recognized Benedict's voice. "I just want to make sure she is resting comfortably."

"And I told *you* that nothing has changed since this morning." She immediately recognized Jonathon's voice.

"I would like to see for myself."

"Why? She is just sleeping," her brother retorted in a frustrated tone. "Besides, you should not be up here."

Eliza started to sit up, because she assumed Benedict would eventually get his way. While in the process, her shoulder and stomach seemed to ignite on fire, and she cried out in pain. The door flung open, and Benedict and Jonathon raced to her bed. Her eyes were filling with tears at the intense pain.

Benedict reached her first and he claimed the chair next to the bed. "Do not try to get up. You might tear the sutures."

Eliza lowered her head back on her pillow and waited for the burning sensation to go away. Tears streamed down her face, and Benedict tenderly wiped them away.

"Do you remember getting shot, Eliza?" Jonathon asked, sympathetically looking down at her.

She nodded. "I am sorry, it just hurts." The two men hastily glanced at each other. It was obvious they did not know how to help her, and it pained them. She tried to distract them and herself by asking, "Were you able to rescue the girls?"

"Yes. We found the key on Aaron, and they all went home over a week ago," Benedict informed her.

Eliza turned her head towards him, hoping she misheard him.

"Over a week ago?"

"You lost a lot of blood between getting shot and slashed. Initially, the doctor was not sure that you would survive, then the wound on your shoulder became infected, and you had a high fever." Benedict's voice hitched. "Your condition was precarious for over a week. Fortunately, your fever broke yesterday."

Eliza closed her eyes when she realized how close she had come to dying. Her mind fluttered back to when Aaron Wade kicked her friend. "What about Lady Rachel?"

"Lady Rachel has come calling a few times this week. Aaron broke her nose when he kicked her, but the swelling has gone down since the last time we saw her," Benedict said.

Eliza was relieved that her friend was recovering. "She saved my life."

Jonathon edged closer. "She said the same thing about you."

"All of those girls heard that I am *Shadow*. Will I have to go into hiding?" she nervously asked her brother.

"No, it appears that most of them were too emotional to remember anything that happened that night. The few women that did overhear your conversation, like Lady Rachel, have sworn never to reveal *Shadow's* identity," Jonathon reassured her.

Eliza frowned. She knew that women liked to gossip. Benedict must have seen the worried look on her face because he said, "Mr. Larson also spoke to the girls. He told them that if he ever finds out that they revealed *Shadow's* true identity, he would personally hunt them down, and slaughter them along with anyone they told."

Amused, she smiled. "He did not."

Jonathon and Benedict exchanged a serious look, as Jonathon confirmed, "He did."

Her eyes widened at the thought of Mr. Larson threatening the ladies. She noticed how dry her lips were and asked, "May I have some water?"

Jonathon went to a pitcher on the nearby table, and filled a cup. He handed it to Benedict, who gently put his hand behind her neck to tilt her up, bringing the cup to her lips. After she drank a few sips, she indicated she was done.

Grabbing a chair by the wall, Jonathon dropped it down next to the bed. As he sat down, he asked, "Can you tell us what happened in the cargo hold? Lady Rachel told us what she saw, but we were hoping you could share more details."

Eliza spent the next little while telling them what had transpired in the cargo hold, but she left out one important detail. Once she finished briefing them, she reached for Benedict's hand. "Wade also confessed to me that he murdered Henry."

Benedict clenched his jaw, as a muscle below his ear twitched. His eyes flickered away for a brief moment. "Did he say why?" Eliza bit her lip as she debated whether telling him the truth was wise or not. After all, Henry's death was in vain. Benedict must have noticed her turmoil, because he said, "Please, just tell me the truth."

"Aaron killed Henry because he had him investigated," she stated, wishing she could have spared him the pain.

Nodding slowly, his eyes grew stormy. "I assumed as much."

"I am so sorry, Benedict," Eliza said, squeezing his hand.

For a moment, his face lost all expression, then he frowned. "What a pathetic reason to take a life."

After a few quiet moments, Jonathon put his hand on his friend's shoulder. "All right, you saw her. Let us go downstairs and alert Martha that Eliza is awake."

"I am sorry, Jonathon, but if Eliza will have me, I will never leave her side again," Benedict said, his eyes never leaving her face.

"That was beautiful, Benedict," Jonathon said, pretending to wipe away tears.

"Go away, Jonathon," Eliza ordered. Her brother was making a nuisance of himself, and he was loving every minute of it.

Jonathon put his hands up in front of him. "I am afraid I cannot leave you two unchaperoned, but I will sit over there for a few minutes," he said, as he walked over to the settee against the opposite wall. He picked up a book that was sitting on a nearby table and started rifling through the pages.

After Jonathon was situated, Benedict stood from his seated position and sat on the bed next to her, making sure he was not hurting her. He tenderly wrapped his finger around a piece of her hair. "I was terrified that I was going to lose you. I have never been so afraid," Benedict said, his voice shaking with emotion. "Even though we haven't known each other very long, you somehow have entangled my heart, and my mind. You are the first thing I think about when I wake up, and the last thing I think of as I lay my head down to sleep. Please never leave me again, because my life would have no purpose without you."

Benedict gave her such a tender, heart-felt smile that Eliza's heart ached with love for him. "I feel the same way," she said, hoping her eyes conveyed how deeply she cared for him.

"I know I cannot give you anything that you do not already possess. You already have a title, an estate, inherited lands and a family." He cupped her cheek with his hand. "The only thing I can offer you is my heart, unequivocally and without reservation."

Before she could respond, Jonathon stood up and started slowly clapping. "Now that was the most beautiful thing I have ever heard. I knew those years at Oxford would pay off." He walked to the bed and slapped Benedict on the shoulder. "Welcome to the family."

Rolling his eyes, Benedict smiled. "She has not said yes yet."

Jonathon gave his sister a lopsided grin. "Of course she will say yes. After all, I did handpick her husband for her."

Eliza's brow scrunched up in confusion. "What are you talking about?"

Benedict shrugged. "I guess your brother and Lord Beckett planned a ruse to get us together."

"And it worked perfectly. You are welcome," Jonathon said as he executed a mock bow.

"Can you please leave? I would like to properly propose to your sister," Benedict growled.

Jonathon rested his hands on the back of the chair near the bed, and glanced at Eliza. "Father is downstairs, and he would be furious if he knew Benedict was up here in your room, especially unchaperoned."

"Do you think Father would demand that we should be married as quickly as possible?" she asked, her eyes lighting up with amusement.

"Either that or I would be forced to challenge him to a duel," Jonathon said with a wry smile.

"A duel with you would not be much of a challenge." Benedict chuckled.

Jonathon's eyes narrowed. "You may have a reputation for being a good shot, but I have never witnessed it. I am sure it is exaggerated."

Benedict shook his head. "Perhaps, but I could shoot you with my eyes closed."

Pushing off the chair, Jonathon pursed his lips. "You would think you would be nicer to me, considering I am allowing you to stay up here with my sister by acting as your chaperone."

A mischievous smile tugged at Eliza's lips. "Will you please make yourself useful by going downstairs and telling Father that Benedict is in my room, and that we are unchaperoned."

Jonathon smirked at her playfully. "Fine. I will *slowly* make my way downstairs and into the study where Father and Mr. Larson are. They have been locked in there for over an hour now." He started backing up towards the door and pointed at Benedict. "I am sure Mr. Larson is informing Father of all your misdeeds. After all, nothing happens at Beaumont Castle that Mr. Larson is not aware of." He turned and walked out the door, but left it wide open. "You have five minutes," he shouted from the hallway.

Glancing at the door, she whispered, "He means well, but sometimes he can be annoying."

"I heard that," Jonathon shouted from somewhere outside of the door.

The corners of Benedict's lips curled into a smile, as his eyes twinkled with humor. "You should know that I never wanted the life of a marquess, because it lacked excitement, but then I met you, Eliza. You have brought such adventure into my life that being a boring marquess sounds relaxing."

Eliza started to laugh, but groaned when her stomach burned. "Please refrain from making me laugh. It hurts when I laugh."

Benedict tenderly tucked a piece of her hair behind her ear. "I love you, and I want to spend the rest of my life with you." He leaned in for a kiss before continuing, "I want to wake up next to you every morning and have lots of babies with you." He kissed her again. "I know you love working as an agent, but perhaps you could spy only part of the time when we have children?"

Her face grew serious. "I think it is time for me to retire from the spy business. I do not want to get shot again," she said with assurance. "Have you been shot?" When he shook his head, she continued. "I have, twice now. It really hurts."

Benedict laughed and brushed his lips over hers. Slowly, he raised his face so it hovered a few inches away, his dark blue eyes imploring. "Will you marry me, because I find myself desperately in love with you?"

Gazing into his eyes for a moment, Eliza basked in his undivided attention. "Yes. I thought you would never ask." As Benedict kissed her tenderly, it felt as if his lips branded her heart and soul, and she belonged to him forever. His love filled her heart, and she finally found where she belonged. "I love you," she whispered against his lips. She then kissed him, pouring all her love into it.

Benedict seemed reluctant as he broke the kiss and pressed his forehead to hers. "I would like nothing more than to spend the day kissing you in your bed, but you are still injured." Then he glanced at the door as they heard voices coming towards them. "And if I am not mistaken, your father will be here any minute demanding satisfaction." He leaned back but did not relinquish his hold on her hand.

At that moment, her father stormed into the room with Jonathon and Mr. Larson on his heels. "What is the meaning of this, Lord Sinclair?" He was shouting, but there was no anger in his voice, and Eliza detected that her father was attempting to hold back a smile.

Arising, Benedict respectfully bowed and addressed him, "Your Grace."

Her father waved his hand, dismissing the formality. "You cannot be alone in Lady Eliza's bedchamber. I demand you marry her at once," he announced.

"Yes, sir," Benedict responded before her father even finished speaking, and it made Eliza smile.

The duke's face softened as he looked over at his daughter in bed. "Does that please you, my dear?"

"Yes, it does, Father. The sooner, the better," Eliza confirmed happily, unable to wipe the smile off her face.

The duke seemed pleased with himself. "Excellent. It is about time." As he walked closer to her, the worry lines etched between his brows were evident. He watched her as if she would break apart at any moment. "How are you feeling?"

Smiling up at him, she tried to ease his concern. "I am in pain, but I will recover soon enough," she said honestly.

Her father nodded his approval at her response, but continued to gaze at her. He hesitated for a moment. "Your mother has been very worried about you. Now that you are awake, she was hoping to come visit you." His watchful gaze suggested he was very nervous about her response.

"I would like nothing more than to spend time with my mother," Eliza replied.

Smiling graciously in response, the duke turned back to Benedict. "I will have the wedding contract prepared and will send it over to your townhouse within the week."

Benedict shook his head. "If you do not mind, I would like my solicitor to prepare the wedding contract."

The duke tilted his head while considering the request. "That is not necessary. You are not aware of any of Eliza's holdings, or the stipulations of her dowry."

"True, but, frankly, I do not care," he said earnestly. "All the money and holdings that Lady Eliza has prior to our marriage will remain in her name," Benedict said, turning to fully address his beloved. "I do not care what you do with your money. You can will it to our children if you would like. I just want you as my wife."

Eliza's eyes fill with tears, as she gazed at the man she loved. How was she so fortunate as to find a man that did not care for her money or possessions, but just wanted her?

Searching her father's face for his reaction, she noticed that there was moisture in his eyes as well. "This is what I wanted for you, Eliza," he said, his voice was husky with emotion. "I wanted you to find a man that would love you, and would treasure you above all else." He extended his open hand to Benedict.

While they were shaking hands, he said, "My boy, take care of my precious daughter. I know it won't be easy, but it will be worth it." With that, her father put his hand on Benedict's shoulder. "I know you want to stay in here, but let us do it the right way. We'll send Martha up here, and she can chaperone you two."

Mr. Larson edged closer to the bed, eyeing her with a wary eye. "I was so worried, Eliza. You need to stop getting yourself shot," he said, attempting a lighter tone, but his eyes betrayed his concern.

"I agree. Although, getting yourself shot is quite fashionable right now," she joked.

Her beloved protector smiled, and gazed at her tenderly. "I hope not, or you are going to send Benedict to an early grave. He kept a round-the-clock vigil at your bedside until your fever broke last night. The duke then ordered him to go home, get some sleep and clean himself up."

"He was starting to stink," Jonathon offered up.

Benedict's lips flattened. "At no point did I smell. If I recall, your slum clothes stunk so badly that the people in the *actual* slums plugged their noses when you passed by."

Eliza smiled up at Mr. Larson. "You should know, I am starting to believe being married to Benedict will be adventurous enough for me."

His face lit up with happiness, and his voice was choked with emotion. "I am truly happy for you." He then turned to face Benedict. "Lord Sinclair, I am pleased that I do not have to kill you after all."

"Pity," Jonathon snickered.

The Duke of Remington's lips were pressed together. His commanding presence now dominated the room, as he looked Benedict directly in the eyes. "Yes, I just became aware of how much time you spent with Eliza. Unchaperoned, may I add. That ends now." He put his arm on Benedict's back and pushed him towards the door. "The next time you spend time with my daughter alone, you will be married."

Benedict allowed her father to escort him out of the room, however, he stopped short at the door. He gave her the crooked smile that she dearly loved. "I love you, Eliza." He quickly glanced over his shoulder. "We should have eloped to Gretna Greens when we had the chance," he said with a conspiratorial wink.

Eliza could hear her father splutter from the hallway. "No daughter of mine will elope to Gretna Greens. Get that ridiculous notion out of your head, young man. Larson, guard the door!"

Mr. Larson grinned wryly as he shook his head. "I'd better go save Lord Sinclair from your father."

Her lips curled up into a smile. "You do like him!"

"I have to admit that he is growing on me." Mr. Larson reached down and grabbed her hand. "Do not ever scare me like that again." Without waiting for a reply, he released her hand and trailed behind the other men.

A few minutes later, Eliza found herself alone, but she could not stop smiling. Even though she was almost killed twice now, she realized that soon she was going to marry Benedict, and she would never be alone, or forgotten again.

Epilogue

Eliza stared back at her reflection in the full-length mirror in her new dressing room at Benedict's ancestral estate. Today was her wedding day. It had been two weeks since she woke up after Aaron nearly killed her. Benedict had wanted to marry her as soon as possible, so the day after she woke up in Jonathon's townhouse, he had secured a special license from the Archbishop of Canterbury.

It took some convincing, but Benedict finally agreed to wait two weeks. It was decided that they would marry at the chapel near Chatsworth Manor, so his father could attend. Sadly, it appeared that the Marquess of Lansdowne would not be on this earth much longer, but his greatest wish was to see his son married.

She fingered the lace on her silver wedding dress, which was embroidered with silver shells and flowers. When Lady Anne brought over the dress to offer it to Eliza, she explained that it had belonged to her mother. Her eyes filled with tears as she acknowledged that she would never be able to use this dress for its intended purpose, but she would be honored if her daughter would wear it.

While Eliza was recovering in bed, Lady Anne spent hours at her bedside making up for lost time. Her mother explained the turmoil she felt when she put her daughter into the care of Duchess Diana, but she knew it was the only way to secure Eliza's future. Now that Eliza was aware of the circumstances, Lady Anne explained it was her greatest wish to have a relationship with her only child. She praised her for all her accomplishments. Eliza finally had a mother that loved her just the way she was, and it felt wonderful.

Eliza was so deliriously happy at this moment that she twirled in a circle like she used to do as a child. She stopped twirling when she heard the door latch, and looked up to see Benedict's intense gaze focused solely on her. She flashed him an easy smile, but his gaze did not waver from her, and his eyes glistened with unshed tears. Dropping the smile from her face, she began slowly wringing her hands together, because she could not discern what he must be thinking.

Finally, Benedict spoke with raw emotion, his eyes never wavering from her face. "You take my breath away."

Eliza hesitantly glanced down. "You need to stop staring at me so, Benedict."

He closed the distance between them in a few strides, and reached for her hands. "I am afraid I cannot do that, my dear. You have bewitched me with your beauty," he said with such love in his voice that it was almost her undoing.

She saw the range of emotions flittering across his face. Oh, how she loved this man. "I can assure you that I have not cast a spell on you," she bantered back, smiling at the memory of their previous conversation after she agreed to be his partner.

"How could you not?" he asked quietly. Benedict put his finger under her chin, and leaned in to give her a kiss. "I have come bearing gifts."

Eliza decided she was not satisfied with a quick kiss. She put her hands around his neck and pulled him down to meet her lips. He tried to pull back, but she refused to release her hold on him. Chuckling against her lips, he carefully removed her hands and placed them in front of her.

"My lady, you need to stop tempting me, or I will not be able to wait till our wedding night to make you my own," Benedict said, as his lips curled upward into a seductive smile. She blushed at his brazen comment and Benedict chuckled again. "I do so love to see you blush."

He slowly dropped her hands and reached into the pocket of his black coat. As he pulled out a necklace, the sun reflected off the flawless diamonds, and Eliza gasped. Tentatively, she reached out and touched the large diamonds. "It is beyond exquisite."

Benedict motioned that she should turn around so he could put the necklace on. "This was my mother's, and I want you to have it as the future Marchioness of Lansdowne." As he clasped it on, he took a moment to trail warm kisses along the back of her neck. Gently placing his hands on her shoulders, he said, "There is one more gift I wanted to give you."

Eliza shook her head. "No, you have given me enough." She was embarrassed that she had not even considered getting him a wedding present. She bit her lower lip before saying, "Besides, I did not get you anything."

Benedict turned her around to face him, but she diverted her eyes. He tenderly put his hand on her cheek to force her to look at him.

"You have given me everything, Eliza." As his eyes filled with tears, he continued, "I think I started falling in love with you when Jonathon read your letters to me. That girl was full of life and had the wildest adventures." She wiped away a tear that was sliding down his face.

"When I gazed upon you at Lord Vernon's ball for the first time, I knew my life had just begun. With you by my side, we will have the grandest adventure." Benedict rubbed his thumbs over her cheekbones and whispered, "You saved me."

Eliza tilted her head slightly, so she could kiss his palm on her cheek. "It was you who saved me. I would have been lost if you had not helped me."

He smiled tenderly down on her, and Eliza thought her heart might burst from the love she held within for this man. "Since we cannot seem to agree on who saved whom, I want to tell you about your second gift. After all, I worked hard to acquire this steward."

Eliza looked baffled. "You are giving me a gift of a steward?"

Dropping his hand from her cheek, Benedict gave her a crooked smile. "Not just any steward, a highly recommended and sought-after steward. In order for me to convince him to leave his current employer, I had to double his salary, and gift him a small cottage on our property.

Eliza lifted an eyebrow. "He does not seem very loyal if he could be swayed so easily by more money."

"Oh, I assure you he is very loyal, almost to a fault," Benedict chuckled.

Turning away from him, she looked out the window. She was watching their wedding guests approach the chapel near the estate. "I am still not sure why a new steward is worth mentioning on our wedding day."

Benedict came up behind her, and put his hands around her waist, while Eliza leaned into him. "Well, my dear, he did start off as a butler, but he did such a poor job at that," he whispered teasingly in her ear.

Eliza spun in his arms when she realized who he was talking about. "You hired Mr. Larson as our steward?"

He leaned in and whispered, "Surprise," right before his lips captured hers. When Benedict's mouth left her own, he started nibbling on her ear, and Eliza felt pleasure explode through her body. A slight moan escaped her lips.

"Have a care, Benedict," Jonathon's voice resonated throughout the room.

Eliza dropped her face into Benedict's chest to cover her embarrassment. Her brother had caught them in a yet another compromising situation. Benedict laughed at her reaction, but turned his head to address Jonathon.

"Why are you here?" he asked, annoyed.

"Why am I here? Why are you here?" Jonathon said emphatically while leaning against the door frame. "You two are going to be married in less than an hour, and you cannot seem to stop touching each other." He shook his head, feigning disappointment. "We have been looking for you, and I thought you might have slipped in to see my sister." Jonathon tilted his head towards the door and asked, "How did you get past Mr. Larson?"

Benedict smiled. "Well, it appears that Mr. Larson likes me now."

Amused, Jonathon laughed. "I never thought I would see the day that you could win over Mr. Larson."

"It did cost me a lot of money to earn his affections," Benedict said good-naturedly.

Pushing off from the door frame, Jonathon walked into the center of the room. "The good news is that Luke just arrived. The bad news is that our dear mother is sitting in the front row of the chapel, and she is overjoyed with your wedding."

Eliza removed her forehead from Benedict's chest and turned towards Jonathon, hoping she misheard him. "That woman has never been overjoyed at anything I have done."

It must have come out more bitter than she intended, because Jonathon gave her a sad smile. She should be more sensitive towards Jonathon, because Duchess Diana was still his mother. She was lucky enough to find out that she had a mother in Lady Anne, who loved her.

"I am sorry, Jonathon. I know it must be difficult for you knowing that Mother is a spy for the French," she said, giving him a sympathetic glance.

Jonathon shrugged. "I have always known she was not the best mother, but I never thought she would betray her country," he said, his voice resigned. "Remember that we need Mother to continue to think that we know nothing about her treachery, or that we know you are not her daughter," he stated, pointing his finger at her.

"I know that. Uncle Charles explained that it could compromise the mission against Matthew, our dear brother-in-law," she rattled off sarcastically.

Jonathon gave her a knowing smile. "Oh, speaking of that, Lord Camden is in attendance too."

"And Kate?" Eliza asked hopefully.

Jonathon nodded, as his smile grew. "I thought you would be happy about that."

Benedict's grip tightened on her waist. "I cannot fathom why Lord Beckett has not already taken him in for treason."

"My uncle says the case is not airtight. Lord Pembrooke claims he has some documents that will prove Lord Camden plotted an assassination attempt against Prinny, but he is still in hiding," Jonathon said while adjusting his cuff links. "An agent, with the code name of *Hawk*, managed to smuggle the documents out of France and handed them off to Lord Pembrooke in Spain."

"Have you come close to locating Lady Hannah?" Eliza asked.

"No, she has vanished," Jonathon said disappointedly. "If Matthew finds her before we do, then he can use her to blackmail Lord Pembrooke."

"How do we know that Lord Camden does not already have her?" Benedict inquired.

"We do not know for sure, but Lord Pembrooke sent a note to his daughter that gave specific instructions on what to do if she was in danger. I am still holding out that Lady Hannah is following those directions and is in hiding."

"We can help you look for her." Benedict glanced down to see Eliza nodding in agreement with him. "We are delaying our honeymoon to the Continent due to my father's poor health."

Jonathon smirked knowingly at Eliza. "I thought you were retiring from the spy business?"

Her eyes lit up in amusement, knowing she could not pass up another adventure. "I may take on new assignments, but *we* will decide on a case by case basis." She smiled up at Benedict, gauging his reaction.

He gave her a teasing grin. "Why am I not surprised?"

"I will let you two know if I need assistance, but for now, you are needed downstairs," Jonathon reminded the groom.

Benedict started to nudge Eliza forward with his arm on her waist, but she did not budge. He glanced at her with a questioning look on his face. "I think Jonathon meant that you were needed downstairs. I will come down later," she said, as one side of her lips curved up.

He smiled down on her. "I would like for us to go down together. I never want to leave your side again." Benedict dropped his hand from around her waist and held it out to her.

Eliza gladly accepted his hand and let him lead her downstairs. She knew that by Benedict's side, she finally had everything that she had been searching for.

Coming Soon

A Peculiar Courtship

"He would protect her from anything. Even herself."

by

Laura Beers

Acknowledgements

I would like to thank my amazing family and friends for their love and support as I spent hours writing my book, fulfilling a dream of mine. I would especially like to thank Ashley Griffin and Courtney Austin, who literally spent hours helping me recall the basic nuances of the English language.

I am also especially grateful to my wonderful husband, who never complained when meals weren't cooked or the house wasn't clean when I went into my writing mode.

About the Author

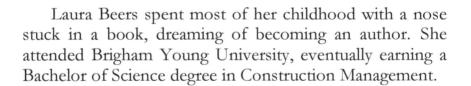

Laura Beers spent most of her childhood with a nose stuck in a book, dreaming of becoming an author. She attended Brigham Young University, eventually earning a Bachelor of Science degree in Construction Management.

Many years later, and with loving encouragement from her family, Laura decided to start writing again. Besides being a full-time homemaker to her three kids, she loves waterskiing, hiking, and drinking Dr. Pepper. Currently, Laura Beers resides in South Carolina.

CPSIA information can be obtained
at www.ICGtesting.com
Printed in the USA
BVHW040508080121
597271BV00006B/241

9 781943 048359